DARKNESS FALLS FROM THE AIR

Nigel Balchin was born in Potterne, Wiltshire in 1908, and educated at Dauntsey's and at Peterhouse, Cambridge, where he was an exhibitioner and prizeman in Natural Science. After graduating from Cambridge he took up various occupations, becoming for a time a fruit farmer, and later an industrialist. During the Second World War he worked as a psychologist in the Personnel section of the War Office, before transferring to the Army Council and becoming Deputy Scientific Advisor. By the end of the war he had risen to the rank of brigadier-general. In 1934 he wrote *How to Run a Bassoon Factory* under the pseudonym Mark Spade. Thereafter he published his remaining novels under his own name, including *Lightbody On Liberty* (1936), *The Small Back Room* (1943), and *Mine Own Executioner* (1945). He died in 1970.

Brightness falls from the air,
Queens have died young and fair,
Dust hath closed Helen's eye ...

DARKNESS FALLS FROM THE AIR

NIGEL BALCHIN

CASSELL&CO

Cassell Military Paperbacks

Cassell & Co
Wellington House, 125 Strand
London WC2R 0BB

First published in Great Britain in 1942
This Cassell Military Paperbacks edition 2002

British Library Cataloguing-in-Publication Data
A catalogue record for this book is available from the British Library

ISBN 0-304-35969-6

Printed and bound in Great Britain by
Cox & Wyman Ltd., Reading, Berks.

ONE

I STOPPED at about seven. There was too much stuff on my desk to have a chance of getting clear that night, and I was tired of it. I felt pretty guilty coming downstairs, and had to tell myself that this was the first time that week that I had stopped before eight.

Two French officers were just coming in the front door as I went out, and I did the bowing and waving act that I always do with them. It struck me as odd that they should still be around – unless they had decided to stay on in England and fight with us.

Going up the street I looked at the balloons and still thought they looked like a shoal of silver fish, and that when the war was over it would be worth while to keep them as decoration. But I'd thought those two things so often that they were getting a bit second-hand as thoughts, and it began to feel as though I'd better find something new to think about barrage balloons. But not tonight because I was damned tired.

I thought about the two French officers and remembered that before the French crack-up I used to think of the French Army and find it comforting. Every morning when I went into the lavatory at the office I used to think of the French Army and tell myself that it was something expert and professional which knew its job, rather like the Navy. It wasn't so much Gamelin or *la ligne Maginot*. They were just catchwords. But I believed in the French Army. Hadn't France seen this war coming for ten years? Well – there we were. The two I had seen coming in looked as expert and professional as hell, but that hadn't stopped the Panzer Divisions.

I was damned tired and I suddenly didn't want to go home. I turned into a telephone box and rang up Ted Ransome and asked him to come and have a drink. He hummed and hawed and said he hadn't got any money. I said I'd pay and he hummed and hawed some more and then said he'd come, in an unwilling sort of way. I felt more tired than ever and nearly told him to go to hell. I got a bus and went up to the Royal.

It was pretty full. There were the usual tarts and the usual collection of one-pips and airmen and a naval bloke in a beard who looked like George V, and the usual young wide boys and me. I had a drink while I waited for Ted and it went down very well and I had another, and that went down very well too. I told myself that I was beginning to drink too much and ordered another and shut my eyes. The one-pips were all very cheerful about something. I wondered whether they had one joke between them or one each. Anyhow, I wished I thought it was funny. Sometimes when they glanced at me I thought I caught that look again, and wondered how long it would be before we got to the stage of handing round white feathers and throwing stones at dachshunds. Anyhow, it would be all right to be in the Army or the Navy or something. If you got killed – well, that was all right, and if you didn't you sat round with tarts and laughed your head off. Better than working your guts out trying to get Lennox to do his job.

Ted turned up just as my third drink arrived. He was tired and looked fed to the teeth. I asked him how his outfit was getting on and he told me. It might have been a description of our joint – or any other Ministry, I dare say.

I asked Ted to have another and he said No and looked all grim.

I couldn't do with it any more and I said, 'For Christ's sake don't sit there, looking so damned disapproving. You give me a pain.'

Ted looked even grimmer and said, 'Well, Bill, we've got to face up to it, and if people like you and me don't, who's going to? This war's costing God knows how much and . . .'

'I know,' I said. 'If we have another drink there'll be a gap between the country's expenditure and revenue which can only be filled by inflationary borrowing. Then we shall get the Vicious Spiral in wages and prices and lose the war or the peace or something. Hell, d'you think I don't read the papers? Have another.'

He shut his mouth up like a trap and said, 'No, thank you.'

'OK,' I said. 'Then I will. The trouble with you is that you're a prig and an economist. Either's bad enough but both's just terrible.' I called a waiter and ordered two more drinks. Ted

6

grinned rather painfully but he didn't say anything.

I was beginning to feel a lot better, so I told him about Lennox. He wasn't very helpful. He'd got too many people just like Lennox around in his own Ministry. And anyhow you should never tell your troubles to Ted. He's too good at being reasonable about them when you want somebody who'll stop being reasonable and help you curse.

He said, 'How's Marcia?'

I knew what he meant, but I just said, 'Oh, flourishing,' and that ended that.

He told me he was damned hard up. I couldn't see why he should be. His Ministry salary was nearly as much as he got at Parks', and he'd only got himself to keep. But he said he'd told Parks he didn't want a retainer. Heaven knows why, but it was very characteristic.

Ted wasn't happy, and when he said he thought he'd go I didn't stop him. He can be the devil in that mood. He asked me if I was coming and I said No, though I hadn't an idea what to do.

The one-pips were getting on nicely. One set of four had only one girl between them and she was having a wonderful time. I thought of the story about the St Cyr cadets, and that brought me back to the French Army again.

I still didn't want to go home, but it was past eight and I was getting hungry. I went upstairs and rang up the flat. Marcia answered, and I asked her to come up West and meet me at De Vrie's for dinner. She hesitated and I knew why.

I said, 'If Stephen's anywhere about, bring him along.'

'Well, as a matter of fact he's here,' she said.

'Fine,' I said. 'Well, put him in a suitcase and bring him along. Tell him it's all right. I'll pay.'

'If I tell him that in that voice, he certainly won't come,' said Marcia, going a bit stiff.

'All right,' I said. 'Then don't tell him. Just imply it. And don't worry about me, honey. I'm a trifle tight.'

Marcia giggled. 'I thought so. Darling, you mustn't take to solitary drinking.'

'It wasn't solitary. I've been with Ted. Anyhow, buck up, because I want my dinner. Take a cab.'

Marcia said all right and we rang off.

7

There weren't many people in De Vrie's, but Tony seemed quite cheerful and said business was fair. I looked at the menu and it looked pretty good – except the prices. But I was tired of that stuff about the inflationary gap and I didn't care. I'd averaged seventy hours a week for the last month and I wanted some dinner. Marcia and Stephen turned up about five minutes after I got there. I thought they made a pretty pair, and didn't much like it. Marcia was all smoothed out and sparkling like women are after that sort of thing, and Stephen was looking big and handsome and haunted and so like a creative artist that you wouldn't have thought he'd have the nerve to go around looking like that. They were very much together, and I felt like a stockbroker uncle taking the engaged couple out.

I said, 'I've ordered you some smoked salmon, honey. Right?'

'Lovely,' said Marcia. 'Bloody day?'

'Average,' I said. 'I think I shall commit suicide soon.'

'You can't do that,' said Stephen. 'I thought of it first. Besides, why worry? If you wait a week or two you'll probably be killed anyhow.' He drank some sherry and looked haunted.

'I'm tired of waiting for Adolf,' I said.

'You certainly look darned tired of something,' said Marcia. She was looking at me with her anxious expression. What with looking at me anxiously and looking at Stephen anxiously, Marcia's anxious expression was doing heavy overtime.

'I am,' I said. 'I'm tired of using all I've got to overcome a lot of bloody incompetence and gutlessness. By the time you've fought your way over the dead bodies of the Civil Service, you haven't got time or energy to do anything useful.'

'Lennox being difficult?' asked Marcia.

'It isn't only Lennox. It's the man higher up every time. Lennox is an incompetent but he knows the Ministry. He knows all the reasons why you can't do things. If you get a thing past him against his better judgement it simply sticks higher up.'

'Look, darling,' said Marcia. 'Why do you stand it? It isn't as though they're paying you or as though your career depends on it. There must be thousands of other things you could do in a war.'

8

'It's the same everywhere,' said Stephen. 'Did I tell you what happened to me?'

'No,' I said. I didn't want to hear what happened to him.

'I wrote to the Censorship people and told them I had French, German, Italian, Spanish and a bit of Russian, and was I any good? Unpaid, of course. They waited six weeks and then sent back a printed slip telling me that there were no vacancies. So now I suppose the only thing for me is to go and carry a rifle.'

He drank the rest of his sherry and looked haunted some more.

'Oh bunk!' said Marcia, coming in pat on her cue. 'There must be something more useful than that.'

'They don't seem to think so,' said Stephen gloomily. 'Not that I shall be much good to them anyway, with my knee.'

I didn't say anything, but this made me a bit cross. It was exactly like Stephen to have a ready-made dud knee. The wine waiter came up and I chose a Chateau Yquem. I was still savage about Ted and the inflationary gap.

The waiter said, 'The sirens have just gone.'

'Another caterpillar in the machinery,' I said.

'No. There is guns firing, sir. But a long way away.'

He went away. Marcia said, 'I hope something *is* happening. I'm sick of waiting.'

We listened but we couldn't hear anything. You're about thirty feet underground in De Vrie's so we hardly should.

I said to Stephen. 'How's work?' He shrugged his shoulders. 'It isn't. You can't write in the middle of this.'

'Oh come,' I said. 'The spontaneous overflow of powerful feeling and so on. Why, for the last ten years all you boys have been saying you couldn't write good verse on the brink of a war because it didn't mean anything. Hasn't the start of the thing made it easier for you?'

'No,' said Stephen curtly. 'I'm not Kipling or Leconte de l'Isle.'

'You might try being Siegfried Sassoon,' said Marcia. 'But I don't see why you should.'

I looked at Stephen and he was looking pretty done. I suddenly felt sorry for him in the contemptuous way I always did.

'Why on earth didn't you clear out before the war started?'

9

I said bluntly. 'This isn't your show. You'd got the money. Why didn't you clear off to America or something?'

'And leave the war to you practical people?' said Stephen bitterly.

'Well, Christ, why not? I don't seem to be getting a lot done about it myself.'

'You've never known what it is to be useless,' said Stephen, using his profile and looking more haunted than ever. 'With your brilliant practical ability, you can't understand what it feels like.'

I glanced at Marcia. She was looking at him with large worried blue eyes. I decided that she must be a long way gone if he could get away with that stuff. Stephen's eyes were full of tears and that always embarrassed me, so I said, 'All right. Have it your own way. I don't understand how it feels,' and filled my glass up.

'What country's that?' asked Marcia in a low voice, looking towards a chap in uniform who was just being served with an escalope.

'Polish, I should think,' I said.

'It's extraordinary,' said Stephen, pulling himself together with a click which could be heard all over the room, 'the way these odd people come over here and want to go on fighting.'

'No odder than the International Brigade in Spain,' said Marcia, starting a conversation.

'Very noisy up above,' said the wine waiter, passing. 'Nice and safe here. Deep down.'

'Look here, if there's really anything happening let's go up and have a look at it,' said Marcia, quite excited.

'Not till I've had coffee,' I said firmly. 'This may be the last dinner like this you'll have, my girl, if the thing's really starting. It certainly won't be the last air-raid.'

'I keep having the last dinner I'm going to have,' said Marcia. 'Do you remember the first one? The night after the war started? You ate a whole lobster.'

'Yes,' I said. I suddenly felt pretty fed-up with sitting drinking Chateau Yquem and eating that sort of food in De Vrie's.

'How was Ted?' said Marcia, coming down, as usual, slap on what was on my mind.

'Very grim,' I said. 'He doesn't approve of me. You can't wonder. I don't approve of myself much.'

'Why?'

'Because this sort of thing is pretty disgraceful in wartime.'

'You mean we can't afford it?' said Marcia.

'God knows. I've given up reckoning whether I could afford things. But even if I can afford it the country can't.'

'I think that's bunk,' said Marcia.

'You would, darling.'

'No, but seriously, Bill. You can't work as you're working now without doing this sort of thing occasionally.'

'You mean I don't want to.'

'No. I mean you can't. It's like the Lancashire man and the kid – You can't do that sort of thing on bread and jam.'

'Ted manages to.'

'Rot. Ted doesn't do the same sort of thing as you. He's the sort of person who sees that we don't lose the war. You're the sort of person who wins it.'

Stephen was getting a bit restive over Marcia doing this stuff with me. 'There's one war job,' he said bitterly, 'that rather appeals to me. Rear gunner in a bomber. I believe it's as near suicide as no matter.'

'It doesn't appeal to me,' I said firmly. 'If I'm going to be killed I'd rather do it without being sick first.'

'Oh, I don't know,' said Marcia. 'If you felt sick enough you probably wouldn't mind being killed so much.'

I grinned because I knew that would rattle Stephen.

'I believe they're finding it so difficult to get people that they're taking volunteers up to any age,' he said, 'and I don't suppose you have to use your knees on that job.'

He went into profile again and looked very haunted indeed.

I looked at Marcia to see how that one had gone across. It had been quite a fair success and she was registering anxiety again. Then it struck me that Stephen was the sort of bloke who might go and do just that and leave you feeling rather a fool.

I gave up and called for the bill. It hadn't helped the inflationary gap a bit.

There was no commissionaire outside and no cabs on the rank. We were quite bitter about it until suddenly Marcia said, 'My God, look!'

We looked. The whole sky over East London was bright copper colour.

I said, 'It wasn't a caterpillar in the works that did that. I thought there didn't seem to be many people about.'

'Where is it?' said Marcia.

'Docks, from the look of it.'

A bobby in a tin hat came by. Stephen said, 'Is the raid still on?'

'It's been quiet for the last half-hour,' the bobby said. 'But the All Clear hasn't gone. I'd get home as fast as you can.'

'Any excitement up here?' I asked.

'Not very near. All down east. Plenty of noise though.'

He went on.

'And there we've been sitting eating and not heard a thing,' said Marcia disgustedly. 'D'you think we might get down there somehow? We might be able to do something, and it looks pretty bad.'

'Probably be more nuisance than we were worth,' I said. 'There'll be far too many people there with no equipment but good intentions already. Come on. We're going to have to walk home.'

'I shall leave you now,' said Stephen abruptly.

'All right,' I said. 'Goodnight.'

'Goodnight. Goodnight, Marcia.' He hesitated and then said, 'I may ring tomorrow,' as though he might and might not.

'All right. Goodnight, Stephen.' Marcia patted his arm and he went off. Suddenly he turned round and came back past us. He didn't look at us as he went by.

We walked up Regent Street. There wasn't a soul in it.

'That's a ghastly colour,' said Marcia, jerking her head back towards the glow.

'The colour's all right,' I said. 'It's what it's the colour of.'

There was a faint bump down East.

'Bomb or gun?' said Marcia.

'Gun, I should think. D'you mind walking about in air-raids?'

'No. Do you?'

'No. But then nothing's happening. Otherwise I should run like a rabbit, I expect.'

A cab came along. I hailed it and it stopped.

'Just not taking any notice?' I said as we got in.

'Naow,' said the driver. 'Goin' to get you it will. Business as usual. Where d'you want?'

When we were in the cab Marcia hooked her arm inside mine. I let her, but I didn't do anything else. 'Angry with me?' she said.

'About what?'

'This evening?'

'No. Why should I be?'

'I don't suppose you wanted Stephen,' she said rather wretchedly.

'Not particularly,' I said. 'But I thought you'd like to have him so I ordered him for you. Like the smoked salmon.' I looked back through the window. The glow seemed brighter than ever.

Marcia said, 'Poor Stephen.'

'That's the bit I can't understand,' I said.

'What?'

'The poor part of it. I should have thought that was the last thing he was.'

'I suppose so. He has a pretty bloody time though, Bill. Honestly.'

'Of course,' I said. 'He sees to that. But so what?'

Marcia didn't say anything.

I said, 'My main grouse about the whole thing is that it's made Stephen do tense close-ups all the time. Before he knew you he used to stop sometimes and be rather good company. He never is now.'

'Not when you're there,' Marcia said. 'But he still is with me.'

The cabby was driving as if he wanted to get home soon, and we went over in the corner in a heap as he went round Marble Arch.

'I'm a bitch,' said Marcia.

I said, 'Well, bitches are warm-hearted anyhow.'

'You're quite right about Stephen. Of course he loves being miserable. But somehow I can't help—'

'Somehow you can't help helping him?'

'Bill?' said Marcia, squeezing my arm and going intense.

'Yes, darling?'

'Can I – can I really have this and get away with it? Because if so, I'll make it up to you. I will really.'

'There's no charge,' I said. 'You can have anything you can get.'

'But how much do you mind?'

'When I mind enough to matter I'll tell you,' I said.

'But you do mind, all the same.'

'Just enough to preserve your self-respect,' I said.

'Not more than that – honestly?'

I said, 'I told you long enough ago about that. I love you and I think you love me. If so, we don't have to take people like Stephen seriously. If it meant anything to you, I assume that you'd stop, and stop quick.'

'Of course,' said Marcia. 'But not many people would see that.'

'Pure conceit,' I said. 'If I were five feet two and spotty, or if I thought you were doing me a favour by being married to me, I should probably mind a lot. As it is, I'm just amused.'

'By me?'

'Yes. You're rather sweet being all bad and sinful. But I think it's rather bitchy of you to let Stephen think you take him seriously.'

'I suppose so,' said Marcia. 'But he *likes* it like that.'

The All Clear went just as we got to the flat.

'Like some tea?' asked Marcia.

'Yes. It's only about eleven.'

I lit the gas fire and sat down while she went and got the tea. There were seventeen cigarette stubs in the ashtray. Two had lipstick on and the other fifteen hadn't. Stephen must have been there quite a time. Marcia came back with the tea. She had put on a dressing gown. I could see Stephen's point of view. But then I always could. The sirens went again.

'I wish they'd make up their minds,' said Marcia. 'Anyhow I vote we just stay here, don't you?'

'Sure,' I said. 'If a bomb lands within a hundred yards of this place it'll fall down anyhow, and if it's going to fall down I'd rather be on top of it than underneath.'

There were a few bangs and bumps, but still a long way away.

'I suppose when the local batteries start we shall be deafened,' said Marcia.

14

She sat down on the floor and leant her head against me. I stroked her hair. It was queer, thick, smooth stuff and nice to stroke.

'Oh God,' she said. 'I wish I knew about us. And more particularly about you.'

I lit a cigarette.

'Stephen's going to leave Peggy,' she said.

'Why?'

'Says he can't stick it any longer. And yet it's odd, you know, Bill. He's very fond of her.'

'What can't he stick any longer?' I said. 'It doesn't strike me that he does a lot of sticking now.'

'Do you hate him?' said Marcia suddenly, turning and looking at me.

'Lord, no!' I said. 'I don't hate people much, you know. Is Peggy making a fuss about you?'

'Oh no,' said Marcia. 'She's used to it.'

'Then what can't he stick?'

Marcia shrugged. 'I don't know. I think he has a conscience about her.'

'Stephen doesn't deny himself anything,' I said.

'I wonder if you're right about that?' said Marcia thoughtfully.

'About what?'

'About his liking to be miserable and conscience-stricken and so on?'

I thought this was going a bit far and anyhow I was tired.

'No,' I said. 'Of course not. It's just that there's a conspiracy against him. That and the artistic temperament.'

'That's badly below your standard,' said Marcia. 'Anybody could have said that.'

'Sorry,' I said. 'But it isn't a very subtle subject.'

'Oh *damn* Stephen,' said Marcia. 'Why in God's name do we talk about him?'

'Everybody likes a bit of scandal,' I said. 'Why shouldn't we?'

It struck me that the thing was changing on us slightly. But I was too tired and I didn't go into it.

15

TWO

THERE WERE thirty-two letters, fourteen files and two Parliamentary questions that needed something done about them. Doris had them all sorted out. I said she was a good girl and smacked her bottom approvingly and she blushed. It isn't every secretary who can still blush when you smack her bottom after working for you for five years. I knew she must be having a thin time. She hated the Civil Service as much as I did, and nobody really approved of my having a secretary anyway – even though I had brought her with me and they didn't have to pay her.

I went at it hard. I knew Lennox wouldn't be in till about ten, and Doris and I could clear a lot of it in an hour.

About half past nine a girl with a Cockney voice rang up from the Stationery Department. She said, 'You sent us through a requisition.'

I said, 'Yes.'

She said, 'You sent the requisition through in an envelope with a label over the old address. You aren't supposed to use those reconstructed envelopes for internal correspondence. An old envelope with the address crossed out is quite good enough.'

I said, 'Who told you to ring up?'

'Mr Meadows,' she said. 'We always ring people up when they do that.'

I rang off and said, 'This place will drive me cuckoo.'

Doris just smiled.

We did the Parliamentary replies first. The first asked if the Minister was aware of something which wasn't so. I couldn't remember whether the bloke was an Honourable and Gallant Friend or the Honourable and Gallant Member, but I said politely that it was bunkum. The second asked if the Minister was aware of something which we'd funked tackling for months, and I said the Minister was lying awake at nights about it and maybe something would happen sometime.

I said to Doris. 'I don't suppose either of those will get

16

past Knox. He'll say they're too definite.'

People kept on ringing up. It would have been easier just to have headphones and keep them on. I tried Lennox, but there was no reply, so I started on the letters.

Pearce rang up from Establishments and said, 'Do you still want a man?' I said, 'No. I want three men. I told you so four months ago.'

Pearce said, 'Well, I've got a man who might suit you.'

'Fine,' I said. 'What like?'

'Past middle age. But he's had a lot of experience.'

'What of? Pole jumping?'

'No. He had his own business. He was a broker. Then he was in the States, and then—'

'Don't tell me,' I said. 'He was in business and he went bust. He's been fired in nearly every country in the world, and now he's nearly seventy and doesn't look that. I know.'

'Well of course if you don't want him there are plenty of other people who do,' said Pearce huffily. 'I thought you were short of staff.'

'So I am. As I told you months ago I'm short of three young, well-educated men or women with a lot of intelligence and no experience of anything.'

'Well, do you want Clynes allocated to you or not?'

'Listen,' I said. 'How on earth can I tell you whether he's any good to me or not without seeing him first? He sounds about as different from what I asked for as he could be. But he might be all right. How can I tell?'

'We've engaged him. So of course he'll have to be allocated to somebody. Anyhow you can ask for him to be transferred if he's no good.'

'All right,' I said. 'Send him along. How old is he really?'

'About sixty,' said Pearce. 'You don't realize how difficult it is to get staff.'

'I do not,' I said. 'I'm used just to paying them in the ordinary way. When you want them for cigarette money it makes it harder. Anyhow, are you getting me those cabinets?'

'We got you one,' said Pearce, a bit hurt.

'I know, and it was marvellous – except that it was locked and there was no key. But how about the other five?'

'Cabinets are difficult,' said Pearce.

17

Lennox finished reading my minute and said, 'I think that's completely admirable.'

I didn't say anything. I was used to Lennox.

'In principle,' he said, as though he'd just invented the words, 'I entirely agree with you.'

'How about in practice?' I said.

Lennox bit his pipe and thought a bit.

'Now what's the next step?' he said.

'Do it,' I said. I could see the way it was going and it made me a bit savage. 'We ought to have done it months ago. If we don't get going soon we shall be in a mess.'

'Do you think the trade interests will accept it?' said Lennox. 'It's a big step, you know. A very big step.'

'It depends what you mean by "accept it",' I said wearily. 'If we just tell them that the Minister's decided to do it, they'll accept it all right. There won't be anything else they can do.'

'Ah, yes,' said Lennox, taking off his glasses and gazing in a bleary sort of way. 'I dare say. But you know we can't do that sort of thing.'

'I know we *don't*,' I said. 'But for the life of me I don't see any reason why we *can't*.'

'No, no, no!' said Lennox. He got up and started to walk about the room frowning. I could see that I was under his skin as usual. 'You know quite well it must be the iron hand in the velvet glove.'

I said, 'Well, we've had just about a year of velvet glove. Isn't it about time we got through to some iron hand?'

'My dear Sarratt,' said Lennox, going all patient, 'this is a democracy. We must never forget that. Democracy has its disadvantages, but after all, it's what we're fighting for. One of the disadvantages is that we must proceed by nego-tiation. We can't do these sweeping things that they do under dictatorships. In Germany I don't doubt they would do this and more and think nothing of it. But we're not in Germany.'

'No,' I said, 'but if we don't stop saying that soon we *shall* be in Germany – or rather Germany will be in us.'

'Apart from anything else,' said Lennox, 'the Minister would never stand for it. The Minister is a democrat and a business man. He hates bureaucracy and he's absolutely determined not to be a dictator or to interfere with usual business methods any more than he can help. If you took him a proposition like this the first thing he would say is, "Have you consulted the people likely to be affected?" And if you said "No," he'd tell you to go away and not waste his time.'

I said, 'Well, that makes it all delightfully simple.'

'Simple?' said Lennox.

'Yes. Here we've got a position in which a group of people are getting away with murder at the expense of the taxpayer. If we can't stop it unless they give us their blessing, then we can't stop it, and that's that.'

'No, no, no!' said Lennox going irritable again. 'You work too much in blacks and whites. There's probably a perfectly simple compromise which will protect everybody.'

'Such as—'

Lennox put his glasses on.

'We could probably reach agreement with them regarding profit margins.'

'And have an Order limiting them?'

'Oh, we don't want an Order. Some sort of gentleman's agreement would do it.' He took out his watch. 'I'm overdue at a meeting. Think it over on those lines, will you? Not too *sweeping*, you know.'

He grinned and we got up.

'All right,' I said wearily, going to the door.

'By the way,' said Lennox. 'I take it that you agreed on this minute with Harness?'

It was so obvious that for a moment I thought of just going out without replying.

'No,' I said, smiling at him. 'I haven't shown it to Harness.'

He didn't like my smile. 'Well, I certainly think he should be consulted, Sarratt. It never occurred to me that this was not agreed with him.'

'You must have thought he'd had a change of heart then,' I said.

'I should be glad if you would consult Mr Harness,' said Lennox stiffly.

'I certainly will,' I said. 'I'll tell him you agree in principle.'

Then I came out.

There was a rather used-up looking old boy waiting in my office.

19

He said, 'Mr Sarratt? My name's Clynes. I've come from Mr Pearce of Establishments.'

We shook hands. I should think he had been a handsome man once, but that was a long time ago. The whites of his eyes were bright yellow and very bloodshot, and he had a bald head with smuts on it.

He said. 'Of course I've been used to running my own business. But I thought it right to offer my experience to the Government in any capacity. Any capacity.'

'Yes,' I said. 'We're very short-handed here. This Department's a sort of waste-paper basket for the whole place. Any job which doesn't actually belong to anybody else is shoved on to us.'

'Don't you worry about that, Mr Sarratt,' said the old boy, as though he thought I was worrying about it. 'I'm adaptable. I always have been. There's nothing like width of experience.' He looked at me as though he were trying to figure out whether I was really as young as that or just youthful looking.

'Of course,' he said, 'I've been used to my own business.'

I cursed Pearce quietly to myself. I could see it was going to be sticky.

'Quite,' I said. 'You were a broker, weren't you?'

'I was a general merchant. I had a fine business. Many's the year my turnover's been over a quarter of a million.'

I decided that it was the invention of the steam engine that had finished him.

Doris came in and said, 'Mr Sarratt, Mr Thomas Percy's been on the telephone. He asked if you'd ring him at Grosvenor House as soon as you came in.'

'All right,' I said.

'And will you ring Mrs Sarratt?'

'Right.'

She went out.

The old boy said, 'I understand that they wished me to start in this department. Perhaps you could outline my duties.'

He leant back and put his finger-tips together. His finger-nails were black.

'Perhaps the best thing would be for you to have a look round first,' I said, feeling pretty helpless. 'Just to get an idea what we cover and who is who. Then we could have a word about it tomorrow.'

The old boy nodded. 'I agree. I agree entirely. I am willing to fall in with whatever you suggest.'

'Right,' I said. 'Then I'll get Giles in and get him to take you round.'

I rang for Doris and told her to get Giles.

'There's only one thing I want to say,' said the old boy, waving his hand.

'By all means,' I said.

'I regard myself as having put my experience at the disposal of the country *unconditionally*,' he said. 'When I give, I give without reservation.'

'That's nice of you.'

'Not at all, Mr Sarratt. It is the only thing to do. Please understand that I am completely at your service. There's no need to feel that because I am a senior man and widely experienced and have been used to my own business that I must be given only large issues to deal with. I am not one of those old fogeys who won't work with a young man.'

'That's fine,' I said. There wasn't much else to say.

Fred Giles came in.

I said, 'Fred – this is Mr Clynes who's been sent over by Establishments in answer to our SOS's.'

'I am glad to know Mr Giles,' said the old boy, shaking hands.

'Will you show Mr Clynes round and tell him what it's all about?' I said, all breezy. 'And then we can all be thinking where he'll fit in best.'

'Sure,' said Fred. I could see what he was thinking.

The old boy gathered up his hat and they went out. I caught Fred's eye and it said a lot.

I sat down and was just wondering what on earth I should do with the old josser when he came back.

'I left a gasmask,' he said. He picked it up and waved it. 'Remember,' he said. '*Where* you like, *what* you like and in whatever capacity – even the most junior.'.

'I appreciate that,' I said.

I rang up Pearce, and said, 'Look – that old boy Clynes. What have you taken him on as?'

'Grade II Clerk,' said Pearce.

'Well, good God, why didn't you say so? I thought from what you said he was administrative grade.'

'Oh no.' said Pearce.

'But I don't *want* a Grade II Clerk. And certainly not one like that.'

'I thought he might be useful,' said Pearce. 'He's had a lot of experience.'

I wasn't sure whether to ring up old Percy or Marcia first. I had an idea that what they wanted might overlap.

Finally I tried Marcia.

'Hullo, darling,' she said. 'Having a bloody time?'

'Average,' I said. 'Did you want me?'

'Yes. Look – would you think I was a beast if I went out tonight?'

'No. Of course not.'

'Sure, Bill?'

'Of course. I'm probably going out myself.'

'Who with?' said Marcia, jealous.

'A blonde,' I said. 'Old Percy to be exact.'

'He's not a blonde, darling. He's a bald.'

'Where are you going?' I said.

'I don't know yet. Why?'

'I was only going to say don't make it Grosvenor House.'

'We're not likely to. Stephen's paying.'

'Huh,' I said. 'Got any money?'

Marcia giggled.

'Yes, why? Don't you think he will?'

'If he's still there when the bill comes. But you never know with Stephen. Look – where are you likely to go? Luigi's?'

'I should think so.'

'Be back tonight?'

'Of course.'

'All right. I shan't wait up. Goodbye.'

'Bill?'

'Yes?'

'Darling Bill.'

'Goodbye, sweet.'

I rang up old Percy and arranged to meet him at Grosvenor House at 7.30. He was very matey and I knew something was coming. It had been coming for a long time.

The sirens went just after lunch and there were guns in the distance. Once, looking out of the window I saw a sudden puff of cotton wool against the blue of the sky, far away down the river. I couldn't see what they were firing at. Fred came in and said, 'Are you going down?'

'I don't think so,' I said. 'If we start having a lot of warnings and go down below for all of them we might as well pack up altogether.'

'The girls asked me,' he said. 'Most people are going down.'

I went along the offices. Everybody was staring out of the windows. I said, 'The instructions are that anybody who wants to go down to shelter can. If any of you want to go down, try to take any work you can.'

Three or four went. The rest might as well have gone. They didn't do any work while it was happening anyway.

I went back to my office and rang up two or three people but they'd apparently gone to ground. I said to Doris, 'Well, I suppose it wouldn't be right to risk valuable personnel like the crowd we've got here.' I felt a bit savage about it. The whole thing was miles away.

I carried on for a bit, but I wanted some stuff from Edwardes and as I couldn't get any further without it, I thought I'd go and have a look at the suicide squad in the basement.

It was funny. The place was one very big room with pillars all over the place. There were a couple of typists pounding away, and in one corner Lawrence and four or five more were going on with a meeting round a table, taking no notice of the row. In another corner little Rogers was dictating. Most of the rest were wandering about gassing and doing nothing. I didn't see Lennox or the Secretary or any of the very senior people. I don't know whether they were carrying on upstairs or whether they had an exclusive dug-out of their own.

I found Edwardes sitting on the floor with his back propped against a pillar, reading the paper.

I said, 'With selfless devotion to duty, and utterly ignoring personal risk, the Civil Service carries on.'

'I wish they had a bar down here,' said Edwardes with a grin.

'Listen,' I said. 'This raid's never been within twenty miles of here. How about a spot of work?'

'Just whatever you say, o'boy,' said Edwardes. He got up and we started for the door. As we passed Lawrence's meeting

23

one of them was saying, 'That seems to me a very dangerous doctrine, Mr Chairman.'

Edwardes said, 'God help us, they even see danger in a dug-out.'

'It seems to me a bloody dangerous doctrine to stop the whole place like this every time there's a warning,' I said. 'We didn't get all that much done before.'

'Ah well,' said Edwardes. 'Maybe if we just stop doing anything everything will go on better.'

I said, 'No German in his senses would drop a bomb on this place. He'd let well alone.'

The lifts had stopped working so we had to walk up seven floors. Then Edwardes couldn't find the stuff and wanted his girl, and she was still down in the basement. I wanted him to go down and get her but he wouldn't. He said that since his life was in danger he wanted to meditate on higher things, and got out his paper again. I gave him up.

After about an hour the All Clear went, and I thought I'd go and see Harness. I went in and put a copy of my minute to Lennox on his desk.

I said, 'Lennox wanted you to see this.'

Harness glanced at it.

'Ah yes,' he said, looking up at me in his queer sidelong way, with his head on one side. 'I've been wanting to have a word with you about it. Lennox told you what I felt?'

'Well, no,' I said. 'He didn't. He just suggested that I should talk to you about it.' This was getting interesting.

Harness leaned back in his chair and looked at the minute rather like a kid looking at the dinner it doesn't want to finish. 'Mother!' I thought. 'Constipated child needs California Syrup of Figs.'

'Well,' said Harness. 'In the first place, Sarratt, to be frank, I wish you'd showed it to me before putting it to Lennox.'

'To be equally frank,' I said, 'I think that was up to me.'

'Oh quite,' said Harness, looking up sideways. 'But in my capacity as his Personal Adviser—'

'Quite,' I said. '*His* Personal Adviser on what he does. Not mine on what I put up to him.'

'Anyhow,' said Harness. 'This is a technical matter, and not one which the Civil Service side ought to handle without proper advice.'

24

'Exactly,' I said. 'Well, that minute is proper advice.'

Harness shook his head. 'From your point of view,' he said. 'But there are other points of view, you know. I told Lennox at once that the thing needed a lot of thinking about.'

I said, 'When did he show it to you?'

'Oh, I happened to be in his office,' said Harness vaguely, smelling a rat. 'Why?'

'Nothing,' I said, 'I only wondered whether you'd had a chance to think it over.'

'Not fully,' said Harness. 'Not fully.' He turned his head sideways and looked at the minute out of the corner of his eye. 'Undoubtedly there's a lot in what you say. But I don't think I could recommend industry to accept the proposal as it stands.'

'But does that arise?' I said, keeping my temper. 'I mean, if the thing were a part of Ministry policy, I take it that as an officer of the Ministry you'd try to put it across?'

'Ah,' said Harness cocking his head. '*If* it were. But it isn't. In fact, Sarratt, if that minute were accepted as Ministry policy, it would reverse all the patient work of months.'

'Which work have you in mind?' I said. Harness waved a hand.

'You know we have our industrial committees. What would they say if they were suddenly confronted with a thing like this?'

I said, 'Well – what would they?'

'They'd say, "Harness – the Ministry has asked for our co-operation. We have given it unstintingly. Now we are suddenly confronted with a purely theoretical scheme which takes no account of the facts of business, and told that it is to be forced on us".'

'Listen, Harness,' I said. 'The snag about that scheme from their point of view is that it takes a darned sight too much account of the facts of business to be comfortable. Why can't we be frank?'

He leaned back in his chair and squinted at me like a man sighting a rifle.

'Sarratt,' he said with a sigh, 'I can't understand your attitude. You are not a professional Civil Servant. I should have expected that you and I would have made common cause in educating these Civil Servants on matters of this kind.'

I said, 'I don't think it needs two of us. You manage quite nicely by yourself.'

'But it isn't pleasant for me,' said Harness pathetically, 'always to seem to be holding a brief for the business man.'

I said, 'Then why do it?'

Harness went dark red. 'Are you suggesting that my advice is not impartial?' he snapped.

'Of course I am,' I said wearily.

'I could sue you for slander for that,' said Harness.

'You could,' I said. 'But you won't. Why should you? You've got the justification of your own conscience and you've got Lennox in your pocket. Why worry about me? It doesn't matter what I think.'

Harness got up and walked over to the fireplace.

'Look here, Sarratt,' he said quietly, 'can't we get away from this sort of thing?'

'Apparently not,' I said. I was feeling sick.

'I confess I don't understand your attitude,' said Harness. 'But I think you're being unduly cynical.'

'Maybe,' I said.

'I'm not opposing what you want to do. I'm only opposing the way you want to do it. These big firms aren't easy to handle, you know. They've got power. They've got influence. You've got to bring them with you. No government department can fly in the face of a dozen big industries. You ask any experienced Civil Servant. Lennox, for example. He saw the danger at once.'

I didn't say anything.

'You're a young man,' said Harness. 'And if you'll allow me to say so, a brilliant one. But you mustn't try to change the structure of society overnight.' He picked up the minute. 'Now this. I've every sympathy with what you're trying to do—'

'You agree in principle?' I said.

'Exactly,' said Harness, pleased with the brand new phrase. 'I agree in principle. But it's got to come *gradually*. You've got to give me time to bring my committees with us, and for them to bring industry with them. I think it can be done – most of it – all the essentials. But we must have *time*.'

'We've had a year already.'

'Quite. And during that year a great deal of spadework has

been done. Soon now we can begin to sow the seed – to prepare them for what's coming.'

I didn't say anything. I was feeling sicker than ever.

'Don't think I'm trying to stall it off,' said Harness, sighting me again with his rifle. 'I give you my word that what I'm suggesting is the quickest possible way to get what you're aiming at.'

He tossed the minute down on the table.

'I know you think I'm just looking after the business man,' he said brightly and matily. 'But I can't help that. I can only speak and act as I think.'

'We're all in that position,' I said.

'Of course we are,' said Harness. 'As a matter of fact,' he added confidentially, 'you'd properly put the wind up Lennox over this.'

'Why?' I said.

'He could see the force of your argument,' said Harness out of his left eye, 'but he was scared stiff of where it would lead him in practice. I told him, "Don't worry. The basis is right. *Solvitur ambulando*. Let's feel our way and it'll be all right."'

I decided that I was feeling sick enough to make it worth while trying to be sick, and I went along to the lavatory, but it was no good. I put my head against the tiles and they were beautifully cold. I kept it there and wondered why Lennox took the trouble to do that sort of thing. He was quite entitled to show my minute to Harness. Why lie about it? There was no doubt that these old men understood one another. I looked at my watch. It was half past five.

I went back to my office, had Doris in, and got on with it.

Old Percy was waiting in Grosvenor House. He greeted me like a long-lost brother, and asked after Marcia and so on. We went up to the bar and had some drinks. I came to my usual conclusion – that for a real old scoundrel he was a remarkably decent old boy. The trouble about old Percy was that, while of course he didn't ask me out to dinner because of my *beaux yeux,* he did really quite like me.

While we were having a drink a hell of a blonde came and talked to him. He introduced me and she had a drink and then pushed off.

27

'Very intelligent woman that,' said old Percy. 'Her husband's a chartered accountant.'

I nodded. Hell, I should have nodded if he'd said her husband was a rural dean. It was nothing to do with me.

'Have another?' said the old boy. 'How's the Ministry?'

'No, thanks,' I said. I'd had dinner with old Percy before, and I fancied I was better without too many White Ladies. The Ministry's much as usual.'

'You know,' said the old boy, 'I don't believe half these people realize what's coming to them. Sure you won't have another?'

'Quite sure, thanks,' I said.

'They seem to think everything can go on as usual and that no government will dare do anything to them.'

I just nodded. I was prepared to do a lot of nodding.

'Well, you know that can't be and so do I,' he said. 'With this French business the government *must* tighten things up. The country won't stand it if they don't.'

'I think you're probably right,' I said.

'No doubt about it,' said old Percy. He waved a hand to an acquaintance. 'I saw Harness the other day,' he said casually.

'Oh yes,' I said.

'How d'you get on with him?'

'Quite well.'

Old Percy chuckled. 'Funny Harness having that job. You know I put him into it?'

'No. I didn't know.'

'Oh yes. I was dining with the Minister and he said he'd need somebody. I think he rather wanted me to take it on. But I wasn't having any. Too busy. So I suggested Harness.'

I reckoned there was about one chance in thirty that that was true, but it might be. Old Percy has a hell of a lot of pull.

'He's a good fellow,' said Thomas. 'But he can't see beyond the end of his nose.'

'He's a business man,' I said.

Old Percy laughed like hell.

'That's right,' he said. 'A business man first, last and in the middle. Well – after all, what's your Minister beyond that?'

'I think he's a good Minister as they go,' I said. 'It isn't a possible job to do well, but he does it better than most.'

'I've known Clive Baxter for forty years,' said old Percy. 'He's all right.'

He drank up and said, 'Come on – let's go down and have dinner.'

We got up.

'And remember,' he said with a grin, 'if ever you have any trouble with Harness you know where to come.'

'Oh, we get on quite well,' I said.

I knew where to come all right but I was waiting to hear what it cost to get in. I reckoned that part of it would crop up about with the fish.

It was just getting dusk and as we went downstairs the darned sirens started wailing again.

'We're off again,' said old Percy. 'Don't mind having dinner in an air-raid, do you? I should think this is as safe as anywhere.'

'Good Lord, no,' I said. I was thinking of that damned tumbledown joint of Luigi's up in Soho.

The row started while the sirens were still going. I'd never heard it so noisy. It seemed to shake even that elephant of a place. There was one very loud wallop that certainly wasn't far away, but that was the only bomb I could swear to. Of course it seemed to me to come from a Sohoish direction.

Old Percy was rather good about the raid. He just sat there and ate and talked and took no notice.

I said, 'You don't mind air-raids?'

The old boy shook his head.

'Too old,' he said. 'Can only make a year or two's difference anyway. So what's the good of worrying?'

I thought it was queer that he should feel like that and yet go on wire-pulling hard. If it didn't matter being killed, why should he care about his bloody business and all the other stuff he played with?

I'd meant to make him buy me the hell of a dinner. But I was sweating a bit about Marcia, and the one thing I wanted was to get the party over. I don't know what we ate.

He didn't get back to the Ministry until the coffee came – but then I think he was reckoning that there was the whole evening to come.

He said, 'You must find your company a bit queer sometimes.'

'Why?' I said.

'I shouldn't have thought you had much sympathy with red tape,' he said, warming his brandy with his hands.

'No,' I said. 'It's a bit like swimming in a barrel of treacle sometimes.'

'Harness reckons he can work through a lot of committees,' he said. 'He's committee-mad. That's no way to do anything.'

'It's a bit slow,' I said.

'Slow? It's worse than that. It just leads to a lot of gas and no result.' He lit a cigar. 'I've been in business for forty-five years,' he said. 'Shall I tell you something, Sarratt?'

'Yes?' I said.

'The important things in this country – yes, and in this world – aren't done by committees. They're done between men – over a dinner table or a lunch table.'

I nodded. It looked as though we were getting to it.

'You've no need to go winding yourself in red tape,' old Percy went on. 'There are too many people who'd be prepared to cut through it for you. I've known your Minister for forty years. He trusts my judgement.' He put down his brandy. 'And I trust yours,' he said.

'That's very nice of you,' I said.

'No,' said the old boy, putting his hand on my arm. 'I'm not flattering you. I've watched you and I know what I think. You're not in the Harness class.'

This would have been good at any other time, but it was too loud outside. I wriggled my toes in my shoes to try and keep myself still.

'Take this sub-contract price business,' said the old boy suddenly. 'There'll be control, won't there?'

I looked at him for a moment and didn't say anything.

'I give it a month,' he said. 'Am I right?'

Damn it, I thought, it's not fair to eat the old blighter's dinner under false pretences.

'I think it's still being discussed,' I said.

'What, the date?' he said.

'No – the whole thing.' I had a sudden wild urge to say, 'Listen – what's it worth to you to have an hour with that file – cash down – no cheques?' I'll bet he'd have taken it like a bird.

30

He didn't mind my stalling. I knew he wouldn't. He was like that. He just said, 'Nothing decided, eh?'

'God knows,' I said. 'They don't tell me when they decide things like that.'

The old boy laughed. 'And if they did, you forget it, eh? Quite right.'

He called for another brandy, and said, 'You don't mind my talking about these things? I've known Clive Baxter all my life. We talk a lot. He knows I keep my mouth shut.'

I said, 'Lord, no. I like it. Particularly as I never know anything that matters. It means you don't have to be careful.'

He laughed. He saw it was no go, but he was quite cheerful. He always was.

'I'll bet you'll know whatever is decided about contract prices before I do,' I said. 'I get most of my information about the Ministry from you.'

He was pleased with that.

'That's the Ways and Means Society,' he said.

'I'm damned if I know how you do it,' I said. But I knew all right. I even knew what some bits of it cost.

'Have another brandy,' said the old boy.

'No thanks,' I said.

I was reckoning that in about another five minutes I could make a bolt for it.

It had quietened down for a moment as I came out of Grosvenor House. There was still a bit of gunfire but it was very distant. There were no cabs in Park Lane so I started to walk. It was only just on nine, and I reckoned they would still be at Luigi's.

I cut down into Mayfair, intending to go along Curzon Street, up Hay Hill, across Bond Street out into Regent Street and so into Soho. It was a bit eerie and I decided I'd better think about something, so I thought about old Percy. The thing that puzzled me was why he should waste a perfectly good dinner failing to get tips out of me, when he could obviously get them for nothing from one of his other pals. I decided that he just couldn't help it. Show the old blighter a wire and he had to pull it, just for fun.

Just as I got to the corner of Clarges Street and Curzon Street all hell started again. The guns started firing like mad at something slap overhead. There were three or four sharp

31

cracks as splinters came down on roofs on Clarges Street, and I cursed not having a tin hat. About fifty yards on I met a girl. She was walking quite slowly, smoking a cigarette.

She said, 'Hadn't you better come in out of the rain, my dear?'

I was rather tickled. I stopped and said, 'What in God's name are you doing wandering about in this?'

She said, 'I'm cooling off. I've just been with Michael.' She was tight.

I said, 'You'll get cooled off all right if you're not pretty careful. You go home, like a good girl.'

I don't think she was a tart, but she may have been. Anyhow, I was in a hurry. A warden turned the corner as I got to it, so she'll have been all right.

The guns were barking away like dogs on a rabbit and once there was a hell of a wallop behind me which I reckoned was about a quarter of a mile away. I thought it was in Park Lane. I found out afterwards that it was in Earl's Court, which just shows.

There was a lot of glass about in Regent Street and some AFS people were working a trailer pump. There didn't seem to be a fire, so I thought a main had probably gone or something. There was a biggish looking fire up north though.

Three or four searchlights in that bit of sky were doing a get-together on something, but I couldn't see what. Whatever it was, the guns didn't seem to think it was worth firing at.

Just as I was crossing into Soho a window fell out of a shop on the corner of Burlington Street. Nothing was actually firing at that moment. It just fell out by itself. I went about a foot into the air at the smash – I suppose because it was an unexpected sort of noise.

There was a bobby walking along Beak Street. I said, 'Did that fall or was it pushed?'

He said, 'They often do that.' He didn't seem to be going anywhere; or if he was, he wasn't hurrying about it.

Luigi's had the word 'Open' showing in blue light. I was glad about that. It had occurred to me about halfway that they might have packed up.

I went in and looked round. There were only two lots of people there – two officers in khaki and a man and a girl who looked as though they'd been left over from before the war.

32

The soldiers were pegging away at gnocchi, but the other two had got to the coffee stage. As I passed them the man was saying, 'He may have left Matte, but Matte never left him – not even in the Marquesas.' I thought that was pretty good for a bloke in a plum-coloured shirt even though I didn't agree with it.

Luigi came forward looking as oily as ever, and said, 'Good-evening, Mr Sarratt. A table?' I suddenly realized that it was better in there with lights, even though it was a damned sight safer outside.

I said, 'I'm looking for Mrs Sarratt. Has she been in?'

'Mrs Sarratt? No. Not here, Mr Sarratt. Not tonight!'

'Or Mr Ryle?'

'Mr Ryle? Not tonight.'

'Well, it's tonight I'm talking about,' I said. 'Not last night or tomorrow night. They haven't a table booked?'

Luigi shook his head.

'Damn their eyes,' I said.

'You want a table, Mr Sarratt?'

'I've fed,' I said. 'But I'll have a black coffee and a fine.'

I sat down and thought about it. Luigi brought the coffee and fine himself.

'Terrible night,' he said comfortably.

'Bad for business,' I said.

Luigi shrugged. 'Oh *business*—!' he said as though there wasn't much left you could do to that. I don't suppose there was.

I sipped my fine and thought.

'I tell you about my bomb?' said Luigi.

'No,' I said. 'And you aren't going to now. Otherwise I shall show you my operation. Where's the telephone in this joint?'

I rang up Stephen's flat and ours but there was no answer from either. I came back and finished my coffee. It struck me that Italy coming in might have made it difficult for Luigi. I wanted to ask him but he'd vanished downstairs. The man in the plum-coloured shirt was still talking about Gauguin but the soldiers had gone. It was warm enough in there, but I was beginning to feel a bit shivery sitting down. My shirt was wet through.

I drank up my fine and went out again.

It seemed darker outside after being in Luigi's, and it was

33

still thudding and bumping about, though a lot farther away. I thought I'd go home. There didn't seem to be much else to do. As I came out into Regent Street a taxi drew up and put some people down at the Café Royal. I sprinted down and nabbed him.

'That'll cost you six bob,' he said when I told him the address. The fare's usually half-a-crown from there.

'All right, you old pirate,' I said. I didn't care. I could see his point of view.

But he didn't like it.

'Pirate!' he said. 'Risk my bloody neck. You bloody well walk.'

'Can it,' I said, getting in. 'Let's die together, George.' He didn't say any more.

There was hardly a sound all the way home.

'There you are,' I said, giving him seven bob. 'Money for old rope.'

'Thank you, sir,' he said. 'Now I shall push off 'ome. I've 'ad enough.'

'Don't blame you,' I said. 'Goodnight.'

I went up to the flat. There was no light under the door. Marcia hadn't blacked out before she went and I had to go scrambling about in the dark doing it. I was annoyed to find that I was quite shaky, which was rather odd, because except when the window fell out in Regent Street I'd been quite happy. I got the black-out contraption up, switched the light on, lit the fire, and got myself a drink. It was just after ten and there didn't seem to be much point in going to bed. I put a record on the radiogram but it made an awful row and seemed a bit irrelevant, so I switched off and started to read.

This was fine for a bit. I think I nearly went to sleep. Anyhow the next hour went very quickly. But just after eleven Jerry, having gone away and thought the thing over, came back and started to do some real plain and fancy flying all over London. You could hear that he was coming in from the east. There'd be silence for a few minutes and then a couple of very distant thuds. Then a few more, not quite so distant. Then another one quite close. And then a gun would start yammering and oincking away, apparently on the door-step. I heard plane engines every now and again, and once there was the unmistakable sound of someone doing a power-dive. I thought perhaps they were dive-bombing, but I heard him flatten out and there was no explosion afterwards so I suppose he was just diving out of a searchlight.

They seemed to be dropping a hell of a lot of stuff – far more than earlier in the evening. I heard several sticks of three land, and once two fell close enough to leave me waiting for the third with a lot of interest. But that time there wasn't a third. Actually, there was nothing so very near, though I saw next morning that they'd written off a pub in Notting Hill.

I didn't like this part of the evening at all. I wished to God Marcia were in, and it wasn't only for her sake. Air-raids are a game for two or more players.

I decided that if she wasn't in by one I ought to start looking for her pretty fast, but for the life of me I couldn't see how. I tried her again at Stephen's but that was no good. I knew the names of one or two of the people they sometimes went to see, but I was damned if I was going to ring up and ask them for her there – not yet, anyhow.

On recent form, she might just have decided to stay out all night. I considered that, told myself that if she did she'd be sure to ring up, and then wondered whether it followed. I was having a lot of trouble knowing just what to expect with Marcia just then. Marcia as I'd known her until the war began would have rung up. But then Marcia as I'd known her until the war began wouldn't have stayed out all night, wouldn't have been out with Stephen, and wouldn't have a hell of a lot of other things. So it didn't follow.

I got all morbid eventually, and started to work out how you found people who'd been killed in air-raids – whether you went to the morgue or the police or hospitals, or where. And anyhow I didn't know where there were any morgues.

Marcia came in in the middle of this. There wasn't a feather out of place and she not only didn't look dead but didn't even look as though the idea made sense.

She said, 'Hullo, darling. Lot of row going on tonight.'

I said, 'Where have you been?'

'Out with Stephen,' she said, surprised. 'You knew I was going, sweet.'

'You told me you were going to Luigi's,' I said.

'I said we might. Why?'

'I went along to see if you were there.'

35

'Oh, darling, what a shame!' she said. 'We nearly did, too. I wish we'd known.'

She meant she was sorry we'd missed each other.

Marcia said, 'I thought you were hob-nobbing with old Percy.'

I said, 'That finished early.'

She sat down and started to straighten up a stocking which had got twisted. It seemed to me that we weren't making a lot of contact.

I said, 'Where did you go eventually?'

'Oh, to a new place Stephen wanted to try in Greek Street. Not very good.'

'How was Stephen?'

Marcia said, 'Oh, he was all right. At least he was all right most of the time.'

Marcia finished straightening the stocking and started to pull it up. I found myself as interested as though I'd never seen her pull a stocking up before. I thought maybe it was because we didn't seem to know one another very well just then.

'What was he like when he wasn't all right?' I said.

'Oh, you know Stephen's stuff,' said Marcia. I could see this wasn't going to be one of her expansive evenings.

I was still feeling pretty fed-up about the whole evening. What made me more fed-up than ever was that there wasn't anything much to go for her about. I'd known she was going out. She hadn't been at all sure about Luigi's. And she wasn't really very late even.

'Listen, honey,' I said. 'I just want to tell you something. Ever since that raid started I've been having the jitters about where you were and what was happening to you. Next time you go out and a raid starts I'll take it as a favour if you'll ring me up and say where you are.'

She looked at me with those Siamese cat coloured eyes very wide open.

'Oh, my sweet!' she said, leaning across and putting her arms round my knees. 'What a terrible shame! I never thought—'

'You never do,' I said.

'Is that why you went to Luigi's?' she said.

'For God's sake!' I said. 'Why the hell else should I? I don't usually come and play gooseberry, do I?'

'But, Bill – I was quite all right. Of course I was!'

I said, 'And as long as you were all right, everything was fine.'

'What d'you mean?' Marcia said.

'It doesn't seem to have occurred to you that I mightn't be.'

'You know that isn't fair,' said Marcia. She looked away and said, 'As a matter of fact I very nearly came to find you as soon as the sirens went.'

'Quite,' I said. 'That's just the trouble.'

'What?'

'At one time you used to do things. Nowadays you nearly do them and tell me about it afterwards. You're catching it from Stephen.'

'Oh, damn Stephen.'

I said, 'It'd interest me to know if you care as little about me when you're talking to Stephen as you do about Stephen when you're talking to me.'

Marcia said, 'You know perfectly well I don't discuss you with Stephen.'

'Oh Christ, Marcia!' I said in some disgust.

'But it's true. And you know perfectly well it's true.'

'I don't know anything of the sort,' I said. 'In fact, it sounds extremely improbable.'

'Well, if you think I'm such a bitch as that—' said Marcia.

I said, 'I don't know what degree of bitch you are. That's my trouble. I thought I did a year ago – to a hair. But so many things have happened since then that I've been forced to conclude that I had it all wrong.'

We lay a long way apart in bed at first. I could tell Marcia was crying. I was pretty fed-up, and didn't do anything about it for a bit, but she snorted about in the way that always gets me, so after a bit I went and collected her. We didn't say anything, but we hung on to each other.

There were still occasional bumps going on outside, but not many.

THREE

THE NEXT morning Marcia said, 'I don't think we want Stephen for breakfast as well as for supper, but I just wanted to tell you that I've made up my mind.'

I said, 'Your what?'

'Don't be an ass,' said Marcia. 'I mean I'm going to finish it.'

I just nodded.

'And I'm going to get a job,' she said.

'As what?'

'I don't know yet. But it's not having enough to do which has made this mess. I must be some use somewhere.'

'The Stephen part of it is up to you,' I said. 'But I quite agree with you about the job.'

'I shall go and see Estelle Rich and ask her what jobs there are.'

'All right,' I said. 'I'd avoid the women's organizations if I were you. I doubt you'd like it, and there are plenty of other things.'

Marcia said, 'I'll do anything that doesn't involve uniforms and saluting.'

I was rather early for once, so I walked to the office. I thought I might see a bit of what had happened the previous night. It must be quite a couple of miles but I only saw one place that had been hit. That was a five-storey house just north of the park. A bomb had cut the front of it off very neatly, so that it looked exactly like a doll's house with the front open. The ground floor was all bunged up with rubble, but up above the parts of the rooms which were left seemed hardly touched. There were pictures still on the walls, and in a bathroom I noticed a glass tooth mug still in a holder on the wall. There was a bit of smoke going up further to the north-west which might or might not have been a fire, and in one place there was a very small crater in the road. That was all.

They had hauled down a barrage balloon. It was a bit deflated and the tail fins were flopping down. End on, the whole

38

thing looked exactly like an elephant in a vile temper flapping its ears. I remembered that people who ran barrage balloons were said to get very fond of their own balloon. You could see that they would. This particular one had a lot of personality.

Lennox had called a meeting at ten to talk about appropriation of factory premises. Lennox had two lines of defence against anything which was proposed. His first was to try to get it shelved. Then, if he got kicked off that, he called a meeting. I didn't see much what we were meeting about. I'd seen the papers. The Minister had got fed-up about the whole thing and had actually sent down some quite specific instructions for once.

I sat next to Edwardes. As we sat down he said, 'Another good useful morning, I expect.'

I said, 'I wish to God most of these people had some work to do. Then we should have less of this stuff.'

Lennox was in the chair and there were about twenty people there. Lennox started by spending about half an hour explaining what it was all about, just exactly as though none of us had heard about it before. Everybody got very bored except Carter, who kept on correcting Lennox's figures.

'The exact figure's neither here nor there,' said Lennox at last, getting fed up with it.

'Nor is the inexact one if it comes to that,' Edwardes said to me.

Lennox waded on and then read out the Minister's note about it. Then he leaned back in his chair with the air of a man who's started something. Nobody seemed to think he had. There was just silence.

'I should like the reactions of this meeting to the implications of the Minister's note,' Lennox said at last. I thought its reactions were pretty obvious – it wondered why the hell Lennox didn't just get on and do as he was told. Still nobody said anything for a bit. But just as it was getting funny an awful little Assistant Secretary named Rogers, who wears a toupee and always talks as though he were addressing a meeting in the Albert Hall, gave tongue, and started to point out why what the Minister wanted couldn't be done. That started them off and we had the usual shattering exhibition of cold feet that we always got when someone wanted to do something.

Edwardes wrote, 'Charge of the Fright Brigade' on a bit of paper and passed it to me. I took it and wrote underneath:

'We are descendants, we are heirs
Of Britons who stood fast in squares;
And broke the forces of a faction
Which thought that wars were won by Action.'

Edwardes was very pleased, and started to write the next verse.

After about half an hour of this I got fed-up. I knew the stuff would be piling up on my desk, and we could have gone on like that all the morning. I said, 'Mr Chairman, I'm getting a bit confused. Is this meeting supposed to discuss whether we are to do this, or *how* we're to do it? They're not quite the same thing.'

Lennox looked at me in the tight-lipped way he does when peeved, and said, 'We are entitled to consider it from every aspect.'

Then good old General Parks waded in and said, 'Under favour, Mr Chairman – but are we?'

'Why not?' said Lennox.

'I should have said we'd received an instruction,' said old Parks. 'The Minister isn't asking for our advice. He's telling us.'

'Hear, hear!' said Edwardes and I.

'Oh quite,' said Lennox with a nasty little smile. 'But we all know that instructions from higher authority don't always take account of the difficulties.'

There were a few sniggers. It always struck me as odd that people like Lennox, who never had the guts to give their Minister any positive advice, went in for that sort of sneer at him when they thought it was safe. Old Parks was pretty fed-up.

'Well, it's up to you, Mr Chairman,' he said. 'If you feel that we're not bound by the Minister's instructions—'

'Oh no, no!' said Lennox, panicking at once. 'You misunderstand me. There's no doubt that the Minister has made up his mind. It is our business to find ways and means of carrying out his instructions.'

'There you are,' said old Parks nodding across the table at me with a grin. 'There's your answer, Sarratt.'

40

'Fine,' I said. 'Well, could we start talking about that part of it soon?'

Lennox went a bit red, but kept his temper.

'Well, have you anything to propose, General?' he said, ignoring me.

'I?' said the old boy. 'Lord, no. It's nothing to do with me. I should have thought it was purely for your department.'

'We've got the whole thing worked out,' said Edwardes in a bored kind of way. 'It's only a question of taking powers, sending round a circular, and getting on with it.'

'But based on what information, Mr Chairman?' said little Rogers, throwing back his head till I thought he'd jerk his wig off 'Gentlemen talk as though this were a small matter. But where are the figures? Where are the facts?'

'In my office,' said Carter gently. 'They've been there three months.'

Everybody laughed.

'The Minister talks about October 1st,' said Lennox. 'That's only about three weeks away. I take it that that's out of the question?'

'Why?' I said.

'Perfectly simple' said Carter. 'Do it next week if you want me to.'

'I dare say,' said Lennox angrily. 'But we don't work that way.'

'Hear, hear' said Edwardes. Lennox looked at him sharply, but Edwardes was sitting with his arms folded looking as grave as a judge.

'I'm going to have a pint of beer,' said Edwardes at lunch. 'So are you.'

'All right,' I said.

'It's a solemn thought,' Edwardes said, 'that the sort of thing we've seen this morning is going on everywhere.'

I said, 'It'll break us if we're not damned careful.'

'Sure it will. But what d'you expect. We organize our peace-time Civil Service on the basis that there's only one sin – to do something. Because that something may be wrong. And then when an all-in war starts, we hand ourselves over to people like Lennox or Rogers or the Secretary, who've got where they are by carefully avoiding action of any sort—'

'Listen,' I said. 'Any man who tells me that bit about the Civil Service mind again is no friend of mine. What I want now is somebody who can see what to do about it. Where's that beer?'

'We might try bumping a few of them off,' said Edwardes. 'The Home Guard has just been issued with ten rounds each. I could do a lot of good with ten rounds, judiciously distributed.'

'It'd be a patriotic gesture,' I said. I was rather wishing I'd lunched alone. I was too fed up to enjoy reading the usual Commination Service.

The beer was good. After a bit Carter came in and joined us. He was a cheery little bloke with a gift for having funny things happen to him – or else with a gift of making them up. He told us he'd just had in a file from another Ministry. It was marked to him, but the stuff in it was arranged differently from our files, and Carter couldn't find where it began and ended. He read bits of it and saw something about a firm of merchant bankers, so he marked it out to Cardwell with a slip pinned on it saying, 'I think you should reply.'

'The obvious step,' said Edwardes. 'What did Cardwell do?'

'The bastard wrote, "I agree with the views expressed" under my note and sent it back,' said Carter.

Edwardes roared with laughter. 'Don't you think that's marvellous?' he said to me, seeing I didn't laugh.

'Bloody marvellous,' I said.

'Have another pint,' he said. 'You take it all too seriously, Bill.'

He said to Carter, 'Bill's all worried about it.'

'Who isn't?' said Carter.

'I'm not,' said Edwardes. 'I would be if it were any use but it isn't.'

'Ah, that's the trouble,' said Carter. 'You can always do just enough to make it worth while trying.'

'Exactly,' I said. 'If you pushed with all your might and nothing at all happened, it would be different. But as it is you push with all your might and the thing moves one millimetre a week.'

'I don't push,' said Edwardes. 'I just stand by and cheer. Did you notice my nice "Hear, hear!" this morning when

Lennox said, "We don't work that way"? He looked quite annoyed. I was only agreeing, damn it.'

Edwardes pushed off. After he'd gone Carter said to me, 'That's a bright lad.'

'Too bright for me today,' I said. 'It doesn't feel as funny as all that.'

'So I gather,' said Carter.

'I think it's rather important to win this war,' I said.

'I agree,' said Carter. 'But I think we shall, you know. I doubt if we shall deserve to, but still—'

'What makes you think so?' I said.

Carter looked at his cigarette.

'Because I believe the mess we're in here is probably less than the mess in Germany. After all, imagine a country where the government runs everything—!'

I said, 'Yes. But remember you throw out incompetents there. We don't do that.'

'That's true,' said Carter. 'But there aren't all that number of competent people in any country.'

I said, 'Any ideas about *how* we shall win?'

'Oh, the usual formula,' said Carter. 'Mastery of the air with American help. Bomb their factories to blazes. Stir up trouble in the occupied countries, and there you are.'

'Time factor for this process—?' I said.

'Oh, God knows,' said Carter with a grin. 'We leave that bit out.'

I said, 'Oh well, we always do win things.'

'Yes,' said Carter. 'Between ourselves I think that's really the best argument at the moment.'

Lennox came in. He never goes to lunch till about quarter to two.

'Hallo,' he said in a cheerful sort of way. 'I thought that was a good meeting, didn't you? Cleared the air.'

'Very useful,' said Carter.

Lennox went on to his table. Carter said, 'The curious thing is that he probably really thinks it did.'

Doris was looking very decorative in a tight little blue blouse affair and a short black flared skirt.

'Nice,' I said, looking at her. Doris blushed. 'It's new,' she said, looking down at herself.

43

'You ought to wear your hair behind your ears,' I said.

'I look awful if I do.'

'Nonsense,' I said. 'You try it. I'll bet he'll come at you with bared teeth.'

I knew she would try it, too. Doris had great faith in my beauty hints.

I started off on some notes for the Area Unit Scheme which I'd had about in my mind for some time. It seemed to hang together rather well. After about half an hour I began to get quite thrilled with it.

I said, 'Pull your frock down, Doris. You're taking my mind off my work. Am I kidding myself, or is this a hell of a good idea?'

Doris didn't say anything. She wasn't supposed to. I went on and it still held together.

Fred Giles came in. He said, 'Listen – that old bloke Clynes—'

'What about him?' I said. 'I've got a thing I want to tell you about.'

'He's tight,' said Fred.

'Tight?'

'Absolutely sozzled. He always is. That's the point about him apparently.'

'Oh God!' I said.

'I wouldn't have bothered you if he'd been quiet about it,' said Fred apologetically. 'He's no good anyway and we could just have propped him up somewhere and left him. But he gets amorous with it."

'The old goat,' I said.

'All round the place,' said Fred. 'He's been making passes at Miss Chase.'

'He must be very drunk,' I said. 'Did you catch him at it?'

'No. Miss Chase came and complained. She was livid about it. She pointed out that she was an established Civil Servant.'

I said, 'For God's sake what's that got to do with it?'

'She seemed to think that it came in somewhere,' said Fred.

'Perhaps she believes in racial purity,' I said. 'No contact between the Established and Non-Established races. All right. I'll ring up Pearce and have him shipped back to Establishments.'

'I'd be glad if you would,' said Fred. 'He's rather upsetting

44

things. Incidentally he's told several people that he's here to keep an eye on you.'

'Well, he isn't doing it very well then,' I said. 'I haven't seen him since he came.'

I rang up Pearce.

'You noticed that he'd had one or two when he was in here the other day?' said Fred.

'No,' I said. 'Had he?'

'Oh yes. I thought you'd spotted it.'

'No. I thought that was his natural manner.'

'It is,' said Fred. 'Being a bit tight *is* his natural manner.'

Pearce came on the line.

I said, 'Hallo, Pearce. This is Sarratt. Listen – your old boy Clynes. He gets tight and makes passes at my girls. Take him away, will you?'

'Good heavens!' said Pearce. 'Not really?'

'Yes, really,' I said. 'He's already torn the clothes off the backs of two Grade III Clerks and he's standing outside the ladies' lavatory and kicking to be let in.'

'No, seriously,' said Pearce. 'Does he drink?'

'He does.'

'Are you sure? He has a rather odd manner.'

'Giles says that his manner's odd because he's always tight. Anyhow he's been making passes at an Established Civil Servant.'

'Oh, Lord!' said Pearce. 'We can't have *that*!' He seemed to agree with Miss Chase that the Established part of it settled the thing.

'Would you like him back?' I said.

'Well,' said Pearce, a bit doubtfully. 'Of course we can't keep him if he's like that. He'll have to go.'

'You said he was a very experienced man,' I said. 'He seems to be as experienced as hell. Surely there's somewhere in the Ministry where a lifetime's practice in assaulting typists would be useful?'

'Just a minute,' said Pearce. 'I'm thinking.'

'Well, get him out of here for Pete's sake,' I said. 'He's upsetting Giles' department and they're busy.'

'Do you mind if I ring you back?' said Pearce.

'Not as long as it doesn't mean we're left with him. Don't ring me. Ring Giles.'

45

'All right,' said Pearce.

'And while we're talking, has anything happened about my cabinets?'

'I've been on to them again,' said Pearce. 'They're urging the order. But cabinets are difficult.'

I hung up. 'Pearce is going to ring you back,' I said. 'I expect they'll send a plain van to collect the old boy.'

'Bet you they palm him off on someone else,' said Fred.

'Of course,' I said. 'They wouldn't let a valuable man like that go. Incidentally, is he any good at all when sober?'

'I haven't had a chance to see.'

I said, 'Well, anyhow, I've got something I want to ask you about.' I told him about the Area Unit Scheme.

'Sounds all right,' said Fred a bit doubtfully. 'But why is it better than a central scheme for the whole country? That's the obvious thing.'

'Possibly. But they'd never look at it. There'd be all the usual cries about nationalization of industry and using the war to bring about Socialism.'

'Do we really have to bother about that?' said Fred. 'Hell — what we've got to do is to win the war.'

I grinned. 'It does me good to talk to you,' I said. 'It gives me an idea what it must be like for Lennox to talk to me. Of course we have to bother about it. You don't have to go to these bloody meetings or you'd see. You think this doesn't go far enough. Let me tell you that even as it stands we should need a charge of dynamite to get it through.'

'Well, you know more about that side of it than I do,' said Fred.

'What's more,' I said. 'I think for once the kickers would be right. A central scheme would be lovely on paper but it just wouldn't work out. The variation in local working custom's too great. You could do a thing like this for an area like Clydeside, and another for London and another for Bristol. But you'd never get one to fit all three.'

'Maybe you're right,' said Fred. 'Anyhow it'd be better than the present free-for-all.'

I was a bit disappointed that Fred wasn't keener, but I went on with the thing. The more I saw of it the more I liked it. What was more, I thought for once it ought to get by the stone-

46

wall boys without much trouble. They'd got to have something, and they ought to like the area idea.

Marcia rang up and said, 'Look, darling, I've seen Stephen.'

'You surprise me,' I said.

'I mean I've told him that I'm going to finish it.'

'Mm?'

'I've also said I'd ask you to go to dinner tonight with him and Peggy. How about it? Think you can face it?'

'I don't see why not,' I said. 'Sort of Last Supper, eh?'

'Yes,' said Marcia. I thought she sounded a bit doubtful.

'All right,' I said. 'What time?'

'I said about eight, unless you were working on.'

'No. I'll pick you up at the Green Bay Tree at quarter to and we'll go on from there.'

As Doris was going she said, 'Have you heard about the typewriters, Mr Sarratt?'

'No,' I said. 'What?'

'Establishments have just sent round a note asking each typist to type the model and number of her own machine on a piece of paper and her own name underneath. I don't know what it's for.'

'Easy,' I said. 'All the slips are then placed in a hat, a member of the audience chooses one, and Pearce says which it is, blindfolded. It's amazing what these boys in Establishments think up.'

Pearce rang up and said, 'About Clynes.'

'Isn't he gone yet?' I said.

'No,' said Pearce. 'But I've just told Giles to send him over.'

'Fine,' I said.

'I've been thinking it over,' said Pearce. 'And I think he ought to have one more chance. Have you any objection?'

'Not at all,' I said. 'On your head be it. Where are you sending him?'

'There's a vacancy in Transport. And they're all men in there.'

'Sounds all right,' I said. 'His tastes seem to be entirely heterosexual. Pity they aren't all teetotallers, too, but you can't have everything. Now, how about a replacement for him?'

'I'll have to see,' said Pearce. 'You're a bit difficult, you know.'

'Difficult?' I said. 'What d'you mean? You send us one

elderly drunk and then when we throw him back at you, you say we're difficult. Snap out of it, Pearce.'

'I'll do my best,' he said. 'But you don't realize how difficult it is for us.'

I settled down to a batch of letters to the Minister. The second one began, 'A certain Right Honorary Gentleman said in yesterday's paper—' It was pretty sarcastic about the Ministry, but I think that bit was accidental.

Just about quarter-past seven, when I was getting cleared up nicely, Harness came in. He said, 'Well, I put your contract prices proposition up to my committee this morning, but I'm afraid they wouldn't look at it.'

'You told them the idea?' I said. It seemed to be going a bit far even for Harness.

'Of course,' he said, tipping sideways. 'Lennox and I were quite agreed that it had to be put to them.'

I thought that old Percy might have saved himself the cost of that dinner.

'And you just asked them if they'd like it?' I said.

'I asked them if they thought it was practicable. They were unanimous that it wasn't.'

'Extraordinary thing,' I said, 'Still – it may have done a bit of good even telling them about it. They may decide to moderate the racket a bit, just in case.'

'On the other hand,' said Harness, swinging his face hard a-port, 'they were quite willing that there should be a general exploration of the possibility of a voluntary scheme.'

'Isn't that rather rushing things?' I said.

'I don't think so,' Harness said, perfectly seriously. 'The time has come when the matter should be examined.'

I said, 'Perhaps you're right.'

'They've appointed a small sub-committee,' said Harness, rolling out the words. Harness might be a pest in some ways, but there was something rather touching in his love of appointing a small sub-committee.

'That'll be all right then,' I said. 'Private show? Or Ministry to be represented?'

'It was agreed that I should represent the Ministry. Lennox has agreed.'

'Good,' I said a bit vaguely. I was sorting the stuff on my desk into two piles and rather wishing Harness would go.

48

'I'm sorry it hasn't proved possible to give your very in-genious suggestion a trial,' said Harness sadly.

I looked up at him. He was sighting me carefully and there was a rum look on his face. Slightly disappointed, I suddenly realized that this was a gloat. He'd come in to tell me my scheme had been sunk and that he'd got what he wanted, and I wasn't reacting properly. Hence the mention of Lennox having agreed.

I suddenly felt a bit savage. I'd got myself so wrapped up in the Area Unit idea that I'd almost forgotten about this other thing. Certainly I didn't care a damn whether it was sunk or not. I'd written it off as dead anyhow. But Harness looked pretty repulsive, and I remembered that it was a damned good idea which I'd taken a lot of trouble over and which was now being chucked out by a bunch like that.

'That's all right,' I said. 'I'm used to it. It's my job to have ideas. But as long as this Ministry takes its orders from big business I can't expect anybody to use them.'

I wished I hadn't said it as soon as it was out. It was just what he wanted.

'I think you make unfounded statements of that kind too easily, Sarratt,' he said gently. 'They might get back to the ears of – of the authorities.'

I decided to make a job of it. I said, 'If by the "authorities" you mean Lennox, I know they'll get back to him all right. If you mean anybody higher up, then I˙think it would be quite a good thing if they did.'

'You're always looking for trouble,' said Harness.

'I'm always looking for somebody with guts,' I said. 'And never finding him.'

'Thomas Percy's a friend of yours,' said Harness suddenly. It wasn't a question.

'Yes. Why?'

'He mentioned you at this meeting,' Harness went into an almost vertical bank. 'He seemed to grasp the basis of your scheme very quickly.'

'Odd,' I said. 'He doesn't usually grasp anything quickly.' I was wondering in a vague way if this was where I hit him. The implication was clear enough.

'As a matter of fact,' I said, 'I rather wish I'd known you were going to spill the beans today. Old Percy was trying to pump me at dinner last night. I might as well have let him.'

'Good Heavens!' said Harness. 'Surely you wouldn't think of discussing Ministry affairs of that kind with an interested party?'

I just roared with laughter. It was too much.

I said, 'You're a marvel, Harness.' He went very red.

'What exactly is amusing you?' he said.

'Nothing,' I said. 'I get these hysterical spasms at times. Sorry, I must go now. Goodnight.'

I picked up my hat and coat and came out. As I went down in the lift I remembered that there was a lot of stuff still on my desk. But there was nothing that I minded his reading anyhow.

FOUR

I WAS a few minutes late, but nothing to matter. We got to Stephen's flat just after eight.

Stephen was giving his impression of a man who has received a blow which has numbed him. I must say it was good. That was one of the snags about Stephen. His repertoire was limited, but so polished that it fascinated you. If you'd asked any intelligent person to look at Stephen as he handed round the sherry and say what had just happened to him, they would have said, 'Well, obviously, Tosti's "Goodbye" and all that.' It isn't anybody who can get all of Tosti's 'Goodbye' into handing round sherry without letting one or the other slop over.

Peggy was exactly as usual. I never knew what to do about Peggy. She was at least fifteen years older than Stephen, very plain, and no particular shape. She had two moods – vivacious and serious, of which the one you were having was the worse. Stephen was sometimes rather touchingly nice to her and about her; but usually he made it quite plain that he was as surprised that he'd married her as you were. I found this odd, because I always saw exactly why he married her. We had about a quarter of an hour with Peggy being vivacious and Stephen being emotionally concussed and Marcia being social and me being bored. Then Stephen said pointedly, 'Look – there's no beer. I'm going round to get some. Coming, Bill?'

I said, 'Well, clearly somebody's got to get beer.'

It was only a couple of hundred yards to the pub. Stephen didn't say anything as we walked along. I was wondering what Marcia and Peggy were saying to one another. I know Marcia found talking with Peggy a bit difficult – not that the atmosphere was strained but because it was so unstrained. As Marcia once said to me. 'I can quite understand Peggy not minding if I sleep with Stephen. But what I can't understand is that she can't understand that I can understand it.'

Stephen said, 'We may as well have a drink now we're here.' We ordered pints. Stephen said, 'I want to tell you that I quite see your point of view about Marcia and me. I've been expecting it, of course.'

'Expecting what?' I said.

'That it would have to end,' said Stephen sombrely. 'It's indecent to expect happiness of that order from life. As I say, I naturally see your point of view.'

'I'm glad of that,' I said. 'I've never seen it much myself. Tell me about it.'

'At the beginning,' said Stephen firmly, 'you succeeded in convincing yourself that you didn't mind. Now you feel that you must protect your own life and happiness. It's perfectly reasonable.'

'Perfectly,' I said.

'You couldn't do anything else,' said Stephen. 'You've been marvellously patient and understanding. I want to thank you for that.'

'You're welcome,' I said, raising my glass. 'Bungho!'

Stephen took a sip of his beer and gazed moodily round the bar.

'I think you'd better tell me what's been happening,' I said. 'I'm a trifle behind the band on the facts. I gather you and Marcia have been hatching something?'

'Hatching something!' said Stephen, making a disgusted face. 'Why is it that a man with your gifts deliberately uses foul words?'

'We'll go into that some other time,' I said. 'What's been happening?'

'What you had arranged should happen,' said Stephen bitterly.

'Quite,' I said. 'But what *had* I arranged should happen?'

Stephen gazed at the beer-pulls.

'Marcia came to me this afternoon,' he said in his lovely deep voice. 'She said it must end – at once. I knew she was right, of course, but I fought. Damn it, a man must fight for his own life.'

'Yes,' I said. It seemed a reasonable idea.

'It was no good,' said Stephen. 'Marcia's strong. Stronger, probably, than you know. I knew I'd lost.' He threw up his head and pointed his chin defiantly at the beer-pulls.

'I did my best to face it. So did she. For a while we talked about it quite calmly – even happily in a way. It was only after quite a long time that we broke down.'

'Both of you?' I inquired.

'We sat beside one another on the sofa, holding hands like a pair of frightened children,' said Stephen.

I decided that it wouldn't do to let this get too visual.

'Frightened of what?' I said, trying to make it sound a rather deep question.

'Frightened of life,' said Stephen. 'What else is there to be frightened of?'

'I shouldn't have thought that was one of Marcia's fears,' I said. 'Have another?'

Stephen smiled. 'It's a damned presumptuous thing to say,' he said, pushing his glass forward. 'But in some ways – in *some* ways, mark you – you carry your deliberate misunderstanding of Marcia dangerously far.'

'I agree,' I said.

'You do?'

'I agree that it's a damned presumptuous thing to say,' I said.

Stephen waved a hand. 'Was that worth while?' he said. 'You can't hurt me, you know. I'm pretty well numb.'

I was glad I had been right about his being numb.

'Tell me more about these undiscovered depths,' I said. 'It's quite possible that I just don't know about them at all.'

Stephen said, 'I was necessary to Marcia. You won't like that, but I was.'

'Of course,' I said. 'Even I see that.'

'And what's more,' said Stephen, banging his glass down on

52

the bar, 'I still am. And she knows it. But I can't expect you to agree.'

'Does Marcia say so?' I said.

'*Say* so?' said Stephen. 'Of course not. What's the use, when she's made up her mind to – to finish?'

'You just know it instinctively?' I said.

'We held each other's hand,' said Stephen softly.

I took a longish drink of beer and thought it over.

I said, 'I still haven't got this quite straight. If Marcia is necessary to you and you're necessary to her and she knows it, and you know it, why all this business of sitting holding hands and feeling numb?'

'What d'you mean?' said Stephen.

'Why, if it's such a good show, are you busting it up?'

'Do you really enjoy this sort of thing?' said Stephen.

I said, 'My enjoyment is neither here nor there. I'm asking for information only, just why two people, who apparently don't want to, are indulging in agonized partings. Do *you* enjoy *that* sort of thing?'

'If what you want is an opportunity to be sarcastic,' said Stephen with dignity, 'I'll give it you. We are doing it because Marcia loves you, and you are my friend, and we do not wish to ruin your life.'

'I thought that might be it,' I said.

'What other reason could there be?' said Stephen wearily.

I took another drink and thought some more. 'Just what makes you think that you're likely to ruin my life?' I said. 'Did Marcia say so?'

'Not in so many words.'

'Did she imply it?'

'Naturally. She made it perfectly clear that you felt that it must end. As I say, I quite understood.'

I said, 'Listen, Stephen – stop quite understanding my point of view, there's a good chap. Or else understand it properly. Marcia knows perfectly well that whether you and she part or go on or what not is simply and solely up to the two of you. There's no more question of stopping for my sake than there was of starting it for my sake. I haven't *got* a sake in this matter. And as for ruining my life, it would take more than you two to do that.'

Stephen stared at me for a moment and then shook his head.

'I don't understand,' he said. 'I hear the words but they don't convey anything to me.'

'That's because you're numb,' I said. 'Stop being numb and then it will all be quite simple. But don't let's have any more of this Babes in the Wood stuff with me as wicked uncle. It's funny.'

After a bit Stephen said. 'You have the most extraordinary self-control of anybody I've ever met.'

'That's right,' I said. 'I hide a bleeding heart so skilfully that often I'm not even sure it's bleeding myself.'

'Either that or else you're damnably clever,' said Stephen.

'The possibility that I might just be saying what I think doesn't strike you,' I said.

'I don't know what you think,' said Stephen. 'We don't approach things in the same sort of way.'

'There's positively no deception,' I said, getting a bit tired of it. 'If and when it becomes necessary to my happiness to stop this particular business between you and Marcia I'll tell Marcia so and stop it, without leaving anybody to read between the lines and make noble sacrifices for my sake.'

Stephen said, 'You're very sure of yourself – and of Marcia.'

'Quite,' I said. 'That comes of not realizing how difficult and complicated everything is. Hadn't we better be getting back?'

We drank up, took a couple of quarts of beer and started back. It was just getting dark.

'Curse this bloody black-out!' said Stephen, falling over the curb. 'I nearly dropped one.'

'Life's greatest tragedy,' I said.

Stephen said, 'I think I underestimate your cleverness at times.'

'Maybe,' I said. 'But most of the time you make me so subtle that I get all conceited about it.'

'This, for example,' said Stephen, 'is damned clever of you.'

'Oh, Christ!' I said. 'What is?'

'You are clever enough to realize that if you stopped Marcia from seeing me now it wouldn't pay in the long run.'

I said, 'It doesn't pay now. It costs a hell of a lot of money.'

'God damn you!' said Stephen. 'I wish you wouldn't be so bloody facetious.'

'What you mean is that Marcia couldn't live without you,' I said. 'Maybe you're right. But if it's like that why should she?

I like her to have what she wants, as long as she doesn't make herself sick.'

'I've done what you couldn't do to her,' said Stephen exultantly. 'And you know it. I've woken her up. I've made a woman of her. You're just Pygmalion. You made her, but you couldn't bring her to life.'

'Pipe down,' I said. 'It's nothing to do with the neighbours.'

Peggy and Marcia were pottering about in the kitchen when we got back. Marcia looked at me and raised her eyebrows, but I just put out my tongue at her. Stephen had come all unnumbed and was as cheerful as hell. I was glad he'd got that last bit off his chest. It left him feeling that he'd triumphed, and he was much better company like that. Besides, it had put the thing back on a satisfactorily complicated basis. Stephen always got miserable if anything was simple. As it was he was charming – more charming than I'd known him be since the Marcia affair started. He laughed and his eyes shone and he looked handsome and showed off like a child of fourteen. You'd never have known he'd been all emotionally concussed about half an hour before. During dinner he quoted Langland, 'Urn Burial', Marston, Leopardi, Ronsard, Crashaw (wrongly), Banjo Patterson and Cornelius Whur. He proved that Gerard Hopkins' metrical stuff was by Campion out of the obvious, and claimed to be the only man in England who realized the greatness of Coventry Patmore. This was all more for my benefit than Marcia's. He even asked my opinion once. As a matter of fact it was quite good stuff that he talked. As long as Stephen was being professional and not artistic, he was good. Marcia was obviously a bit puzzled by all this, and I could see she was wondering what on earth had happened in the pub. She didn't say much. I think she was feeling a bit nervous. She always hated it when Stephen showed off to me. Peggy loved it, of course. She kept looking proudly at me to see if I was being suitably impressed, and every now and again she weighed in and prodded Stephen on if he stopped long enough to eat a few fragments of his food. A warning went in the middle of it, and what with the sirens and Stephen declaiming a bit of the 'White Devil', and Marcia looking like that, it was one of the more peculiar parties.

After a while Stephen began to get distinctly tight. He'd only had a couple of pints of beer, but Stephen could get tight on water when he gave his mind to it. He said, 'Seriously now, what do you think of me?'

Like a fool, I said, 'I don't think I've ever really given you much thought. Sorry.'

Stephen was on to it like a knife. He cocked his head on one side and looked at me with a grin. 'Now isn't that odd?' he said. 'Odd and interesting!'

'There are other subjects for thought, you know,' I said, having rather a poor shot at being crushing.

'Oh no,' said Stephen gently. 'You misunderstand me. I didn't mean it was odd that you shouldn't think about me. I meant that it was odd that you should say that so promptly. I ask you a rather difficult question and out comes that silly answer, click. Just like getting a ticket on the underground.'

'The formal lie is an accepted social convention,' I said. 'Meaning I'm not playing.'

'Exactly,' said Stephen. 'The socially conventional reply to any request for the truth.'

'Was that a request for the truth?' I said. 'It sounded like the beginning of a soul-scratching match.'

Stephen shrugged his shoulders. 'You have a passion for using slang as an argument,' he said. 'Shall we say it was a request for something more than a tube ticket?'

He took another drink of beer. 'I'm sorry you never think about me,' he said. 'Because I think about you a lot.'

'I had an idea we were moving towards that,' I said.

'It's quite true,' said Peggy, as though she thought I doubted it. 'He often talks about you.'

I didn't say anything. Stephen grinned at me and said, 'The penny seems to have stuck in the machine that time. The proper answer to that is, "I'm flattered".'

He leaned back in his chair and looked at me for a long time. I just looked back. There was a very distant bump, but otherwise it was very quiet. Marcia fidgeted a bit. I didn't think she was liking this much.

'How far is your life a settled policy and how far is it an accident?' said Stephen suddenly.

'Go on,' I said. 'There's an explanatory footnote to that, isn't there?'

'I mean this superman stuff? This ridiculously exaggerated emotional control?'

56

I said, 'You think everybody who doesn't spend his whole time laughing or crying has exaggerated emotional control.'

'Possibly,' said Stephen. 'Personally I don't believe in emotional control. I am liable to be had up at any time for being drunk in charge of my emotions. I like it like that.'

'You're telling me,' I said. 'But I don't.'

'Sure of that?' said Stephen, cocking his head on one side and grinning.

'Yes,' I said wearily. 'Quite, quite sure.'

'But what are you afraid of?'

'Afraid of?' I said, getting a bit fed up. 'I'm not afraid of anything.'

Stephen said, 'No. But you're most damnably afraid of nothing, aren't you?'

That made me mad, but before I could say anything Marcia chipped in and said. 'What you don't seem to realize, Stephen, is that Bill happens to be a completely grown-up person, while you're not.'

Stephen gave a sort of crow of delight. 'Exactly,' he said. 'Adult. Grownup. Older. The older you are the more control you have. And then finally you're dead and then everything is *completely* controlled.' He pointed to himself. 'Drunk in charge and driving furiously,' he shouted. He pointed at me, 'Under complete control, because stationary.'

Marcia flushed and said, 'You're slightly tight, Stephen.'

I was feeling pretty savage with Marcia for butting in. I said, 'D'you mind stopping protecting me, honey? I can do my own trousers up now that I'm a big boy; honest, I can.'

Marcia looked at me in a hurt sort of way and then looked down and started to crumble a bit of bread.

'Over-orderly,' said Stephen. 'Over-conscientious. A passion for organization and control, expressed rather assertively. You'll find it in all the text-books.'

'Of course,' I said. 'Those of us who aren't on page forty-seven are on page ninety-two. I know.' I like them to burst a bit farther away than that.

'You mustn't take any notice of Stephen,' said Peggy. 'He says the rudest things to people.'

'Oh, he won't take any notice of what *I* say,' said Stephen. 'He knows about himself. Don't you, Bill?'

'Naturally,' I said. 'And I know it's all true. Why, you told me yourself.'

'Click,' said Stephen. He chucked himself back in his chair and roared with laughter.

I let it go at that, but I felt like kicking everybody present, including me. Chiefly me, in fact, for letting him in like that. It wasn't as though I didn't know all Stephen's leads backwards.

After dinner I went out and helped Peggy wash up. I thought maybe Marcia and Stephen wanted to sit on the sofa and be frightened children again.

I said to Peggy, 'Is Stephen doing any work?'

'No,' she said very seriously, 'he isn't, Bill. That's what worries me. If Stephen isn't working, it's always a sign.'

'What of?' I said.

'The thing gathers up,' said Peggy. 'The pressure inside him rises. He gets depressed.'

'Sort of egg-bound,' I said.

'It's the war,' said Peggy. 'How can he speak beauty in a world like this?'

'Oh, I don't know,' I said. 'The trumpet that sings to battle, you know.'

'Ah, I dare say,' said Peggy. 'But Stephen feels atmosphere so strongly.'

I gave up. I've never known quite what to do about Peggy.

'Marcia looks very beautiful tonight,' said Peggy.

'She usually does,' I said.

Peggy said, 'I like to hear you say that.'

'Shall I say it again?'

'No – but, seriously, Bill, it's nice to hear a man admire his wife.'

'Uxoriousness,' I said. 'Horrible word.'

'What does it mean?'

'Love of one's wife,' I said. I was beginning to think that if Marcia and Stephen wanted to do any frightened children stuff they'd better get on with it quick. We weren't going to be long washing up and making the coffee.

When we got home Marcia switched on the light, turned straight round to face me and said, 'Look, Bill—'

'Half a mo',' I said. 'Are you going to make a statement?'

'Yes,' said Marcia.

'Then for Pete's sake let's be comfortable about it,' I said. 'Take your clothes off and put on a dressing-gown or something while I make some tea.'

'Oh, damn tea!' said Marcia. 'I want to say it *now*.'

'Then say it,' I said. 'And see if it sounds all right. Then when I come back you'll have got it right.'

I went out to the kitchen and made the tea.

When I came back Marcia had put on a dressing-gown and was sitting curled up on the floor beside the fire.

I gave her her cup.

Marcia said, 'Bill – why did you do that?'

'What?' I said.

'Go out and make tea then?'

I said, 'In dealing with you and Stephen, one gets tired of always playing away matches.'

'I don't understand,' she said.

'You both like to choose your ground,' I said. 'And the setting and the lighting and how the furniture is arranged.'

'I still don't understand.'

'You'd obviously made up your mind as we walked up the street to make an intense announcement as soon as we got into the place – before you even took your coat off. Whatever you're going to say, it won't be affected by having a dressing-gown on instead of a coat – unless we're just playing charades. I wanted you to have a chance to see whether we *were* playing charades.'

Marcia didn't say anything. I lit a cigarette and said, 'Shoot.'

Marcia said, 'Stephen told me what you'd said to him when you were out.'

'Well?' I said.

'You don't give me much help, do you?'

'Don't I?'

'No. In fact – you made me look rather a fool.'

'That's mutual,' I said. 'You certainly made me look one.'

'How did I?' said Marcia.

I said, 'Well, I've only got Stephen's word for it, which doesn't mean much. But, according to him, you seem to have implied that there must be agonized partings for my sake.'

'Nonsense,' said Marcia. 'I never said anything of the sort.'

'I don't imagine even you'd have quite the nerve to *say* that.

59

But that's what he thought. In fact he was kind enough to say that he saw my point of view.'

'Stephen cheats,' said Marcia wearily.

'Of course he does,' I said. 'Any fool knows that. Stephen is a completely reliable person. He'll always let you down on every issue with absolute consistency.'

'What did you say?'

'I said that I hadn't got a point of view – that the whole thing was completely up to you and you knew it.'

Marcia said, 'I'd just like you to know that I neither said nor implied that you were anything to do with it. I simply said that I'd made up my mind to finish it.'

'Giving what reasons?'

'I didn't give reasons. I just said I thought it was best.'

'After which,' I said, 'I understand that you sat and held hands like frightened children.'

'*What?*' said Marcia.

'According to Stephen. Didn't you?'

Marcia said a bit viciously, 'I can't answer for Stephen. Personally, I've seldom felt less like a frightened child in my life.'

'After which,' I said, 'or maybe before which, I can't remember – you both broke down. Anyhow the whole thing was heart-rending. I was deeply moved.'

'Look here,' said Marcia, getting up, really angry. 'This is just damned unfair, and you know it!'

'My dear girl,' I said. 'I'm simply reproducing the story, word for word, as Stephen told it. *Didn't* you break down?'

Marcia said, 'You probably know just about what happened. Stephen got into a state and cried and said he'd commit suicide and so on.'

'And you?'

'Well, short of being quite unnecessarily beastly I couldn't do anything else but try to – to comfort him. Besides,' she said defiantly, 'I was sorry for him. I dare say I'm a fool but I always am sorry for him when he gets like that.'

'Quite,' I said. 'But as it was quite certain that he'd get like that anyway, why do it?'

'How d'you mean?'

'If you really care a damn whether Stephen cries and threatens to commit suicide or not, why make him do it?

Apart from the laudable desire to give him a good time?'

Marcia said, 'You're trying to make me out as a worse bitch even than I am.'

'Not at all,' I said. 'I'm simply trying to find out what you did it for.'

'I did it,' said Marcia wearily, 'because I thought it was high time the thing stopped. I still do. You say you've no opinion about it. Well I have. I'm not going to muck our marriage up for the sake of Stephen or anybody else.'

'Fine,' I said. 'Then why not tell him so and stop it?'

'I did,' said Marcia.

'Bunkum,' I said. 'You know perfectly well that what you did was to throw an emotional parting scene. I don't mind your trying to kid me, Marcia, but why on earth try to kid yourself?'

Marcia thought for a bit.

'Look here,' I said, 'I'm going to ask you a question, and I think the answer matters quite a lot. Are you in love with Stephen by any chance?'

'Good God, no!' said Marcia, too quickly.

'How sure are you of that?'

'Quite sure. Why?'

'Because you're beginning to act as though you were.'

'How am I?'

I said, 'As long as you're not in love with a person it's reasonably easy to stay sensible about them. But if you *are* in love with them you can't see them any longer, and then there's no knowing what may happen. I wouldn't fall in love with Stephen if I were you. Otherwise you'll start taking him seriously, and that would mean a lovely mess. Stephen's all right as farce, but he'd be poison as drama.'

'Bill,' said Marcia, 'will you be hurt if I'm frank?'

'Do you imagine I shall?'

'I don't know,' said Marcia bluntly. 'But I think I've got to risk it. I've *liked* having Stephen to – to play with.'

'That isn't being frank,' I said. 'That's being platitudinous.'

'I dare say. But it's like this. I'm not in love with Stephen, but I know we ought to stop. I know that whatever you say you hate it. I know I'm taking the most frightful risks with both our lives. And I'm pretty sure that one of these days you'll get fed-up and just throw me out.'

'So what?'

'So I start off quite sensibly deciding I'll finish it, like I did today. And then Stephen gets all fussed and cries and so on and – and I don't know what to do.'

'No,' I said. 'That's just my point.'

Marcia said, 'Damn it – don't you see Bill? You don't cry or say you'll commit suicide. You just stay quite calm and patient. So, like a bitch, I just let you.'

I thought about it.

'Well,' I said, 'that's fair enough.'

'It isn't,' said Marcia. 'It's damned unfair.'

'No,' I said. 'I reckon that my attitude is a better one than Stephen's. I'm not prepared to do that stuff. It seems completely bogus to me, and as I've got to live with myself I can't do it. But if it happens to appeal to you, that's just my bad luck. If you like a lot of third-rate emotional ham-acting, that's something I can't and won't give you.'

Marcia said, 'But I know perfectly well it's bogus. Of course it is. But I like playing with it.'

'All right,' I said. 'Then why worry? As long as you don't think it's genuine, it's all right.'

'But you hate it – and hate me when I do it. Don't you?'

I said, 'No. I find it a bit disappointing and a bit childish, but that's all.'

'Disappointing? You mean you're disappointed with me?'

'Yes. I don't like to think that your life with me's so unsatisfactory that you have to have that stuff. But I can quite see why it is.'

'Then tell me,' said Marcia, 'because I can't.'

I said, 'Well, I'm out all day and buried in work. Even when I'm here I must be pretty dull.'

'Nonsense,' said Marcia. 'The un-dullest person I know.'

I said, 'Why kid ourselves? The only thing is, I wish you'd picked something a bit less cheap and obvious.'

Marcia said, 'I don't think you can call Stephen that.'

'I not only can, I do.'

'Why?'

'Well, damn it,' I said. 'The man's a caricature. He's a perfect specimen of a spoilt child grown up. He's never done a stroke of work in his life. He's got one interest and one interest only – his own precious ego. All he wants a woman for is to help him admire it and play with it.'

I suddenly thought this was all coming a bit too easily and stopped. I had a nasty feeling that while it was all true it wasn't quite all the truth, and that we both knew it. But Marcia was looking stubborn and that made me a bit savage.

I said, 'That doesn't seem to me a reasonable job for you. And even if it were it doesn't seem a reasonable job for my wife.'

Marcia said, 'Look, Bill – would you rather I went?'

'Not unless you've got somewhere else you'd rather be,' I said. 'But I'm not too sure that you haven't.'

'Of course I haven't, ass.'

'I dare say. But it begins to look a bit like it. I know any baby who squalls loud enough can get anything you've got. But you can't take that too far, sweet.'

'No,' said Marcia thoughtfully. 'What you're saying is that I've got to stop. Which is what I'm saying.'

'I'm not telling you,' I said. 'I'm merely advising you. I believe you're beginning to take Stephen seriously. And if you do, then you and I will be talking different languages.'

'Stephen's so damned good at making you feel *helpful*,' said Marcia. 'He's completely shameless about it. He talks as though I were Mary Queen of Heaven and so on, and of course I fall for it.'

'Of course you do,' I said. 'What you don't realize is that whoever's being Stephen's damp shoulder at the moment is Mary Queen of Heaven. There's no patent involved.'

'I think I must be mad,' said Marcia.

'It's the war,' I said. 'Or the weather.'

'Kiss me?' said Marcia.

'Sure,' I said. 'Whatever you say.'

I kissed her.

'Listen,' said Marcia, 'I haven't told you yet what I wanted to say when we came in. I don't know what you'll think about it.' She stopped and thought.

'Well?' I said.

Marcia said. 'When you came back from the pub Stephen was bubbling over. He said you'd said it was all rot and that you didn't care a damn about him and me.'

'A reasonable distortion,' I said.

Marcia said, 'You won't like this bit. He said you'd realized that if we parted I should resent it and that it would muck us up.'

63

'Yes,' I said. 'I thought you'd get that. He thought of that bit coming down the street. He was so pleased that he nearly dropped the beer.'

'That was pure added content?'

'Oh, yes. It wasn't enough that I preferred you to run your own love affairs. Stephen's convinced that there must be something Machiavellian in it somewhere. So he thought that one up.'

'What did you say?'

'I told him not to shout. He was absolutely bawling.'

Marcia said, 'He does bawl when he's excited. Well, of course he came back to me quite sure that that settled the whole thing and that everything would just go on as usual.'

'Yes?'

'I said it didn't make any difference,' said Marcia slowly. 'That I still thought we'd come to the end.'

'Whereupon he wept some more?'

'No, he didn't. He asked why, and I said I hadn't suggested it because of you, but because of me.'

'What a liar you are, darling!' I said. 'Still – it was rather nice of you. So what?'

'Oh, he was frightfully hurt and so on and started to work up a state. But I stuck to it. And then he asked me if I'd do a – a sort of final party with him.'

'Another?' I said. 'I thought tonight was to have been the fond farewell?'

'Yes, but that was before he talked to you.'

'Well, what did you say?'

Marcia said, 'I said I would.'

She looked at me and giggled rather tentatively.

'Oh, Marcia!' I said.

'Well, darling, he was getting into a state and I thought after what you'd said to him you wouldn't be very surprised—'

She stopped suddenly and grabbed my hand.

'Look, Bill – this is the end of it. I swear it is. Honestly, *honestly* I think I'm through. If I can end it like this instead of in a beastly way – I know I ought not to ask you, but if you could just bear this bit—?'

'What exactly is the idea?' I said.

Marcia took a breath, and said, 'He wants me to go down to the cottage with him next weekend and then finish.'

I said, 'All right.'

Marcia said, 'But how about you? You can't stay here by yourself.'

'Why not?'

'Well, who's going to feed you?'

'Christ!' I said. 'I can boil an egg. Or I might go to Ted's.'

'Would you?' said Marcia. 'I'd much rather you did.'

'I dare say,' I said. 'I'll see. Anyhow it doesn't matter.'

Marcia said, 'You're too bloody good to me, Bill.'

'The same thought's often struck me,' I said. 'Think I'd do better with a horsewhip?'

'Yes,' said Marcia. 'Miles better. Bill!'

'Yes?'

'Are you furious about this weekend business? It is the last thing, really.'

'Lord, no!' I said. 'What does it matter – if it's the last thing? Last things never matter. But I'd make sure it *is* the last thing if I were you.'

Actually, I thought she was asking for something you ought not to ask for. It was the first time I'd felt that.

FIVE

MARCIA'S weekend began on Friday morning, and there was a general vague suggestion that it would finish sometime Tuesday. I wondered once or twice what were the chances that Marcia wouldn't come back at all. But I didn't worry much. The longer anybody stayed with Stephen the less likely they were to want to go on staying with him. And I thought the thing had reached the stage where it had to be settled anyhow. I stayed at the flat on Friday night but it wasn't a success. In fact it gave me a large size in humps. I'd decided that, what with work and Marcia and one thing and another, I was getting out of touch with the war. So I got out an atlas and *Whitaker's Almanack* and so on and studied the war. That took about ten minutes. Then I tried forecasting the next bits. The last time Ted and I did that was at the beginning of the year. Ted put down that Germany would invade Switzerland, and that Japan would have a crack at Burma. I said that Germany would attack Hungary and Rumania and that Turkey would join up with us. The next morning Russia invaded Finland. An experience like that takes the heart out of you as a prophet. I shoved down something about a German invasion of Sweden but it wasn't worth anything. There were so damned few places left for her to invade that it was getting too easy. Then I played the piano and then I went to bed. The whole thing was so grim that next morning I rang up Ted and invited myself to stay with him until Marcia showed up again. Ted came quietly.

As usual Lennox suddenly realized at about lunch-time on Saturday that there was a certain amount of work to do. He kept me there until about five, explaining why the Area Unit Scheme wouldn't work. He seemed quite sorry that it wouldn't. He kept on shaking his head and saying, 'It's a great pity, because the idea in principle is excellent.' I decided that with Lennox as keen as all that I could probably get the thing through.

I went back to the flat and collected some pyjamas and then went round to Ted's. Ted had been throwing a sort of enemy aliens' tea-party. There were Hans Schott, a nice old Bavarian doctor who was an old friend of Ted's family; his daughter; a rum little German Jew who'd come with them; and another German bloke with a wizard Viennese wife who'd been brought by Laurie Gardner. The Viennese girl was a pip.

I couldn't do with them much. Old Schott was all right. He was always a dear old soul. But the rest were a bit too creakily cheerful and much too patriotic – the little German Jew particularly. He was the late Lucy Houston and the British Israel World Federation all in one.

It was particularly bad when they listened to the news at six o'clock. They hung on every word in a way I'd never seen English people do. They really minded like hell. When it was announced that we'd shot down twenty German planes I thought they were going to cheer – all except old Schott. He just sat and smoked his pipe and said nothing.

I didn't like it. I could understand their hating Hitler and the Nazis, and wanting us to win the war. After all, if we didn't, God knows what would happen to them. Still, I didn't like them to be so bucked about German planes being shot down in flames. After the news they started to talk about Germany, and that was even worse. It wasn't only Hitler, it was the German race. They were mad. They were hopeless. The little Jew announced that when the war was over there was only one hope for Germany – to send over English governors for every district.

This was a bit too much for me. Maybe these people were refugees and maybe they had had a rotten time. But this stuff was just masochism. They were crawling and they liked it. I could see that Ted and Laurie Gardner were feeling pretty uncomfortable too.

I said patronisingly, 'Oh, no. You mustn't be too hard on your race. After all, you've got a lot of virtues even if you have your limitations.'

They all looked at me. The Viennese girl's husband said, 'The German people have virtues, have they?' in a hard sort of voice.

'Of course,' I said. 'All the small ones. But you must blow them up and try to make them look like the big ones.'

'And you,' said Fraulein Schott. 'What have you got in England?'

I said, 'We have no small virtues at all. We're lazy, complacent, undisciplined and generally deplorable. We only manage to carry on at all because we've got a certain genius for living in the world. It must be very irritating for other people who have to work hard for their effects.'

It was pretty crude, but it worked like a charm. They fell over one another to get at me first. In about ten minutes they were saying 'Germany' in that mystic way and arguing amongst themselves as to whether they'd produced the ten greatest men who ever lived or only the first nine and the eleventh. Even the little Jew explained to me that it was all a mistake about Germany losing the last war. Old Schott just sat and smoked his pipe and smiled to himself.

When they'd gone I said, 'Sorry, Ted. But I just couldn't bear that stuff that they were doing before. It's bloody bad for them and uncomfortable for us.'

'Poor devils!' said Ted. 'They're just like kids. I wondered what the hell you were playing at for a moment.'

Laurie said, 'Everybody says Hitler's done a marvellous job in uniting Germany. Personally I think he's put up a mediocre show in losing so many of them. Any spellbinder worth his salt could collect that lot in ten minutes.'

'Old Schott's different,' said Ted.

'He's old,' I said. 'I don't think you belong to any country in particular when you're old.'

'Oh, surely,' said Laurie. 'More than at any time.'

'No,' I said. 'When you're old you live somewhere. But I don't think you belong to anything as big as a country.'

Ted said, 'They'll all be scared stiff now.'

'Why?' I said.

'Well, they're all worried about being interned. Even old Schott is worried that they'll take him, even though he's been here twenty years. Now they'll think they've shown pro-German sympathies.'

'Oh, God,' I said. 'I never thought of that.'

'It doesn't matter,' said Ted. 'I don't think the Home Office takes much notice of people's views. It just shuts its eyes and grabs.'

'Oh, bunkum!' said Laurie suddenly. 'I'm sick of all this fuss about internment. We're fighting for our lives. Far better intern twenty people like old Schott than leave one Fifth Columnist. Look what happened in Holland. And Norway.'

Ted said, 'I quite agree with you in theory. Only the theory comes unstuck when you know the people personally.'

'Not for me,' said Laurie.

I said, 'Well, Karl there and his wife are friends of yours. Would you intern them?'

'Yes,' said Laurie.

'Oh, not Anna,' said Ted with a grin. 'Intern Karl and leave Anna under Preventive Detention with me.'

I said, 'She's a pip.'

'You saw what happened,' said Laurie, taking no notice. 'They may not like Hitler, but they've all got the German megalomania. They must either crawl or kick, and you never know when they'll stop licking your boots and start kicking you.'

'There's a certain amount in that,' said Ted. 'But there are exceptions. Old Schott, for example. And I doubt if the little Jew is very pro-German.'

'The Jews are pro-Jew,' said Laurie curtly. 'In England or Germany or anywhere else. It's a pity we don't realize it.'

I said, 'Oh God, Laurie – do we have to have a pogrom as well as interning old Schott?' I've got a bad conscience about Jews, and it makes me a bit touchy about them.

Ted said, 'How about some sherry?'

Laurie told me he thought he'd got into the army at last. He'd been trying for months.

I said, 'I envy you in a way.'

'I don't,' said Ted. 'Too damned dull. Particularly now there's no front in Europe.'

'It's a very difficult business,' I said. 'Am I doing more good where I am or am I kidding myself and ought I to go and fire a gun?'

Laurie said, 'It's perfectly clear to me. A war is a thing where you fight.'

'What are you hoping to get into?' said Ted.

'Guards, I hope,' said Laurie.

'Characteristically willing to die as long as it's in good company,' I said.

'I know a lot of fellows,' said Laurie, flushing slightly. Ted said, 'Tonight there is an expedition to the Artists. Coming, Laurie?'

I was a bit surprised about Ted. He was quite cheerful. Laurie shook his head. 'Can't, thanks.' He said to me, 'How's Marcia?'

'Gone and left me,' I said.

'Serve you right,' said Laurie. 'On holiday?'

'For a day or two,' I said. 'I'm grass widowering with Ted.'

'She ought to have gone to the States with Dolly,' said Laurie. He'd sent his wife to America a year ago. Laurie never took an optimistic view of the war.

'It would certainly have saved a lot of trouble,' I said, looking at Ted.

'She'd never have gone,' said Ted, refusing to see it.

'You should have insisted,' said Laurie. 'I wouldn't have my wife in England. Certainly not in London.'

'You take a gloomy view of the prospects, Laurie,' said Ted.

'I do,' said Laurie. 'I sincerely hope I'm wrong.'

'Dolly having a good time?' I said.

'Oh, yes,' said Laurie vaguely.

I suddenly had a vision of Marcia having a good time in the States with me in London. She'd go mad. Then I thought, 'Well, hell, that's funny in the circumstances.'

69

Laurie said, 'I must go.'

After Laurie had gone I said, 'I rather admire Laurie's attitude about this war. At least he knows his own mind.'

'When you've got a mind like that it's fairly easy to know it,' said Ted.

'Still – there's something in the argument that a war is a thing you fight in.'

'Quite. Oh, he's all right. He'll get a commission in the Guards eventually – and be perfectly happy. Judging from his ideas about internment and Jews he's practising for the job now.'

I said, 'Laurie's the perfect Conservative.'

'Yes,' said Ted, 'but he does it on purpose, which makes it worse. He'd make an admirable Fascist if the thing could be put on a gentlemanly basis.'

'I dare say,' I said. 'But at least he's trying to make a contribution. I'm not sure that you and I are.'

Ted shrugged his shoulders.

'Who's coming tonight?' I said.

'Don't quite know,' said Ted. 'The Peters. Anne. Nesta. Phil. Possibly Mike and Susan.'

I said, 'How about the inflationary gap?'

'The inflationary gap won't get much wider,' said Ted. 'This is essentially a cheap do.'

'Listen,' I said. 'You don't have to be nice to me because I invited myself here.'

'Bunk,' said Ted. 'I owe you fourteen meals and about a couple of hundred drinks. I therefore propose to spend half a crown on taking you to the Artists and then to call it square.'

I said, 'Will Jeff be coming with Anne?'

'Good Lord, no!' said Ted. 'Didn't you know? Jeff was shipped off abroad a couple of months ago.'

'Where?'

'Canada,' said Ted, grinning.

'*Canada*? What in God's name have they sent him there for?'

'To defend it against Greenland, I expect,' said Ted. 'Anyhow they told them they were going to Canada and issued them with pith helmets, so just where Jeff is nobody knows.'

'And Anne's living alone?'

'Yes. She still does her job, of course.'

'Bloody for Anne,' I said.

'I don't know,' said Ted. 'She and Jeff were queer. She doesn't seem to mind much.'

Ten of them turned up eventually and there were two cars. I collared Anne to sit on me.

Anne said, 'Where's Marcia, Bill?'

'Gone away for the weekend, the cad,' I said.

'Weekend!' said Anne. 'That's nothing.'

'Heard anything from Jeff?' I said.

'He's in Egypt,' said Anne. 'But I haven't heard from him for weeks, I thought she seemed a bit depressed.

I looked round the party when we got there. Anne and I were the only loose ends. I was pleased as hell, but I wasn't too sure that it was a good thing.

The Artists was much as usual. I used to love it, but I'd been there too much. Besides, Anne was rather getting me and I didn't know quite what to do about it. I always had thought she was damned attractive, but previously Jeff had always been there, and the shot wasn't on the table. Anne cheered up a lot after a couple of drinks. She'd never been to the Artists before. Several times she looked at me as though we were together, which didn't help at all.

It struck me that of course she'd think I was safe but dull. Everybody always thought of Marcia and me as about the only completely satisfactory set-up in the town.

After the show was over we danced. That again didn't help. I don't think Anne noticed. She was just doing her ordinary stuff, and I don't think she thought it meant any more to me than it did to her. She was a bit cutting about Nesta. She was very fond of Ted and never thought his girlfriends were good enough.

'Another of Ted's little blondes,' she said, watching them dance. 'How the hell does he know them apart?'

'I don't suppose he does,' I said. 'They all fulfil the same function anyway.'

'Does this one scrounge things from him?' said Anne.

'I don't think so,' I said. 'She's quite a nice kid. Dumb, of course.'

'I don't mind her being dumb if she's decent to him,' said Anne. 'Most of his women are such bitches. They let him take them out and spend God knows what on them, and what does he get out of it?'

'Oh, come,' I said. 'They're seldom quite the same after.'

'Oh, I know he sleeps with them,' said Anne. 'But if that's all he wants he takes too much trouble to get it.'

'I think he's gone all serious now,' I said. 'He says he's hard-up.'

'Good,' said Anne. 'Perhaps if he is he'll stand a chance of getting someone decent.'

I said, 'Look here, Anne – will you come out to dinner with me on Monday?'

She was very surprised.

'Mutual consolation of the deserted,' I said, a bit weightily.

'All right, Bill,' she said. 'Thank you. I'd love to.'

'Savoy?' I said.

'Certainly not.'

'All right. De Vrie's.'

'If you like.'

I thought of saying, 'Owner's risk,' but I thought if I did she would have to say she wouldn't come.

Then Ted came up and asked her to dance.

Ted took Nesta and a couple of others home. The other car was going out into the wilds, so the rest of us piled into a cab. I thought up a good circular route which left Anne and me with a longish drive by ourselves.

Anne said suddenly, 'How long's Marcia gone for?'

'Only for a few days.'

'Are you having a bloody time?'

I said, 'Moderately. Not as bloody as you must be having.' After a bit I put my arm round her and said, 'Listen – this isn't making passes at you in a taxi.'

Anne said, 'Poor Bill. It's all right – I know just how you feel. Help yourself.'

We huddled up. She was warm and alive. I didn't kiss her or anything. We just went on talking about this and that. It was quite different from when we'd been dancing, and a much better thing.

As we were getting near her place, I said, 'What time on Monday?'

'When you like, as long as it's not before half past seven.'

'Half past seven, then. At the bar in De Vrie's.'

Anne said, 'Why am I coming?'

'That's between you and your conscience,' I said.

'Oh no – I don't mean from my point of view,' said Anne.

'I never refuse a meal as long as there's no obvious catch in it. But why are you asking me?'

'For the same reason that I'm doing this,' I said.

'I see,' said Anne. 'Well, that's all right. You're welcome.'

'You're a nice person, Anne,' I said.

'Bunkum,' she said. 'I like it. Only it's not a game you can play much unless you know people very well.'

The taxi stopped outside her flat. We disentangled ourselves and got out.

Anne said, 'Goodnight then, Bill. Half past seven on Monday.'

'Fine,' I said. 'Working dungarees of course. Goodnight, Anne.'

We shook hands and I took the cab back to Ted's.

We didn't do anything on Sunday. We got up late and just lay around reading things. About teatime Marcia rang up from Penn.

She said, 'Are you all right, Bill?'

'I'm fine,' I said. 'We went out last night and I took Anne home. I've been wanting to take Anne home for years. You must go away again.'

'Was it nice?'

'It was grand. How are you getting on?'

'Oh, quite well. This is a nice place.'

'How's Stephen?'

'Stephen's all right.'

'In a state?'

'No. Quite calm. Look, sweet – I shall be back on Tuesday night.'

'All right,' I said. 'What time?'

'I don't know exactly. Will you go round to Ted's and I'll come round and pick you up? Then I shan't have to worry about time.'

'Right,' I said. 'I'll wait here.'

We rang off. Ted had just gone on reading.

'Can you do with me until Tuesday night?' I said. 'I shall be out tomorrow.'

'Sure,' said Ted. 'It's nice for me, having you. I get fed-up by myself.'

'I can't think why the Pete you don't get married,' I said.

'Nobody to marry,' said Ted. 'All the people I'd like to marry have bloody-well married someone else.'

'Women are thoughtless,' I said.

73

We sat for a bit and then Ted said, 'Look here, it's nothing to do with me, but aren't you being a BF?'

'You mean about Marcia?' I said.

'Yes.'

'Maybe,' I said. 'Do you think I ought to do the heavy?'

'Well, it's pretty silly,' said Ted.

'So what?'

'She doesn't give a hoot for Stephen. She can't.'

'I wouldn't be too sure of that,' I said, 'in view of recent developments.'

Ted said, 'Well, I hardly know the man. But we've all seen dozens like that. He's funny. Marcia must see that.'

'I think she does,' I said. 'But she's very fond of him. She thinks he has a rotten time.'

'Rotten time my foot!'

'Anyhow, if anything happens that he doesn't like he cries and says he'll commit suicide. Marcia's afraid he will.'

'Be a bloody good thing if he did. Shall I tell you something?'

'Tell me anything,' I said.

'Marcia's got a damned sight too soft a heart. That's her trouble. She's about the kindest person God ever invented. Anybody who likes to bawl for it can have what they like.'

I said, 'Yes. But there's a bit more than that in it. Marcia rather wants her bottom smacked about the whole thing.'

'Then smack it.'

'I've thought of that,' I said. 'But to tell you the truth I've always been expecting it to die a natural death.'

'What I dislike,' said Ted rather savagely, 'is that it's all wrong for people like that to get away with it. Apart from whether you mind.'

'Yes.'

'You try to be reasonable,' said Ted. 'And he takes advantage of it.'

I said, 'Well, that's my funeral. I know what to expect.'

'But you're playing a different set of rules. It's like boxing with a man who kicks.'

'Well, that's all right. I prefer to box.'

'But damn it,' said Ted. 'Even if you do, can't you see it's all wrong? If he gets away with this he'll think he can do it again with somebody else. It wants somebody to tell him he's a tick and rub his nose in it.'

74

'That wouldn't get you anywhere. He'd agree with every word you said and weep quarts.'

'But can't Marcia be shown what he is?'

I said, 'She knows what he is and likes it. That's the trouble.'

'I just don't believe that. She's not a fool.'

'She's more than a fool over this. She's just off her head. By the way, this is supposed to be the end of it – this weekend.'

'And will it be?'

'God knows,' I said.

Ted thought for a bit.

'Look here,' he said, 'supposing I went round and took him apart?'

I roared with laughter.

'No, seriously,' said Ted. 'I know you could do it yourself if you wanted to, but it's awkward for you. But I'd like it. It'd be a pleasant public duty.'

I said, 'And in ten minutes Marcia'd be round putting him together again and drying his tears. Be yourself.'

'There is that,' said Ted. 'Then how about running him out of town? Just telling him he was going away and not coming back for quite a while?'

'Listen,' I said. 'If Marcia wants *that*, she can have it. If I can't keep my wife without taking her boyfriends apart or running them out of town, it's high time I stopped having a wife.'

'Oh, I'm not thinking she'll be fool enough to go off with him or anything like that. But why should you have him snooping round messing everything up?'

I said, 'It's nice of you, Ted, but I think I must do this my own way now.'

'I suppose so.'

'If I'd known there was going to be all this flap in the first place I might have just waded in and stopped it good and early. But I told Marcia it was a thing where she must please herself, and I must stick to it. It won't kill anything that was worth keeping alive anyhow.'

'Well, it beats me,' said Ted. 'A bloke like that.'

'Yes, I find that a bit hard. I tend to look myself over and say, "Well, *Christ* . . .!" '

Ted said. 'I suppose that's the point. If he were a bit less awful she'd make comparisons. As it is, she doesn't have to because they'd be funny.'

I grinned and said, 'You're a comforting bloke to talk to.'

'Well, damn it,' said Ted. 'It's obvious.'

'No,' I said, 'it isn't as obvious as all that. Stephen's a louse, but he isn't a common or garden louse. At his best he's a rather attractive queer. I liked him when I first met him. But the point is that he's completely unscrupulous, completely unprincipled and completely unashamed of it. He doesn't even try to play to the rules because he doesn't admit that there are any. Where I went wrong was in thinking that Marcia would mind that. Being a woman, she doesn't. Women don't care a cuss about principles. They only care about people. As a person Stephen can be very attractive. It's only his methods that make you sick. Marcia doesn't compare us. She just compares what I do with what she knows she can expect of me, and what Stephen does with what she knows she can expect of him.'

'Which is unfair,' said Ted.

'Which is quite reasonable, but makes it a bit difficult for me. Apart from anything else, coping with Stephen makes you feel such a blasted prig. If it goes on I shall start talking about things which aren't done, by Gad, sir, and all that.'

Ted said, 'Well, it beats me.'

Anne was a quarter of an hour late.

'Hey,' she said. 'There's an air-raid upstairs.'

'There always is when I come here,' I said. 'You're looking marvellous, Anne.' She was.

We had some drinks.

I said, 'About this air-raid. Bangs and so forth?'

'I didn't hear any.'

'Ah, well,' I said. 'The night is young.'

Tony came up. He said business was still pretty fair.

'If there is no raid they come. If there is a raid they come because it is so safe.'

'There's no real point in bombing the West End at night,' I said. 'Everybody's gone home except people who're sitting about thirty feet down guzzling. I wish to God he'd drop a few more up here and leave the East End alone for a bit.'

'He don't know whether he bombs the West End or the East End,' said Tony. 'He just drops them – Poom!'

'That's right,' I said. 'He just drops them – Poom! Why

76

the hell don't they do the obvious thing and take places like this for shelters?'

'Now – now,' said Tony.

'Oh, I know,' I said. 'It'd spoil your business and my dinner. What a tragedy.'

This was the second time I'd been in De Vrie's during a raid, and I didn't like it. Of course this was back in the days when people went out a hell of a lot.

'What you like?' said Tony. 'Smoked salmon?' I suppose he thought it must be smoked salmon because Marcia always had that.

'What makes you tightest?' I said when the drink question arose.

'Why?' said Anne.

'I'm trying the alcoholic seduction technique. I've never tried it before. When I was a young chap I didn't think it was sporting.'

'It isn't,' said Anne. 'Only Sir Jaspar makes a girl tight.'

'Or Bollinger,' I said. 'That's why Bollinger costs so much. Did you know?'

Anne said she didn't.

'Well, J. C.,' I said. 'You must have thought there was some reason. It couldn't be the taste.'

I said, 'You were very nice to me on Saturday, Anne. I didn't know you were nice.'

'No?'

'No. I thought you were attractive but firm.'

'I am,' said Anne. 'At least I'm firm. When firmness is called for.'

I looked at her. 'As a matter of fact,' I said, 'I felt a bit low about it.'

'Why?'

'I wasn't really feeling as platonic as all that.'

'Well, hell!' said Anne. 'I didn't think you were being a brother to me. There are degrees in these things.'

I caught sight of myself in the mirror opposite. I didn't look too good. My face was red and I was leering rather.

I stopped leering and said, 'I rather gathered that you were playing elephants with the children.'

Anne said, 'I thought you wanted something to hold on to in a cab. I wanted the same thing so there we were.'

77

Jeff might be in Egypt and Marcia in Penn, but I could see it wasn't getting us anywhere much.

I said, 'Look here, I think I shall give you a lot more of this stuff and then seduce you.'

Anne said, 'Oh, God, not at this time of day, Bill!'

'What time of day?'

'We're both too old for that sort of thing.'

'I'm not. You'd be surprised.'

'Anyhow, since when have you taken up that stuff?'

I said, 'I haven't. I told you. I'd never tried the alcoholic seduction technique before.'

'Flattering,' said Anne. 'But we've both got perfectly good husbands and wives and so on.'

I said, 'Yes, but they aren't *here*. Husbands and wives are never any good unless they're about.'

'No, damn them,' said Anne. 'I wish to God they were.'

'So do I,' I said. 'It'd be fun if they came in together now.'

'French farce,' said Anne. 'But nice.'

Anne said, 'You're wretched without Marcia, aren't you?'

'Moderately,' I said.

'Much more than I am without Jeff. Of course we never travelled together like you do. When's she coming back?'

'Tomorrow night.'

'Tomorrow night!' said Anne. 'Well, damn it, it's nearly that now.'

I said, 'And then everything will be all right?'

'Then everything will be fine.'

I said, 'You're casting doubt on my passion for you, which is not the action of a lady.'

Anne said, 'I don't see why you should have to pretend you've got a letch for me when all you want is someone to talk to and an odd hand to hold.'

I said, 'Sorry, Anne. I am a bastard.'

She said, 'No, you're not, you're sweet. I never liked you much before.'

'Oh, God!' I said. 'I never thought of that.'

'What?'

'I suppose you think I'm having a bloody time?'

'Well?'

'I don't think I can possibly have a female around who understands,' I said. 'Not at the moment anyhow. There are personal reasons against it. Anyhow I'm having a damned sight too good a time compared with most people. That's the trouble.'

'Listen,' I said. 'It is now just after nine. Firstly, are you going to be seduced or not?'

'Not,' said Anne.

'Why?'

'Unnecessary and complicated. You don't want to anyway.'

'Passing over that glaring untruth, we can either stay here or go somewhere else or go home and make tea with Ted.'

'Where else?'

'Oh, around and about. Petty's.'

'Full of drunks.'

'Vics?'

'Shut.'

'The Café Regal?'

'Not in an air-raid. They always hit the Café Regal in air-raids.'

'Like the old Alphonse joke. Shoot! Shoot! We *always* bomb the Café Regal.'

Anne said, 'Let's go back to Ted's and make tea.'

We went back. The raid was still on but nothing seemed to be happening. Ted wasn't in the flat and I thought of starting all over again there. But the thing had gone cold now. It had never really been as hot as all that.

I rooted out cups and things and we made tea. Anne sat on the floor and we told one another about our jobs.

About twelve Ted blew in. Ted said, 'Well, look who's here! Have you been out with him?'

'I have,' said Anne. 'I've spent most of the evening fighting like a tigress for my honour.'

'Poor Anne,' said Ted, kissing her. 'Did he disarrange your clothing?'

'No,' said Anne. 'He plied me with drink followed by certain suggestions.'

Ted said, 'So you're not a worse than dead woman? What's that? Not tea?'

I said, 'I don't think this is much of an air-raid.'

Just then the guns started up not far away.

'You shouldn't say things like that,' said Ted. 'It puts them on their mettle. And then they put their metal on us. Ha, ha, funny joke. See darling, mettle and metal.'

'I see,' said Anne.

We drank some more tea. It got quite noisy.

Ted said, 'I think I ought to warn all gents that this dump is liable to fall down if a bomb lands anywhere in the Western Postal area.'

'Let's put the light out and have a look,' I said.

' 'Ware glass,' said Anne.

We put the light out and drew back the curtains. Ted's flat is right up at the top and you can see a long way. There were searchlights and we saw a few tracers go up. Once a flare came down somewhere north.

'Over Highgate, or Hampstead,' I said. 'What on earth are they after up there?'

'Looking for the Navy on Highgate Ponds,' said Ted.

'There doesn't seem to be any fires tonight.'

It quietened after a bit and I took Anne home. I kissed her goodnight in a gentle sort of way. She'd been damned nice.

Just as I got in Marcia rang up to know if I was all right. It had looked exciting from Penn. It always did look exciting from just outside. I suppose it was seeing it end on.

SIX

FRED GILES came in and said, 'Have you heard anything about my being transferred?'

'Transferred?' I said. 'No.'

'You didn't ask for it?'

'No. Why?'

'Well, Pearce asked me to go down and see him this morning and talked about transferring me to Statistics. He hadn't said anything to you?'

'He has not. It's like his infernal impudence.'

'I was a bit surprised.'

I said, 'Would it mean promotion?'

'I don't think so.'

'Well then, what the hell is Pearce playing at? He knows we're short of staff here. You know this job backwards and you're not a statistician. And, anyhow, why didn't he speak to me?'

'Search me,' said Fred.

'Do you *want* a transfer?'

'No. I'd rather stay here.'

'Yes,' I said. 'And I bet Statistics don't really want a man and probably don't know what to do with the ones they've got. Then we should have the perfect circumstances for a transfer. I want you, statistics don't, and you don't want to go.'

I picked up the telephone to ring Pearce. Then I put it down again, and said, 'No – I'll go and see him.'

I went down to Pearce's office and said, 'What the hell's this about Giles?'

Pearce put his glasses on straight and registered soothingness, and said, 'Oh, he told you about our chat?'

'He did,' I said. 'It would have been better manners if you'd told me yourself.'

'I didn't want to bother you. It may never come off. I only wanted to sound Giles.'

I said, 'It damn' well *won't* come off. I'm short-staffed. Giles is the only reliable man I've got. He knows the job backwards. He isn't a statistician. And he doesn't want to go. I'd be glad if you'd make a note of those simple facts and then forget the whole thing.'

Pearce bridled a bit. 'Oh, I quite realize all that,' he said. 'But you must remember that Establishments has to see the *whole future* of staff needs – not just what one department wants.'

'And do you think it'll help your staff problems to transfer Giles from a job which he knows to one he doesn't know the first thing about?'

Pearce said, 'He'd pick it up.'

'And how about me? I should get another novice and *he'd* pick it up, too?'

'Precisely,' said Pearce, pleased that I understood.

'Look here,' I said. 'Am I mad or are you?'

'I don't understand,' said Pearce.

'Well, good God, man, why have two people learning their jobs when you need only have one? Why not give Stats. a new man and leave Giles where he is?'

'That might be possible,' said Pearce. 'Nothing's decided, of course.'

I said, 'It is. Believe me. Giles is staying where he is.'

'Of course if you take that line it's no good talking to me,' said Pearce huffily. 'You must talk to Lymes. I'm only following my instructions.'

'All right,' I said. 'I'll talk to Lymes. Is he in?'

'No. He's in Scotland. Of course we don't accept this idea that a man can only do one job, you know. People soon pick things up.'

'Listen, Pearce,' I said. 'If you people don't forget that expression soon you're going to lose us the war.'

'Oh come,' he said with a silly grin.

'It's not funny,' I said. 'It's true. Maybe in peace-time it doesn't matter much whether people know their jobs or not. A child in arms could pick up most peace-time Civil Service jobs in a fortnight. But there's a war on and there's real work to do.'

'Well?' he said.

'This idea that anybody can do anything means that about half the Ministry is always just "picking things up . . ." instead of knowing its job. Take Potter. He's had five different jobs since I've been here. Which means he's never been the slightest use at any of them. How could he be?'

'It isn't like business,' said Pearce a bit feebly.

'You never said a truer word,' I said. 'It isn't like anything except a wall-eyed mess.'

'Well, anyhow,' said Pearce, 'you are strongly opposed to Giles being transferred?'

'You've got it,' I said.

He put that down in a little notebook.

'All right,' said Pearce in a long-suffering sort of way. 'I'll put that to Lymes.'

I said, 'While you're about it, you might tell Lymes that if Giles *is* transferred without consulting me, I shall take the thing as high as it will go. To the Minister if necessary.'

'Oh, I don't think that will arise,' said Pearce. 'I think we shall be able to arrange it.'

I went back to my office and got on with it. Doris had her hair done behind her ears.

I said, 'There you are – it looks fine.'

Doris blushed and said, 'It feels queer.'

'Have to wash your ears now,' I said. She had nice ears. Girls nearly always have.

We had a straight run at it for nearly an hour and a half. The telephone only rang twice. I did over thirty letters – some of them pretty tough. It's amazing how much stuff you can carry in your head when you're at it all the time.

I threw Doris out at twelve-thirty. There was plenty more for her to do, but I knew she had as much as she would get through, so I went on to files. There was one very nice one with about six 'Urgent' tabs on it. Somebody at the Cabinet Committee had put in the world's damned silliest paper asking a lot of questions about the Ministry's work. They were the sort of questions which could either be answered in about six lines for the lot or else needed a sizeable book. The Private Office had solemnly taken each question and sent it to the appropriate department for answer. The file had already been wandering about the place for about a month. I read the other answers. There were nine of them and only Lawrence's bit meant anything. I decided that the thing needed pepping up so I began. 'The function of this department must be carefully distinguished for anything which it has accomplished or is ever likely to accomplish under present circumstances . . .' I knew that if anybody in the Private Office ever read the thing they would cut it out. If they didn't read it nobody else would, so it wouldn't matter.

Just when I was thinking about lunch, Jacques came in. I said, 'What ho, Jacques!'

He said, 'Hallo,' in a solemn way and sat down. I could see there was something up.

'What's the trouble?' I said.

Jacques said, 'Do you mind if I ask you some questions before I tell you?'

'No,' I said. 'Fire away.' I wondered what the hell was coming. 'How many people are there in your typing pool?' he said. 'Sixteen.'

'*Sixteen?* Not fifteen?'

'I think it's sixteen, but I can't be sure. Somebody may have gone. Shall I get Giles in and make sure?'

'No. It doesn't matter. All girls, of course?'

'Yes.'

'Anybody else here type?'

'My secretary. Miss Hilder.'

'What typewriter does she use?'

'A Royal.'

'A Royal? I didn't think we had any?'

'We don't. It's mine. I brought it when I came. They were such a hell of a time getting Miss Hilder anything to work on that I pinched one from the firm.'

'Your other people use Smiths?'

'I think so.'

He stopped for a bit and looked at some notes.

'What is all this about?' I said. Jacques hesitated and then chucked across a couple of sheets of foolscap.

'Does this mean anything to you?' he said.

I looked at it.

'I mean, was it done in your office? Or might it have been?' he said.

It was a queer sort of document. It gave a sort of lay-out of the place. Starting off 'Ground floor Room 1. Messengers. Room 2. J. R. Cartwright in charge of Cables. Room 3 Cable Room. Here. Nothing else of interest to us. First floor Movement Statistics particularly 24, 26, 27, 28 but all except 30 – 46 which are of no interest' – and so on right through the place.

I said, 'It's not mine. Tried Establishments? It looks as though it might be theirs. Particularly as half of it is wrong.'

Jacques said, 'No. It isn't theirs. In fact it isn't anybody's. That's the point.'

'I don't see quite what it was intended for,' I said. 'One ought to be able to get it from what does and doesn't interest the bloke who did it.'

'Well,' said Jacques slowly, 'that document was picked up in a restaurant in Soho. It doesn't belong to any department here. Now look again at what *does* interest him.'

I looked. Cables. Shipping. Target Plan. Statistics. Private Office. I looked at Jacques and said, 'My God, that's remarkably fishy.'

'It's a damned sight more than that,' said Jacques.

'But why has he got so much of it wrong?'

'Because it was done two months ago. It was right then –

except for one or two details. We've been working on it ever since.'

'And it doesn't belong to anybody here?'

'As far as we can make out nobody's ever seen it before.'

I looked at it again. 'I certainly haven't,' I said. 'And I don't think it could have been done in the department. The interests are all wrong. We're not interested in cables. Or shipping.'

Jacques said, 'It won't have been done *for* your office. But it might have been done *in* it.'

I was a bit startled. 'Well, yes. Or anywhere else for that matter.'

'No,' said Jacques. 'Here or Lawrence's.'

'How d'you know that?'

'Typewriters,' said Jacques. 'The experts say that was done on a re-built Smith. You and Lawrence are the only people with re-built Smiths.'

'Are we, by God?'

'Yes.'

'Sure it was done in the Ministry at all?'

'No. But it's Stationery Office paper.'

I thought a bit.

I said, 'This is cheerful.'

'We're trying to get the actual machine,' said Jacques. 'That's why we had those samples done on every machine in the place last week.'

'I thought that was just one of Establishment's good ideas,' I said.

Jacques grinned. 'That's what you were supposed to think.'

I said, 'Well, what now?'

'I'm checking up on your typists and Lawrence's.'

'Sure it was a typist? After all, I type.'

'It's professional work,' said Jacques.

I said, 'I should think that lets most of my people out. They type like Oxen.'

'I don't suppose you know anything about them personally?'

'Hardly a thing. Giles will.'

'I'll talk to him.'

'Will you tell him the point?'

'No,' said Jacques. 'This is dead confidential, of course.'

After lunch Lennox rang up and I went along to him.

He said, 'About this Area Scheme of yours. I've talked to the Secretary about it and he's rather impressed.'

'I didn't know the Secretary was ever impressed,' I said. I was very bucked.

Lennox smiled. 'He wants a short summary of the scheme on paper. You showed me one. Have you got a copy?'

'Yes. I'll get one down.'

I rang up Doris and she brought it down.

'It's pretty rough,' I said. 'I've got it a good deal further than that really.'

'This will do,' said Lennox. 'We don't want to give him too much detail. I suppose we'd better have a file made and do it in form. The Secretary hates bits of paper.'

'What's he going to do with it?' I said.

'I don't know. He just wants to see it on paper.' He pushed it over to me. 'You'd better sign it.'

'Shouldn't you?' I said a bit stiffly, 'as coming from the Department?'

'Oh, no,' said Lennox in his vague way. 'You wrote it. You sign it and I'll add my comments.'

I signed it. Lennox squiggled underneath, 'I foresee difficulties but the scheme is right in principle. J. L.' I didn't know whether he was covering himself in case the Secretary decided it was a lousy idea, or whether he was just being rather nice.

'By the way,' I said, 'Establishments think it would be a nice idea to transfer Giles.'

'Giles?' said Lennox. 'Why?'

'Presumably because he knows his present job and is doing it well.'

'Can you spare him?' said Lennox.

'Of course not.'

'Have you told them so?'

I said, 'I've told them quite a lot.'

Lennox said hurriedly, 'Well, look here, don't you quarrel with them, Sarratt. It doesn't do any good. I'll speak to Lymes.'

'Thank you,' I said.

'Who have you spoken to?' he said, still anxious.

'Only Pearce.'

'That's all right. I'll speak to Lymes.'

'They *are* a bunch of incompetents,' I said.

'Yes,' said Lennox. 'It's a frightfully difficult job, of course. You don't want to quarrel with them, you know. They're very powerful.'

'They're a public menace,' I said.

'Yes. Still – you must cultivate a philosophical attitude you know,' said Lennox, taking off his glasses and smiling. 'Philosophy. That's what you need.'

'What I need is staff,' I said.

Lennox picked up the memorandum. 'I think we might quite possibly get this through,' he said. 'The Secretary seemed quite oncoming.'

I didn't say anything.

'Have you left him something that he can disagree with?' said Lennox. 'You always want to do that. Something obvious that he can cross out? He'll like it much better then.'

'I don't think so,' I said.

'Pity,' said Lennox. 'You should always remember to do that.'

I said, 'I sometimes wonder if this is a war or a nursery romp.'

Lennox smiled. Usually that would have rattled him but he just said, 'You mustn't expect so much, Sarratt. These people are only human, and it pays to handle them carefully. It's much quicker in the end.'

'Yes,' I said. 'But it means that this place has an efficiency of about 5 per cent. That's the bit that's helping to win the war. The other 95 per cent goes on internal politics.'

Lennox said, 'Ah well – we must make the best of the material we've got. It's no good just saying that it ought to be better.'

Just after I got back to the office Jacques came in again.

'Well?' I said. 'Any luck?'

'Not much. One rather good bit. One of your girls' typewriters was out of action when those slips had to be done, so she did it on another machine. That means we had no sample from hers.'

'Who was that?'

'Miss Orchard.'

'Little Lilly? If she's a bit of the Hidden Hand, God help them. She's a nice kid but terribly dumb.'

'I don't think that means anything,' said Jacques. 'Though of course we've got to try everybody, however improbable.'

'Of course,' I said. 'Now what?'

Jacques shrugged. 'Wait to see if they can identify the machine from the samples, I suppose. It'll take some time.'

I didn't get back to Ted's until half past eight. We had food and I collected my pyjamas and waited for Marcia.

About ten she rang up and said, 'Listen, Bill – do you mind if I go straight to the flat instead of coming round?'

'As you like,' I said.

'Because I may be late. Don't wait up for me.'

I said, 'Look here – are you coming back tonight at all?'

'Yes. But I'm not sure what time.'

'All right,' I said.

I was a bit mad over it. Not that I minded but it made me look a fool with Ted.

It was about half past eleven when I left Ted's. It was a dirty night, raining and very dark, but there were no cabs, so I walked. It's only a few hundred yards anyhow. As I turned in to the flats I saw the outline of somebody, turning and walking away. He'd been standing still before. It was a tall cove.

Marcia was in. She said, 'Hallo, sweet!'

I said, 'Hallo. Look – I think the boyfriend is outside on the doorstep.'

'Oh, God!' said Marcia wearily.

'I think it was,' I said.

'What was he doing?'

'Lord knows. Standing in mute adoration, I think. It's a poorish night for that sort of thing.'

Marcia looked a bit distracted.

'Is it still raining?' she said.

'It certainly is.'

'Well, I can't have this. He must go away.'

'Oh, let him alone. Maybe if we give him time he'll do a breakdown on the guitar and sing "O Sole Mio".'

'But he'll get pneumonia.'

I said,'Well, that's all right. How about some tea?'

'Nice,' said Marcia vaguely.

'All right,' I said. 'I'll make it. You stay by the fire.'

I went out and put on a kettle. Just as I was making the tea,

Marcia came in looking like Lady Macbeth and said, 'Look, Bill, I'm sorry, but I must go down and send Stephen away. I can't have him playing the fool like this.'

I said, 'All right. But put a jerk in it, darling. After all you've had since last Friday to get the hook out of his mouth.'

I went back and drank some tea. In about five minutes Marcia came back looking worried to death.

She said, 'Bill, for God's sake what am I to do? He won't go and he's in an awful state. Crying and shaking and so on. And it's raining hard.'

'Well, if he won't go away bring him in,' I said. I was fed up. 'Tell him that if he stays and cries on our doorstep it'll give the place a bad name.'

'I tried to get him to come in. But he's afraid of meeting you.'

'If he goes on playing the fool like this he'll have reason. Well, look here, Marcia, I'm not going out again even to save Stephen from pneumonia. Either Stephen can come in with me here or he can bloody well have pneumonia.'

Marcia looked as worried as hell and cried a bit.

I patted her and said, 'Listen – here you are. I'm going to bed. Bring Stephen in and park him in the spare room. Then he'll be dry and he won't have to see me.'

She grabbed hold of me and hung on uncomfortably tight. I kissed her quite a lot and then pried her loose and said, 'All right. Push along and get him.'

I went to bed. Marcia turned up about twenty minutes later and said everything was all right. I was nearly asleep by then.

I don't know what made me wake. Usually Marcia can crash round all over the place without waking me. Anyhow this time I even felt her slide out of bed.

I didn't say anything. There wasn't much to say.

She went to the door, opened it quietly and stood listening. Then she jumped rather and said in a whisper, 'Stephen! – Stephen, where are you going?'

I didn't hear any reply. Marcia went out and there were faint mutterings. Then there was a bump as the front door shut, and Marcia came tearing back into the bedroom and started to rustle about with her clothes.

I said, 'What the hell are you doing?'

Marcia said, 'It's all right, darling. You go to sleep.' Then she went tearing out and I heard the front door shut after her.

I switched the light on and looked at my watch. It was just half past three. It seemed to me that the thing wasn't as over as it ought to have been. But I was very sleepy, so I switched the light out and went to sleep again.

I didn't wake up again until just before eight. Marcia was back. I could hear her crashing about getting the breakfast.

I went down and had a bath. While I was in it she came in and said, 'Hallo, sweet.'

She looked damned tired. I said, 'Hallo. Back then?'

'Oh Lord, yes,' she said. 'I've been back hours. Didn't you hear me come in?' She was trying to act as though she thought it was funny.

I said, 'No. I just slept.'

Marcia fiddled about with my razor in a vague sort of way. I said, 'Don't muck that blade up. What happened anyhow?'

She sat down on the bathroom stool and said, 'I'm awfully sorry, Bill. Really I am. But I didn't know what the hell to do.'

'What happened?' I said.

'Well, I had an awful job to get him to come in, for a start. He was just hysterical. I got him to bed at last. I should have given him some dope but of course I couldn't find any.'

'Plenty of veramon in the cupboard.'

'No, there isn't. It's gone. At least, I couldn't find it. Anyhow it was pretty obvious that he wasn't going to sleep, so I kept an ear out for him.'

I said, 'ie, you didn't go to sleep.'

'Oh, I slept a bit, Then I heard him moving about, so I went to the door and listened. As I stood there he came out.'

I said, 'I was more or less awake for this bit.'

'Were you? I didn't know. You spoke when I came back but I thought you'd just woken up. You heard what happened then?'

'No.'

'Well, I asked him where he was going and he wouldn't say. He looked absolutely awful. I tried to stop him but he tore himself away and went rushing out.'

'Whereupon you went rushing out after him?'

Marcia said, 'I was scared of what he'd do. He was absolutely off his head.'

90

'Well?'

'I caught him up at the end of the street.'

'Marvellous how slowly these hysterical people can rush,' I said.

'He kept on babbling about killing himself,' Marcia giggled slightly. 'It was really rather funny. Every time any sort of car came along he'd do a sort of swerve towards it. I had to keep grabbing him.'

'Why?' I said. 'I should have thought you'd have had to let him go out of pure curiosity.'

'It wasn't so much that I thought he'd throw himself under one. But I was afraid one would get him by accident. Anyhow we went miles. Then he said he'd go to his flat.'

'Which he did?' I said, getting out and starting to dry.

'Which he did. I wanted to get a cab but he wouldn't. Neither of us had a bean anyhow. So we walked. It must be about three miles.'

'Quite that,' I said.

'Anyhow we got there eventually. He'd quietened down by then. I think he was tired out. Anyhow he went in like a lamb. I saw him into the house, gave him ten minutes, and then as he didn't come out I came home.'

'Walking,' I said.

'Oh, I didn't mind. It was a relief to have him off my hands. I quite enjoyed the walk back.'

I said, 'Well, I'm glad somebody enjoyed something.'

Marcia said, 'I suppose it's no good just saying I'm sorry, Bill.'

'It is not,' I said. 'I shall be ready for breakfast in exactly ten minutes.'

We had breakfast in silence. When I was smoking a cigarette afterwards, Marcia said, 'I gather that you're livid with me about this?'

'It'd be a bit odd if I wasn't, wouldn't it?' I said.

'I suppose so. But I didn't see what the hell to do.'

I said, 'The idea was that the last weekend was the finish of the whole thing. It doesn't seem as finished as all that.'

'But what *could* I do?'

'You could have made it perfectly clear that you were through, and that if he chose to hang about outside playing the fool he could.'

Marcia said, 'But he's so hopeless. I was afraid he really would go and put his head in a gas oven or something.'

I said, 'Well, let him if he wants to. It's nothing to do with you.'

'But I don't want him to.'

I said, 'Then why on earth kid yourself and me that you want to finish the thing?'

'Oh, bunk!' said Marcia. 'It's two different things. You know that quite well.'

'What is?'

'Well, I'd do quite a lot to stop anybody I knew from putting their head in a gas oven.'

I said, 'Listen, you bloody little fool. There isn't a hope that that cove will put his head in a gas oven. Can't you see that all this stuff is simply emotional blackmail?'

'Up to a point,' said Marcia.

'Well, what else is it?'

'He might do it. People do.'

'Not people like Stephen. If you'd just done nothing about it last night, he'd simply have gone away – registering that it was time he had a new woman who hadn't seen the joke.'

'Possibly,' said Marcia. She was looking stubborn and that always makes me savage.

'I'm glad you think it's possible,' I said. 'Unfortunately you don't want it to happen.'

'What d'you mean, Bill?'

'It's perfectly obvious that you're getting a hell of a kick out of the whole thing.'

'I may be,' she said, looking more stubborn than ever. 'It didn't feel much like that last night.'

I held on pretty tight and said gently, 'Look, Marcia – as I've told you before, there's only one way to finish this – that is finally, firmly, and if necessary, toughly. You can't do a clean sensible quiet finish with a bloke like that. He'll always play the thing for tragedy to the end.'

'But there are some things I can't do.'

'Such as?'

'Leaving him out there like that.'

I said, 'That's up to you. If Stephen crying is more important to you than anything else, you'd better push off with him. Then you'll be able to spend all your time drying his tears and won't have to pretend you want to be with me.'

Marcia said, 'That's unfair and you know it.'

'Unfair?' I said, really rattled. 'What the bloody hell are you talking about? Do you think what you're doing is fair to me? Whatever I give you, you always want a bit more.'

'How do I?'

'First you say you'll stop. Then you say you want a last farewell. I say all right. You say you'll pick me up at Ted's. Then you ring up and make me look a bloody fool by saying you're not coming. Then you come back and spend the evening persuading Stephen to come and sleep here for your sake. You push off and spend the night running after him all over London. Then when I tell you you might as well wash me out and go off with him you have the bloody impudence to say it's "unfair". My God, what d'you expect me to say?'

Marcia said, 'You're quite right, of course. I haven't a leg to stand on. I quite see that. But—'

'Well?' I said.

'It would have been more helpful if you'd said all this before,' she said very coldly.

I looked at her for a moment. I said, 'Right. That's good enough for me.'

I got up and threw my cigarette away, and went out to get my hat.

Marcia said, 'Bill—'

I didn't take any notice. As I was putting my coat on she came running out. She stopped short in front of me and said, 'Bill!' again. I looked at her. She was standing on the stair above me, looking at me with her eyes very wide open and her tragic expression on. I hated her face, and I swung my arm round and slapped it hard. It made a noise like a whip cracking. Marcia gave a sort of whimper and sat down on the stairs. I knew there was a God then and I said, 'Oh, God forgive me,' and went down on my knees and grabbed her. My hat fell off and rolled down the stairs. I hung on to her as hard as I could and kept saying, 'Honey, honey.' She was sobbing. She said, 'I'm sorry, Bill. I'm so sorry.'

I said, 'Oh Christ, darling.' I hid my head on her. Marcia stopped sobbing, and started to giggle rather.

She said, 'It's all right, silly. Come up. It's all right.' After a bit I sat up. We looked at one another. She had bright red finger marks all across her cheek. Her eyeblack had run where she'd been crying. She giggled.

I grinned at her and said, 'What in God's name did that? Darling, I slapped your face.'

Marcia said, 'Of course you did. And quite right, too. Bill, I'm a bitch.'

'Oh, God,' I said. 'It's all red.' I kissed it. It was burning hot.

'I shouldn't think you'll ever forgive me for that,' she said.

'For what?'

'Making you do that. Bill – do try to.'

'Don't be an ass,' I said. 'I must be going off my head. It was a hell of a clout too.'

'It was,' said Marcia, feeling it.

'What the hell are we coming to?' I said. 'We must be catching it from Stephen.' I was feeling limp. 'It was your face.'

'What was?'

'I just saw it and hit it. Oh, God!' I grabbed her and started kissing her hair.

Marcia said, 'Were you going? For good, I mean?'

I said, 'I don't know, I think so.'

'Don't,' she said. 'I will try, Bill. You won't go, will you?'

I said, 'I don't suppose so. But anyhow I must go to the office now. It's damned late.' It was well after nine.

SEVEN

THERE WERE a lot of air-raids going on all the time now. The daylight ones never amounted to anything much but it was getting monotonous at night. We used to stay in bed. It was as safe as anywhere else in the house.

Then one day they popped one down a bit closer than usual and the windows went. I was feeling pretty low at the time and it fed me up. I said to Marcia, 'Listen – why do we stay in this dump? I know all about the mathematical chances against being hit, but I'm beginning to have an urge towards something big made of steel and concrete to sleep in.'

Marcia said, 'We could go to a pub.'

'Well, why not?'

Marcia said, 'All right. I'd rather like to. This place is beginning to get me down.'

'And me.'

'Too many rather bloody things have happened here lately. Besides, we only want one room and a bathroom really.'

'Where shall we go?' I said.

'The Palace,' said Marcia. 'If we can afford it.'

I said, 'We can't really afford to live here anyway, so it doesn't make much difference.'

We couldn't get the windows mended. Anyhow they'd probably just have been broken again. So we just bunged them up with cardboard and Marcia went out and took us a room at the Palace. It was up on the fifth floor, but there were nine floors altogether, and it didn't seem likely that the place would fall down unless something big actually hit it.

I got back from the office rather earlier than usual that evening. Marcia said, 'Let's wander about for a bit. I want to see what's happened in Bond Street. Somebody told me it's an awful mess.'

We walked along Piccadilly. It was just getting dusk. I said, 'We've got about twenty minutes before the curtain goes up, if they're on time this evening.'

We looked at Bond Street. It was a bit messy here and there, but chiefly because places had been burnt out by incendiaries and their shells were still standing. There were hardly any that were just heaps. It wasn't so funny behind though.

I got a bit tired of it and said, 'Look – one joint that has been hit by a bomb is very like any other joint that's been hit by a bomb. It's just about time for Jerry to arrive.'

As we were walking back the sirens started.

'There you are,' I said. 'Dead on time.' The guns had opened up while the sirens were still going. Marcia said, 'Don't let's go in for a minute. I want to see.'

It was still some way down away east. We walked up to the Circus and stood on the pavement outside Swan and Edgar's for a minute or two, watching flashes. Then suddenly a sort of Day of Judgement started up all round. From the tracer and the flashes they were firing at something exactly over our heads. I said:

'Come on – I'm damned if I'm going to be written off by a nosecap through just goofing about.'

We dived into the Piccadilly and ordered some drinks. We stayed on the ground floor. Of course as soon as we went in it quietened down. Air-raids are like that.

There was a pathetic youth sitting a few yards away from us. He was with three hearty blokes, one in naval uniform. His face was the colour of ivory and he was shaking all over. The other three were taking no notice. Marcia said, 'Something ought to be done about that, Bill. The kid's going to faint or something.'

I said, 'He's all right.' I was half afraid Marcia'd wade in and start stroking him or giving him a bun.

'It must be bloody awful to have it take you like that,' I said. 'Maybe it's the first time he's heard the row.'

It went dead quiet for about a quarter of an hour. We had another drink and I think I was telling Marcia something about the job when without warning or guns there were two terrific wallops that shook the whole place. A woman gave a sort of yip and jumped up looking scared to death. We waited for a second or two in case it was a stick of three but nothing happened. Waiting for the third is always a bit nasty.

Marcia said, 'I like them farther away than that.'

'I think those were biggish ones some way away,' I said. 'If they'd been very close they would have been louder.' I told her about the one in Earl's Court that I thought had hit Park Lane. As a matter of fact I was quite wrong about these. They were only up in Burlington Street. I suppose the buildings smothered the noise.

Of course the guns were yelling their heads off again now. We decided to go downstairs and have dinner in the grill.

The grill room at the Piccadilly is two floors underground, and you had to strain your ears to hear anything of the guns. When the band was playing you wouldn't have known anything was happening.

We had quite a good dinner, but we were a bit short of things to talk about. We'd agreed to give Stephen a rest. We only got cross if we talked about him anyhow. We tried talking about the job and about the war situation, but there wasn't a lot to say about either of them beyond the fact that they were pretty bloody. Marcia said she was going job hunting the next day.

We sat there until about nine o'clock. I could see Marcia was getting restless, but I kept her there as long as I could, though I hated it myself. Everyone was saying that it was distinctly rough outside. They were more interested in the West End than usual.

Marcia said, 'I'm fed up with this. Let's go up and see how the war's getting on.'

I thought it was a fool thing to do but we had to do something. Quite a lot of people were settling down for the night there. One middle-aged chap had been sitting in front of a glass of lager when we went into the grill about half past seven, and he was still sitting in front of a half-glass of lager when we came out. As we went up the stairs Marcia said, 'What we ought to do is to go down east where you can't just go thirty feet underground and have dinner.'

When we got up to the door leading on the street I pushed it open, like a fool, and let Marcia go first. I never did that again. She went through and I followed. As we stood for a second under the glass canopy there was a hell of a whistling noise. Marcia said, 'Listen!' and I yelled 'Drop!' and we flopped down in a heap. There was a flash and a mild sort of crack about thirty yards down Piccadilly, right in the gutter.

It was a small incendiary. It started to burn in a discouraged sort of way, but about six blokes in tin hats pounced on it more or less as it hit the ground. They had it out with sand in about ten seconds.

We got up. I said, 'There you are. The war's still on.'

'It made a hell of a whistle for such a little one,' said Marcia.

I said, 'Just as well it wasn't an HE or we should probably have had most of the Piccadilly on top of us.'

We walked round into the Circus. Everything was in full blast – especially across the river.

I said, 'Look, Marcia, I'm sorry but I think we're being rather bloody fools. We haven't even got tin hats and there are a hell of a lot of splinters about.'

'I suppose we are,' she said a bit regretfully.

'I wouldn't mind if we were *doing* anything. But if we do stop one gaping about somebody'll have to come messing about in this to collect us, which is plumb stupid.'

Marcia said, 'All right. I suppose we'd better go back to the Palace. I just want to go to the all-night Boots first.'

We went across to the all-night Boots. I forget what it was she wanted but it wasn't anything to be walking about in that for. There wasn't a soul in the Circus, or any traffic. You could walk straight across.

When we got over to the other side we found three chaps standing under the arch in front of the bank watching the searchlights and the flashes. Marcia said, 'Let's stay here and watch. We've got this overhead.'

'That'll be a hell of a lot of good if they pop one down anywhere within a couple of hundred yards,' I said. But still it would keep splinters off, and it was splinters I was chiefly afraid of. Bombs were an act of God.

We stayed there for a bit and watched the searchlights pick up a plane down to the south. Judging from the way they moved he was flying straight towards the Circus. After a minute or two he was getting about right to let us have it and I said, 'Keep your ears open now.' But nothing happened. He went straight over. We could hear the broken 'Brr – Brr – Brr – Brr' of his engines quite clearly. Nobody seemed to be firing at him, and he wasn't dropping anything. It was a very friendly do altogether.

Nothing much more happened for a while except a few rather distant bangs. We got rather cold, and went back to the Palace and had a drink. I said, 'You know you and I have an entirely different approach to air-raids.'

'I just want to see what's happening,' said Marcia. 'What's yours?'

'Well, they don't scare me much – not half as much as I expected. But I don't see any point in being out unless you're *doing* something. I must get something to do at night. I can't stick this bloody useless feeling.'

'I'm childish, of course,' said Marcia. 'Afraid of missing something.'

I said, 'You won't if you're not careful. If that incendiary had been an HE we should have looked damn' silly.'

'We shouldn't have looked anything, honey. It was a feeble little bomb, wasn't it?'

'It didn't get much of a chance,' I said.

'No. I felt quite sorry for it in a way.'

The Palace was a pretty distressing joint and downstairs it was crawling with people in dressing-gowns carrying rugs and pillows. Marcia said, 'God forgive me, I do hate the human race when it's doing this sort of thing. Could you bear to come out again and have one more drink somewhere else before we go to bed?'

'All right,' I said. 'We'll pop into the Café Regal. By the law of averages they can't hit it again for a bit.'

I went out first this time, but everything had gone as quiet as the grave. We went along to the Café Regal and drank lager. The front of the place looked a bit battered but inside it hadn't got a feather out of place. It was nothing like as full as usual, but the people who were there mostly seemed amused about something.

Marcia said, 'Air-raids always seem to make people get tight.'

'I'm not quite tight enough to be any good, myself,' I said. 'Shall we get tight?'

'I don't think I will,' said Marcia. 'But you carry on if you like.'

I thought about it but it didn't seem a good idea so I ordered some lager.

We stayed there until just after eleven and then went back to the Palace. It was still quiet and we thought we'd go to bed. Nobody seemed to agree with us. The ground floor and basement were all littered up with people sleeping in chairs. A gaunt female in a lot of make-up came up to us and said, 'That's a terrible thing.'

Marcia said, 'What?'

'That woman,' she said. 'Bombed out. She's lost her husband and her two babies. Hasn't a bean.'

'Oh, God!' said Marcia. 'How bloody!'

'I don't know what to do,' the gaunt female said. 'If I were anywhere east of Suez I should know what to do. But here I don't know what to do. These people—!' she looked round very fiercely at everybody.

It dawned on me that she was very tight.

'Which is the woman?' said Marcia.

She led us into another room and pointed to a very fat old girl of at least sixty-five who was asleep with her mouth open.

'I'd know what to do east of Suez,' she said, and walked off.

99

Marcia was looking at the woman in the chair in a puzzled sort of way.

'Does she mean *this* one?' she said in a whisper. 'Because if she's lost two babies they are somebody else's.'

I said, 'Honey, the Suez female is hopelessly blotto. I don't suppose there's any such woman.'

'I hope she just made it up,' said Marcia, glancing round for anybody who looked like a bereaved mother without a bean. None of them did. They just looked uniformly awful.

'Come on,' I said. 'I'm going to bed. There are some things worse than bombs.'

As we passed the information desk the Suez female was leaning against the counter in a used-up way peering at a Bradshaw.

'Booking her passage,' said Marcia.

Just as we were going towards the lifts there was a hell of a shindy out in the main hall. We went out and saw some sort of free-for-all going on. There was a huge sergeant in khaki who was being held back by half a dozen people. He seemed to be trying to get at somebody but I never did see quite who. A little slim chap with dark hair was patting him on the arm in a soothing way and saying something to him. Suddenly the sergeant shouted out something about 'my uniform', tore himself away and pushed the little chap in front of him and started to swing his fists about. The crowd pulled back from him and he lashed out and caught the little slim man in the chest. The little chap was backing away as fast as he could, and I don't think it hurt him much. But it caught him off his balance, and knocked him flying with his head against a big pillar. The crowd said 'Oo!' in a frightened way. The sergeant turned and flung his fists about a bit without hitting anybody and then blundered out of the door which was just behind him.

'Fighting tight,' I said. 'And very nasty too, with a bloke that size.'

Marcia said, 'You'd have thought a place like this would keep a chucker-out.'

Just then the little chap who'd been knocked down came staggering past us. His forehead was streaming with blood and he was quite alone. The crowd was still milling around making a noise like the parrot-house, but nobody was taking any notice of him.

100

'Hey,' said Marcia. 'That's nasty.' We looked at one another for a minute and then turned and went after the little chap. He was just starting up the stairs, hanging on the handrail, and dripping blood all over the place. We got hold of him on each side.

I said, 'Come on, o'boy.'

Marcia said, 'Lavatory, Bill, where I can bathe it.'

'Nothing whatever to do with me,' said the little chap a bit vaguely.

'Of course it wasn't,' I said. 'Rotten luck.'

We got him into a bathroom and he bled into the bath in large quantities. I was surprised at what a vivid red blood stays, even when a lot of water is mixed with it.

Marcia looked at his forehead and said, 'That'll have to be stitched.' It was a cut about three inches long, going right down to the bone in the middle.

I said, 'The only thing is to patch him up and get him along to Charing Cross. I'll see if I can rustle up some bandages.'

As I went out the little chap was saying, 'Ridiculous, man getting drunk like that. Serves me right for butting in.'

I had a hell of a job to get any bandages. You would have thought a big joint like the Palace would have had everything that opened and shut – particularly with air-raids all over the place. But the best they could do was some sort of a little box of stuff and a frightened kid of about seventeen with an armlet saying 'First Aid'. We went back to the bathroom and Marcia tied him up. She has a flair for that sort of thing and when she'd finished he looked like an illustration out of a text-book on bandaging. The little bloke was looking a bit used-up. He'd lost a hell of a lot of blood. He was still muttering about it being nothing to do with him.

Just as she was getting him finished the little First Aid girl came in and said something about the police. There were three of them – two small chaps in War Reserve tin hats and an inspector. The inspector was wearing a roll-necked Jaegar pullover and old flannel trousers. I should think he was about twenty-seven or -eight. He was a lovely thing. I've never seen any human being that moved more beautifully or looked in better condition. He introduced himself as though he'd come to a party we were giving. He said, 'I'm sorry about these clothes. This is my siren suit. I get tired of flopping down

101

on my face in the street wearing anything decent.'

He asked the little chap a few questions about what had happened. He wasn't as nice to him as he was to Marcia and me. Then he looked at the bandages and said to Marcia, 'Are you a doctor?'

'No,' she said.

'I thought those bandages looked very professional,' he said. 'What are you going to do with him now?'

I said, 'Charing Cross, I should think.'

He nodded and said, 'I'll see about an ambulance. Then I think we'd better go and pick up the sergeant.'

I followed him out of the bathroom.

'Do you know where to find him?' I said.

'The doorkeeper says he's in a pub just across the street.'

He looked at me and said, 'You couldn't spare the time to come and see we get the right chap, could you?'

I said, 'Of course I will.'

I popped back and told Marcia I should only be a minute or two. He sent one of the others off to see about the ambulance. As we walked down the street the inspector said, 'Your wife's done a marvellous job patching him up. Is he a friend of yours?'

I said, 'We don't know him from Adam. But nobody was doing anything about him so we thought we'd better.'

'Lucky for him you did.'

I said, 'Marcia loves a lot of blood and so forth.'

'Useful taste at the moment,' he said.

It was a bit noisier outside now. There was some pretty heavy gunfire.

I said, 'Hell of a lot of it tonight.'

'Yes,' he said. 'We had one right on the doorstep earlier in the evening.'

The pub was only just across the road. As we got to it I said. 'This chap may be a bit difficult. He's a very big bloke.' It struck me that the two little War Reserve chaps didn't look as though they'd be a lot of good if things got rough.

'Oh well,' he said, 'we'll have to see.' He seemed quite happy.

The place didn't seem to be a proper pub. We went upstairs and there was a room with a bar in it. There was no real need for me. The sergeant was the only soldier there. As we went in he was sitting on a high stool shouting something. About half a dozen men were sitting round looking pretty scared.

The inspector just walked in and said, very gently, 'Hallo son. I think you'd better come along with me.'

The sergeant got up on to his feet. He must have been a good four inches taller than the inspector, who wasn't a small man. His eyes looked very glazed and queer.

'Who the bloody hell are you?' he said. Then he caught sight of the other two in their tin hats. He said, 'A bloody cop who's afraid to dress like one. Get out of here.'

The inspector just grinned and took a step towards him. The sergeant swung one at him that started somewhere down by his knees. The inspector hit him with a left hook that I'll swear didn't travel more than a foot. It made a noise like someone snapping his fingers. The sergeant went down as though he'd had his feet cut from under him.

I looked down and saw that the inspector was standing right forward on the balls of his feet with his heels clear of the floor. The two others started forward as though they were going to chuck themselves on the sergeant. The inspector put his arm out and said, 'Let him get up.' The sergeant got up quite slowly and looked at him for a moment without saying anything. Then he suddenly grabbed an empty beer bottle off a table and swung it back. The inspector hit his right wrist hard with the side of his left hand and dropped him again with a right which had all his right hip and shoulder in it.

This time he stayed down. He wasn't out, and he still looked at the inspector in a puzzled sort of way. The inspector just said, 'Well son? That do for this evening?'

The sergeant didn't say anything. The inspector said, 'All right. Bring him along. He'll be all right now.'

The two little chaps went and started to pick him up. He was very shaky. The inspector turned to me and said. 'Thanks so much for all you've done. I'm so sorry to have bothered you.' He said it in an almost tea-party way.

I said, 'That's all right. Nice work.'

I went back to the Palace. Marcia met me just inside the door. She said, 'I was wondering where the devil you were. Look here, he wants us to go with him.'

I said. 'Who wants us to go where?'

'The little chap. The ambulance is here and he keeps on asking me not to leave him. He's a bit concussed, I think.'

103

I said, 'We may as well make an evening of it.'

The ambulance was outside. We got in. The little bloke was leaning against Marcia as though she was the only thing there was to lean against in a cold hard world. He looked pretty done. I noticed it was one o'clock and wondered how it had got so late. The ambulance started off.

Marcia said, 'This is rather fun.'

'Colourful at any rate,' I said. She asked if they got the sergeant and I told her about it. The little bloke suddenly said to Marcia. 'I think you're wonderful. I think he's wonderful too. A perfect stranger.'

'We're marvellous,' I said. 'Only a very few of us left.'

We unshipped at Charing Cross Hospital and they took him away. He said, 'You won't go? You'll wait for me?' We said we would. He seemed to set a lot of store by it.

They were a hell of a long time. We must have been there about an hour.

I said, 'You must be dog tired, honey.'

'Me?' said Marcia. 'I'm having the time of my life. It's a damn' shame really, that poor little bloke being so grateful, when he's given us all this fun.'

'You were very expert,' I said.

'I think he's probably rather a nasty little man really,' said Marcia. 'At least I think he would be if he weren't concussed. I've never been in an ambulance before.'

There was a lot of very heavy gunfire going on now. I said, 'There can't be a lot of casualties anyhow, or they'd be coming in here.' No one was brought in the whole time we were there. There was an old chap at a sort of reception desk. We talked to him for a bit, but after a while I began to get very bored. Then who should turn up but the two little War Reserve bobbies. I said, 'Hallo – you again?' They'd come round to see if the little bloke was fit enough to be taken back to the station to tell his everyday story.

They sat down and waited too. I asked them about the sergeant and they said he'd gone back with them like a lamb.

I said, 'Your inspector seems a useful sort of bloke with his hands. That was very pretty.' They looked at one another and grinned.

One of them said, 'Oh, he's a lad, all right. He'd take on six like that. I've seen him do it.' You could see they thought he was a good chap to have about. I thought so myself.

Marcia said, 'I should think your job's tough enough already nowadays without having this sort of thing to cope with.'

They looked pleased and said you got used to it. I gave them cigarettes and they told us some of the jobs they'd had in air-raids. It sounded pretty grim. They didn't look so very tough either.

They brought the little chap back at last. A rather nice young house surgeon handed him over. He'd had to put in six stitches. He was very complimentary to Marcia about her bandaging, and she was very bucked. It was pretty loud outside all this time, and as we were standing there talking I heard one coming. I heard it as soon as the first faint whistle started. It was quite unmistakable. Both the bobbies heard it. Their ears were pretty well trained. One of them just stepped quietly under the arch of the corridor. I caught the other one's eye and we just stared at one another. I had plenty of time to lean against the wall in a negligent sort of way.

It was already coming pretty close, and it finished up with a real howl and a terrific roar that seemed to be just outside. Actually it was about a hundred yards away. Marcia hadn't heard it at all until the last second, and she jumped a foot.

I said, 'That was near enough.'

The little bloke laughed in a silly way and said to Marcia, 'You jumped. It frightened you.'

I was rather cross with him. So was Marcia. She said, 'Well, I didn't hear it coming.'

One of the bobbies said, 'We usually drop when they're as close as that, but I didn't want to alarm the lady.'

There was the question of getting back to the station. They had a police car outside, but they explained very carefully that if we came with them it was at our own risk. They said they'd give it a minute or two to quieten down anyhow.

We all sat and smoked another cigarette. It got a bit quieter, though not much.

I said, 'Well, how about it?'

'It's up to you,' the bobbies said.

I said, 'Would you go now if you were by yourselves?'

They said they thought they would, so we all went out and piled into the car. One of the bobbies drove and the other kept his head out of the side window to listen for whistles. He stopped us once, but it must have been something else he heard because there was no explosion. A couple of bombs fell some way away, but we got back to the station all right. It was very odd and exciting driving like that.

We had to go some way round to get into the station. A biggish bomb had fallen a few doors away from it earlier in the evening. It was the one we'd heard in the Piccadilly. The whole street was blocked by a huge heap of bricks and rubble, and there was broken glass all over the place.

The inspector in the Jaegar pullover was there. 'Hallo,' he said 'So sorry to drag you all down here. You must forgive these clothes. This is my siren suit. It's good for flopping on your tummy in.' He'd forgotten that he'd said that bit before. I looked at his knuckles and saw he hadn't even broken them. He was extremely charming, and got them to bring Marcia and me some coffee from the canteen. We were glad of that coffee. It was quarter to three. Then he took the little chap away and we sat and waited some more.

About quarter past three they came back.

The inspector said, 'Look here, I'm extremely sorry, but I haven't got a car in. Do you think you could possibly get back to the Palace on foot? You're quite welcome to stay here if you'd prefer to, of course. But I thought you'd probably want to get to bed.'

Marcia said, 'Of course we can walk. It's only a few yards.'

'Fine,' he said. 'I'd wait a minute or two until there's a lull. Then I'll send a man with you to the end of the street. One has to climb rather.'

We waited until nothing was actually firing close at hand, and then said goodbye to him and started. A rather surly bobby came with us to the end of the street. We had to climb over a mound of stuff about twelve feet high, and there was broken glass crunching under foot all the way. It was bright moonlight now. We said goodnight to the bobby when we got out into Regent Street, and he went back.

The little chap was rather a trial. He still seemed a bit concussed. Marcia always maintained afterwards that he was tight in the first place and stayed tight throughout. Anyhow he was still distinctly odd and he walked very slowly, so that we had to stroll along at about one mile an hour to keep with him.

When we were about two hundred yards from the Palace

the firing suddenly blazed up again. We could hear splinters pattering. The little bloke couldn't walk any faster, so we had to go strolling on through it. It seemed to take a hell of a time to walk that two hundred yards, and we agreed afterwards that that was the only really nasty bit in the whole thing.

When we got back the little bloke very much wanted us to sit up and have a drink with him, and when we made him go to bed he wanted us to meet him at breakfast. He was being very grateful. We both thought we'd seen quite enough of him, and decided we'd miss him at breakfast, with some care. He went off to bed still being very grateful. We never saw him again.

We got to bed just on four. The raid was still going on quite cheerfully, but we went to sleep at once. I woke up once or twice when it got unusually loud, and I woke again when the All Clear went at dawn. But apart from that I slept very well.

EIGHT

I FELT a bit used up the next morning, but so did everybody else, so it didn't matter. There was a general feeling that it had been a roughish night and that you were entitled to be tired. I walked from the Palace to the office to see if I could wake myself up. There was a hell of a lot of mess about. It seemed to me that the raid had done more damage in the West End than all the previous ones put together. They hadn't had time to clear the glass up, and that always made things a bit desolate. Quite a number of places were still burning or smouldering, and there were a lot of fire-engines about doing their stuff. But it was all quite well under control. My balloon was down again looking more like a disgruntled elephant than ever. There were a lot of traffic diversions.

As I got near the office I suddenly wondered what would happen if they'd written the place off in the night. I thought it might be quite a good thing if they had. Then we could start again. But they'd need to do it in daylight, so as to get most of the staff, if it was going to be any good.

They hadn't hit the Ministry, but they'd dropped a big one beside the next block and blown most of its front in. All our remaining windows had gone. Apart from that only a few queer things had happened. Some of the partitions between offices had shifted or cracked. Lawrence found that his office had got three feet shorter and his assistant's three feet longer. The partition between them had simply moved three feet, perfectly upright. They just left it like that.

Nothing much had happened to my office. The partition was leaning in at the top a bit, and some of the doors wouldn't shut. But then hardly a door in the place would. Apart from that I was quite all right. I even had one little pane of glass left. The messengers said it was the only one in the whole building. The messengers also told me that our bomb blew a chunk of stone nearly a foot square in through the Secretary's window on the fifth floor, breaking the steel frame, and landing in one of his armchairs.

There was an internal envelope on my desk marked 'Immediate'. I opened it. It said, 'The first meeting of the Committee on the Area Unit Scheme will be held in Room 247 at 2.30 PM today. Agenda follows. J. L. Lawrence, Secretary.'

This seemed a bit sudden. I rang Lawrence up and said, 'Is that J. L. Lawrence, Secretary?' He chuckled and said, 'In person.'

'Listen, John,' I said, 'What is this?'

He said, 'You mean this Area Scheme Committee?'

'Yes.'

'Search me, old boy. You know as much about it as I do.'

'Well, who's on it? Am I?'

'Of course. Haven't you had the notice?'

'What notice?'

'Oh, there's been a notice round. Perhaps yours hasn't turned up yet.'

'What does it say?'

'Just says the Secretary has appointed a committee to consider and report on a scheme recently submitted for Area Unit Grouping.'

'Oh Christ!' I said. 'Who's on it?'

'About half the place. Pellew's in the chair. Who put the thing up? You?'

'God knows,' I said. 'I did put up a scheme and it went to the Secretary. But nobody's said a word to me about it. I'd no idea there was to be a committee.'

'That'll be it then,' said Lawrence.

'But look here,' I said. 'We don't want a whacking great committee to talk about a thing like that. And why in God's name Pellew?'

Lawrence said, 'Pellew's not a bad chairman.'

'But he doesn't know the first thing about it. It's right outside his stuff.'

'Well, equally why in God's name me?' said Lawrence.

I said, 'The whole thing's cuckoo. Is Lennox on the Committee?'

'No.'

'And is the agenda going to follow?'

'No, o'boy, it isn't. That was just legal fiction. I can't do an agenda until I know what it's all about.'

'Oh, God!' I said, 'What a joint!'

I went down and saw Lennox. He seemed very bucked.

He said, 'Well, you've got your committee.'

'So I've just been told,' I said. 'Why have we?'

'What d'you mean?'

I said, 'We don't want a committee. What we want is a decision.'

'I think the Secretary has accepted the idea,' said Lennox. 'I talked to him, and he seemed very keen.'

'Then why the Pete has he appointed a committee to gas about it? The whole thing was set out in my memorandum. He'd only got to say "Yes" or "No".'

'He just wanted it discussed to see if any difficulties emerged, I expect.'

'They will,' I said. 'That's all that will emerge.'

Lennox wiped his glasses and said, 'Well, don't worry about it, Sarratt. The Secretary's sold and he can sell the Minister. I don't think he'll really take much notice even if the Committee isn't favourable.'

I said, 'Sounds like a useful sort of committee.'

I went back and cracked through a lot of stuff with Doris. She still had her hair behind her ears. She said she was getting used to it. I had to work fast because I knew this thing would go on all the afternoon.

Haines from the Press Department came in. I said, 'Hallo –
drunk again.'

Haines said, 'Can I have two minutes?'

I threw Doris out and said, 'Make it quick, o'boy. I've got a
hell of a lot of stuff to get through.'

'You write for the *Era*, don't you?'

'No,' I said. 'I used to. I don't write for anybody now. No
time.'

'Do you read it now?'

'No. I never did. The last I ever saw of my stuff was in galley.'

Haines chucked across a cutting. 'This is the third of these,'
he said. 'Run an eye over it.'

I looked through it. It was an unsigned article in a series on
the Ministry, and damned critical.

'You didn't write that by any chance, did you?' said Haines
with a grin.

I said, 'No, I didn't. I rather wish I had. It's damned good.'

'It's a bit too good,' said Haines. 'His nibs is livid about it.'

'I should have thought he was used to it by now,' I said.

'Yes,' said Haines. 'But that's an inside job.'

I looked at it again. You could see it was. Nobody outside
the Ministry could have done it.

I said, 'Treason, eh?'

'Somebody here,' said Haines.

'Or somebody who's been fired,' I said. 'How about
Christopherson?'

Haines snorted. 'Christopherson never wrote anything as
good as that in his life.'

'That's true.'

'There are only three people in this outfit who've got con-
tacts with the *Era*,' said Haines. 'I'm one, and it wasn't me.
You're another, and you say it wasn't you.'

I said, 'No. I agree with what it says. But I don't write articles
about the place I'm working for. Or if I did I'd sign them.'

'Well, that leaves our pal down the passage,' said Haines.

'Who?' I said.

'Lennox.'

'Oh, come!' I said. 'Lennox is a pukka Civil Servant. He'd
never do a thing like that. Besides, damn it, if the thing's a
criticism of anybody it's a criticism of him.'

Haines got up. 'All right,' he said with a grin. 'Thanks very

110

much, Bill.' He picked up the cutting and started towards the door.

'What makes you think Lennox wrote those?' I said.

Haines said, 'I don't think. I know. I only wanted to check up. Wheels within wheels. Bungho, and keep it to yourself.'

He went out. I would have liked to hear more. It didn't seem to add up.

I went to lunch at a quarter to two and was back in twenty minutes. I wanted to get something finished up before this meeting began.

Just as I got back, Marcia rang up. She said, 'Bill, I've got a job.'

'As what?' I said.

'With Estelle. Rest centre for the bombed and weary. Cup of tea, a few kind words and some disinfectant on the cut. You know the sort of thing.'

'Where?'

'Just off Commercial Road. My God, Bill, it's a mess down here. We haven't seen anything up west.'

'Are you there now?'

'Yes. I got here and asked Estelle if I could do anything and she just said, "Yes. Go and get some bandages and bandage anybody in this lot who looks as though they ought to be bandaged." So I've been at it all the morning.'

'Don't they go to hospital or a First Aid place?'

'Apparently not. Not with superficial cuts and things anyhow. Most of mine have been glass cuts.'

I said, 'It sounds grand. What fun you do have.'

'It's lovely,' said Marcia.

'Do you get paid?'

'I shouldn't think so.'

'Poor do,' I said. 'Do you have to pay?'

'Not officially, but you do in practice. I've spent about two pounds this morning on this and that.'

'It sounds the perfect job,' I said.

Marcia said. 'It is, rather. I'll tell you more about it tonight.'

There were fourteen of us at this meeting. All the usual crowd. I said to Edwardes, 'This may be the new Committee on the Area Unit Scheme but it looks just like any one of about six other committees to me.'

111

Edwardes said, 'Dry up. I'm wearing a different coloured tie and Lawrence is sitting next to the chairman. Both quite new departures.'

Pellew was in the chair. I rather liked him. He was a rather sardonic old bird with grey hair, horn-rimmed spectacles and a niceish sense of humour.

Pellew put his glasses on and looked round at us in a resigned sort of way, and said, 'Well, gentlemen, this is the Secretary's new committee appointed to examine and report on a scheme for Area Unit Grouping. For some reason which escapes me I have been appointed Chairman, and for some reason which I understand escapes him, Mr Lawrence has been appointed Secretary.'

'Hear, hear,' said Edwardes.

'Thank you, Edwardes,' said Pellew. 'Well, gentlemen, I am slightly handicapped by the fact that nobody has given me any terms of reference. I don't know anything about this scheme, and there isn't an agenda. Apart from a few little snags like that, it all seems quite clear.'

Lawrence said, 'I'm sorry there's no agenda, but I only heard about this last night.'

'I only heard about it this morning,' I said.

'Probably there are a lot of people who're supposed to come who haven't heard about it at all yet,' said Edwardes.

'God send not,' said Pellew. 'We shall want a bigger room. Seriously – does anyone know what this is all about? All we've got is this document.' He held up some foolscap sheets.

'May I have a look?' I said.

They passed it down to me. It was a Roneoed copy of my memorandum.

'Oh, yes,' I said. 'This is my thing. I wasn't sure if it would be.'

'Ah,' said Pellew. 'We progress. Someone's heard about the thing before. This is your memorandum, Sarratt?'

I said, 'Yes – except the first two lines. I take no responsibility for them.'

The Roneo copy began. 'As the rate of production increases it becomes more and more necessary as the rate of production increases it becomes more and more necessary.'

'The Committee took note of a memorandum by Mr Sarratt and Miss Gertrude Stein,' said Edwardes.

'It gives a nice sense of urgency,' said Pellew.

'Mr Chairman,' said old General Parks in his formal way, 'since we have this document wouldn't the best way be to circulate it and read it first. Most of us don't know what an Area Unit is.'

'An Area Unit is the equivalent of sixty-two and a half Therms,' said Edwardes. 'Or about enough to boil a medium-sized cabbage.'

'Oh, come on,' I said. 'Shove the things round and let's get on with it.'

Lawrence passed round the copies and they read the thing through in silence. There were only four pages of it, but reading took about a quarter of an hour. Committees always read at that pace. I could see Harness scribbling comments and question marks in the margin with great gusto.

Pellew waded through to the end and then took off his glasses and leaned back in his chair.

'And very nice too,' he said gently. 'Now what?' Everybody laughed. It was what all but about three of them were thinking.

Pellew put his glasses on again and said irritably, 'This is the sort of thing which beats me about this Ministry. We're told to examine and report on that. What do they expect us to do? Presumably Sarratt's facts are right. Anyhow it's his job, and if they're not *we* shan't know. Apart from the facts he suggests doing something. Whether we want to do it or not is a matter of major policy which will have to be decided higher up whatever we say. It's damned silly. What d'you think yourself, Sarratt?'

'I agree with you,' I said. 'It's a yes-no decision that we want.'

'Of course it is.'

I said, 'But I think some people may want to pull the idea to pieces a bit. I see Mr Harness has got a lot of question marks there.'

Harness squinted round and said, 'I have a few points to raise, Mr Chairman.'

'Oh, well,' said old Pellew, cheering up a bit. 'If somebody wants to say something that's all right. I was forgetting it was up your street, Harness. Fire away.'

We went on eventually for about three and a half hours. At first the thing was chiefly an argument between Harness and me. Then gradually everybody got bored with sitting round saying nothing, and it became a free-for-all. Of course it was a hopeless waste of time. Out of the fourteen of us, I knew the facts, Harness knew most of them, Lawrence and Edwardes knew a few, and the rest were hearing about the whole thing for the first time. They suggested doing all the things that we'd tried already and found didn't work, plus one or two things which you didn't need to try to know wouldn't. It was exactly like starting the whole thing again from scratch, and as it had taken me nearly a year to get to the point reached in my memorandum, I didn't see how they'd ever get anywhere.

I didn't say so at the meeting. I couldn't very well. But when we broke up I got hold of Pellew and told him. I knew he thought the whole thing was a waste of time too.

'I know,' he said. 'It must be damned annoying for you, Sarratt. It is for me, for that matter. I've got plenty of work to keep me going without this.'

I said, 'I wouldn't mind if we were likely to get anywhere. But we aren't.'

'If I had my way,' said Pellew, 'I'd send in a report saying, "We have examined this scheme as instructed. We recommend that the Minister should make up his mind what is his policy, if any, and act accordingly." That's the only thing we can say really.'

I said, 'We could go on like this for weeks.'

'I tell you what,' said Pellew. 'I'll try and get hold of the Secretary and get some definite terms of reference out of him.'

It was only half past six, but I was so fed up that I packed up and went and had a drink with Edwardes.

Edwardes said, 'I don't feel like a pub. How about going to Liberty Hall?'

'Don't know it.'

'Oh come,' said Edwardes. 'You must know Liberty Hall?'

'No.'

'Then we'll certainly go there.'

'I put myself in your hands,' I said. 'As long as we end up somewhere near the Palace.'

'It's on the way there.'

We walked across the Green Park, across the Mall and up St

James' Street. Somewhere in Albemarle Street Edwardes turned
in and dived down a lot of stairs. A bloke who was sitting at a
table at the bottom said, 'Good evening, Mr Edwardes.'

Edwardes said, ' 'Evening, Harry. This is Mr Sarratt. He's
with me.'

The bloke just looked at me and nodded. We left our hats
and coats and went down a corridor through a door with
'Liberty Hall' printed on it and a naked girl underneath.

It was a big room with a dance floor in the middle. All round
the sides were cubicles, going back quite a long way like a
theatre box, and looking out on the floor. Each cubicle had
horseshoe-shaped sofas and a table. To get into a cubicle you
opened a half-door in front, like going into an old-fashioned
pew. There were curtains in front so that you could shut yourself in completely if you liked. There were a few people there.
We sat down in a cubicle and rang the bell. A waitress came.
She was the usual sort of cabaret beauty, blonde and with a
rather tired skin. She was wearing a little scarlet jacket and
the world's tightest pair of white silk trousers. They were very
thin silk, and she showed pink through them like a white pig
does through its hair. She knew Edwardes and he made a few
conventional passes at her. He said, 'Bill's never been here
before.'

'*Never been here before?*' she said, looking at me with her
eyes very wide open. She seemed to think that was damned
queer. 'How does he spend his time then?'

Edwardes said, 'He works. What's more, he worries. Can't
have that, Sue, can we?'

' 'Course not,' she said. 'What's the odds anyhow?'

'Ah,' said Edwardes. 'But he's a serious sort of cove.'

I thought it was time I said something.

'Listen,' I said. 'Those pants of yours. They interest me.
Do they come off or are they painted on?'

' 'Course they do,' she said, looking down at herself.

'It's quite easy when you know the combination,' said
Edwardes, sniggering.

'You go on,' said Sue.

'Anyhow I'll bet you can't sit down in them,' I said.

' 'Course I can,' she said. She sat down and got up again.
She looked down at herself and said, 'They get awfully dirty.
It's the dust.'

Edwardes said, 'How about a drink? I'm going to have a whisky and soda.'

The girl went off to get the drinks. Edwardes said, 'What d'you think of this place?'

'Quite fun,' I said. 'Do you wear masks later on or just trust to the curtains?'

Edwardes said, 'You've seen this sort of thing before?' He seemed a bit surprised.

'Not in London,' I said. 'But there's a place in the Rue Druot in Paris very like this.'

'It's run by a Frenchman,' said Edwardes.

'Do you bring your own women or are they provided by the management?'

'Liberty Hall,' said Edwardes. 'You please yourself.'

'And the floor?'

'Used for dancing,' said Edwardes with a grin.

'And for l'exhibition, l'attraction et la demonstration, I suppose?'

'More or less. That only happens a good deal later on.'

I said, 'Well, you couldn't expect much of an audience for that sort of thing before dinner. Why Liberty Hall exactly?'

'Because you can have anything you like if you pay for it.'

'I know,' I said. 'Dirty films three hundred francs, Lesbianism five hundred, flagellation a thousand – exclusive of wines.'

Edwardes seemed a bit hurt. 'I've seen some damned good shows here,' he said.

The blonde girl brought us drinks. Edwardes said, 'What's doing tonight here?'

She rolled her eyes and said, 'You wait and see.'

'Shall I see anything if I do wait?'

'You'll see plenty,' she said.

I drank my drink up pretty fast. I knew I should have to stand him another and I wanted to get back and hear about Marcia's job.

'No hurry,' said Edwardes.

'I've got to get home,' I said.

'Aren't you going to stay and see the show?'

'No. I can't. Got to meet my wife. Why? Are you staying?'

Edwardes looked at his watch. 'I may. It's a bit early. I think I shall go away and come back. Nothing really happens for a long time yet.'

'Can you eat here?'

'Oh yes. Damned good food.'

The girl in the trousers was serving drinks in another cubicle. There was a lot of giggling going on. I was feeling a bit straight-run and Lifebuoy Soap myself. I like it a bit more grown-up than that. I drank up my second drink and said, 'I'd like to come in some time and see a show. It sounds amusing.' I didn't want to hurt Edwardes' feelings.

'You must,' he said. 'It's quite good fun. Takes your mind off things.'

'I suppose it's a club of sorts?'

'You have to join. They'll fix it up for you at the door if you want to. It's only a couple of guineas.'

'I might do that,' I said.

Edwardes decided he'd stay. I was just getting up to go when old Percy came in. He was with the blonde I'd seen in Grosvenor House. I should have let him settle down without saying anything, but he spotted me and greeted me like a long-lost brother. So did the blonde. You would have thought we were old sparring partners. Old Percy didn't seem to care a damn about being there with her. He didn't even trouble to say she was a chartered accountant's wife.

He wanted me to come back and have a drink with him, but I was fed up with the place and said I couldn't.

As the girl went into a cubicle old Percy grabbed me by the arm and said, 'How's your committee?'

'What committee?' I said.

'Your Area one? Goin' on all right?' He grinned at me. I looked at him for a moment. He was as pleased as Punch with himself.

'Now listen,' I said, 'just how do you know about that?'

The old boy roared with laughter. 'Ways and Means Society,' he said.

'Seriously,' I said. 'I'd like to know. Come on, you know, I shan't talk.'

He patted my arm. 'It's my job to know things,' he said. 'I'll give you a tip, o'boy. If you know anything, keep where it came from to yourself. I always do.'

I could see he meant it.

'Honour among thieves,' I said with a grin to help it.

The old boy patted me on the back. 'You're a friend of mine,' he said. 'I know I can trust you. But I'd no more tell you who gave me that than I'd tell him if it had come from you.' He patted me again and pottered off after the accountant's wife. Edwardes had sunk back into the shadows of the cubicle. I had an idea that he'd end up the evening in a mask.

It was half past seven when I got back to the Palace, but Marcia didn't show up for another half hour. She looked dog-tired but she was very bucked with herself. We went down into the bar and had drinks and she told me about it. Apparently just after a raid the place was a shambles. Two or three hundred people all milling around for a staff of about a dozen to deal with.

I said I'd thought it was all much more under control than that.

'So did I,' said Marcia. 'But it isn't. I think it would all be fine if they were normal and could think. But most of them are just numb. It isn't any good to tell them to do things. You have to do the things *to* them.'

She told me about an old woman who came in and sat quite still looking in front of her. They asked her if she'd like some tea and she said yes. Somebody put a tray of cups of tea on a table about four feet away and told her to take one. She said, 'Thank you,' but she didn't take one. They had to put it into her hand.

'Many kids?' I said.

'Not as many as I expected. But quite a few. Some by themselves.'

'What exactly do you do with the people?'

'It depends. Sometimes they're quite all right and just come in, have a cup of tea and a sit down and go off again. But most of them just wander in in a dazed sort of way and sit there until someone does something about it. We try to pass them on to the accommodation people as soon as we can. If they can't take them we can sleep about a hundred on the floor.'

'What do *you* do exactly?'

'Well, today I've been bandaging all the time. Nothing much. Practically all glass cuts. I find I'm appallingly out of practice. By the way, remind me to get some bandages to take down tomorrow.'

'What are the hours?'

118

'Whatever you can do. I've told Estelle I'll try to do eight hours a day. If it goes on like this I want to do some nights.'

I said, 'We'll have to think about that.'

'Oh, come!' said Marcia. 'I'm not going to be a sort of day-time-and-when-it's-all-safe performer.'

We had another drink. After a bit Marcia said, 'Look – I just want to tell you that I rang Stephen up today.'

'What for?' I said. We hadn't heard anything of Stephen for a fortnight.

'Just to tell him where I was.'

'Did you want him to know where you were?'

'Not particularly. But I was afraid he'd be ringing up the flat and getting all worked up. He had been, too.'

I just nodded.

Marcia said, 'He wanted me to have dinner with him tonight.'

I said, 'Are you going to?'

'No,' said Marcia. Then she turned and looked at me and said, 'But I said I would on Monday.'

I looked at her and said, 'You did *what*?'

'It was so *bloody* awkward,' said Marcia a bit wretchedly. 'I kept on saying I wouldn't and finally he asked me to say any time and he'd do it.'

We sat for a long time. Then I said, 'Look, darling – we've got to get this straight. I've always said that this was your affair, and it is. But I can't help coming into it to some extent, and I just want to tell you that if you still want Stephen you can't have me too. Not any longer.'

She turned and looked at me.

'You mean you're – through with me?'

'Unless you get this cleaned up. I don't want to be, but I've no option.'

'I suppose not,' said Marcia.

'You see, sweet, you just make me look a fool all the time. And I can't do with that.'

'Do I make you look a fool, Bill? I suppose I do. I never think of it like that. I just think you and Stephen are quite different things.'

I said, 'That one's getting a bit worn.'

She sat for a long time dropping the last drops of her drink on the table.

I said, 'For Christ's sake, stop making that mess.'

119

'All right,' she said at last. 'I knew I was a fool to do it, really.'

'You were, unless you want to finish us,' I said.

Marcia grinned, 'Silly!' she said.

I grabbed her hand under the table.

'What do you want me to do?' she said. 'Ring Stephen up and say I won't come Monday and that I won't see him again?'

I said, 'You must do it how you think.'

She didn't say anything. I could see what was coming. I suddenly felt damned tired and rather hopeless. I said, 'If you'd rather go on Monday and finish it then, I don't care. I can see it's an awkward thing to do on the telephone.'

'Well, perfectly frankly, I would rather do that,' she said. 'It seems – fairer somehow.'

'As you like,' I said.

'If I ring him up and say I'm not going to see him again you know what he'll be like.'

'I do.' I said. 'I know what he'll be like anyhow.'

'Yes, but if I have him out to dinner I can see that he's sensible about it.'

'Fine,' I said.

Marcia said, 'You think this is one more wangle.'

'Don't you?'

'No. It isn't. It's just that I don't like to do it to him quite like that – just ringing him up I mean.' She squeezed my hand. 'Look – you mustn't mind my saying this, Bill – but you see I'm quite fond of him in a way and I don't want to – to be beastly.'

'No,' I said.

NINE

I worked right through the weekend. There was a lot to do, and all the office pests knocked off at 1 PM sharp on Saturday, so you could get straight ahead without people crashing in and ringing up all the time. Poor old Doris was still there plugging away when I knocked off at five on Sunday afternoon.

I got a lot done, but it didn't really get me anywhere, because Monday was a farce. I wanted Lennox. He wasn't in. I wanted Harness. He'd gone to a meeting in Birmingham. I wanted Lawrence. He had meetings all day. It was nearly twelve o'clock before I got a stroke done. Then, as soon as I'd given them all up and got started by myself, the fun began. First of all Pearce rang up with a long tale of woe about being very short of pool typists and tried to scrounge a couple of mine. Then Fred Giles came in and said, 'Oh God, these bloody women!'

I said, 'What's the matter with them now?'

'That girl Foster,' he said in a tired way. 'She's upsetting the whole registry.'

'How?'

'God knows. Two of the other kids have come and complained that she's rude, and Miss Cameron wants to know if she can be transferred.'

'Which is she?'

'The tall dark kid,' said Fred. 'Rather a nice shape. She's only seventeen and she's got a swollen head.'

'Is she any good?'

'She would be if she worked. She's intelligent enough.'

I said, 'All right. Send her in and I'll talk to her.'

Fred went to find her. While he was gone a telegram came from Charnock at SF144. It read, 'Pages two three four five received, page one missing, stopped by tonight if not received.' I got Doris in and told her to get Charnock on the telephone.

The Foster girl came in. She was looking sulky and cheeky.

I said, 'What's all this about your being rude to people?'

She said, 'I don't know. I wasn't rude to anybody. I only asked for a punch.'

'It isn't any good just not being rude,' I said. 'It's whether other people think you are.' I grinned at her and she grinned back.

She said, 'Some of the girls are so touchy.'

'I know,' I said. 'People are darned silly sometimes about what they mind. But one's got to work with them.'

Doris came in and said, 'There's two hours' delay to Northallerton.'

'Get it on Priority,' I said.

'That is on Priority, Mr Sarratt.'

'Oh God!' I said. 'Well then, get it on Special. I must get them or SF144 will just stop.'

Doris went away. The Foster girl said, 'Mr Sarratt, there's another thing. I don't like the work.'

'What's the matter with it?' I said.

'It's just routine work. Anybody could do it. I'd rather do something where I had to think more.'

'How long have you been at it?'

'A month.'

'Well, come,' I said, 'you can't have learnt all there is to know about the registry in a month.'

She looked sulky and said, 'Miss Cameron never gives me anything important to do.'

'Listen,' I said, 'If you get on and do the job properly Miss Cameron will be only too glad to give you things to do.'

'I want to get on and get promotion,' said the kid.

'Fine,' I said. 'But you won't do it by being slack and cheeky. This is your first job, isn't it?'

'Yes.'

'Well, if you want a better one you'll have to earn it like everyone else.'

Doris came back and said, 'I'm sorry, Mr Sarratt, but they won't take it as a Special.'

'Why not?' I said.

'The Exchange says we're not in the list.'

I said, 'Put them through here.'

The Foster kid said, 'I'm not slack. They're all beastly to me.' I thought she was going to cry.

'Now, look here,' I said. 'That's all nonsense. If you cheek them of course they won't like you.'

The telephone rang, and I said, 'Listen Exchange. I want a call to Northallerton. It's very urgent and it'll have to be Special.'

The girl said, 'I'm sorry, but we're not allowed to give you Special unless you're on the list.'

I said, 'Oh, damn the list. There'll be an SF closing down if I don't get through.'

'I'm sorry,' she said. 'But we're forbidden to do it. I'll put you on to supervisor if you like.'

I said, 'Well, buck up for Pete's sake.'

The Foster kid was staring straight ahead of her and picking at her handkerchief.

I said, 'You've got to remember that you're younger than most of the others. That doesn't mean you're not as good at the job, but you've got to prove it. Half the difficulty of doing any job is fitting in with other people.'

The supervisor came on, and I said, 'Listen, I've got to get through to Northallerton within the next ten minutes or we shall have an SF closing down. What are you going to do about it?'

She said, 'I'm awfully sorry but we can't give you a Special. We've got very strict orders about it.'

'Well, what the hell is supposed to happen then?' I said. 'Do I just let the place stop because of some damn' fool bit of red tape?'

'Well, I don't really know what to suggest,' she said. 'I suppose you're not near a telephone which is on the list?'

'You mean to say that I can have the call if I put it through on another extension?'

'Oh, yes,' she said. 'If Mr Lennox or somebody like that would let you use his telephone it'd be quite all right.'

I said, 'No, that's a bit too much. As far as I'm concerned, the damn' place can shut down.'

I shoved the receiver down. The Foster girl was still sitting there.

I said, 'You've got to remember that there's a war on. There isn't time to think about everybody's likes and dislikes. We've all got to plug away as best we can.'

She said, 'Yes, Mr Sarratt,' and smiled. She was an intelligent-looking kid.

'All right then,' I said. 'You go along and have a try. Get the job going well and try to fit in, and then we'll talk about it again.'

She said, 'Yes, Mr Sarratt. Thank you.'

She seemed quite cheerful now, as though something had amused her. When she was gone I went along to Lennox's office and got through to Charnock. Actually it didn't matter, because the rest of his plan had turned up and he was quite happy.

I had lunch with Haines. I tried to get some more out of him about the article in the *Era*, but he wouldn't talk. I doubt if he really knew anything. Haines said, 'How many actual crooks have we got in this place?'

'It depends what you mean by crooks,' I said.

'I mean crooks.'

I said, 'Actual cash on the table crooks. I should say very few.'

Haines said, 'There's dear Sir Geoffrey. He costs somebody a lot of money.'

'Yes. He's one. But he's so darned frank about it he hardly counts. There aren't more than a couple more as far as I know, and they're in a smaller way of business.'

'And after that?'

'After that we've got a hell of a lot of people who aren't exactly crooks but aren't straight. And even more who're straight according to their lights but have rather odd lights.'

'How much tipping off of pals goes on? Not for money. Just leakages?'

'A hell of a lot,' I said, thinking of old Percy. 'Why?'

Haines said, 'This job of mine isn't easy. Sometimes it's a bit tough keeping the Press boys quiet.'

'You mean they're on to something?'

Haines turned and looked at me. 'They've had at least three absolutely copper-bottomed brass-riveted stories about graft in the Ministry. I've seen the evidence, and there just isn't an answer.'

'Then why didn't they spill them?'

'Because I don't let 'em,' said Haines calmly.

'Oh, come!' I said. 'I know you pull a lot of weight in the Press Club, but . . .'

Haines shrugged his shoulders. 'Have it your own way,' he said. 'It doesn't matter. The only thing is, I'm not sure if I can hold them much longer. And if the lid does come off there'll be a nasty smell.'

I thought for a bit and said, 'You surprise me.'

'Of course. There's no graft in England, is there?'

'These things were actual graft?'

'They were things where people have been allowed and helped to make a packet of money for nothing.'

'That isn't necessarily graft. We allow and help people to make money for nothing all the time by just not knowing our job.'

Haines shook his head. 'No. I don't mean that sort of thing. These were actual cases where pals of people high up in this place were given deliberate tips. And in two of them some of the money came here. I think it did in the other, but I can't prove it.'

'Listen,' I said, 'if that's so, why do you kill the story?'

'That's my job. I kill three stories for every one that goes out.'

'But why? Surely the thing to do is to have a showdown?'

'That'd do a hell of a lot of good,' said Haines. 'I should go out on my ear.'

'But if you can prove it?'

'Laddy,' said Haines, 'if you'd been in the newspaper game as long as I have you'd know that proving things never gets you anywhere unless they're things your boss wants proved.'

He drank his beer and looked round the room.

'After all,' he said, 'what d'you expect? If you try to run a thing like this with just Civil Servants it just gets wrapped round with red tape. If you run it with business men it's a racket. So they mix 'em up.'

I said, 'And get a racket tied up with red tape.'

'That's right. You can't blame the business men. They come and work without salaries. Everybody licks their boots and hangs on their words. There's nothing very queer about it if they make a bit on the side.'

'You don't understand, o'boy,' I said. 'They're just serving their country.'

'Of course they are,' said Haines. 'And, hell, we all know that service costs money.'

The place had still got the devil in it in the afternoon. I went out into the calculating room and found them sweating away at a lot of stock figures. They said Fred wanted them. When he came in I asked him what they were for. He said, 'Sutton rang up from the Private Office and asked for them. They want them for the Cabinet Committee.'

I said, 'Cabinet Committee my boot.'

'It's a hell of a nuisance,' said Fred. 'I've had to take them all off the stuff for Wednesday. I suppose we shall have to work them late tomorrow.'

I said, 'The trouble with you is that when people tell you

125

things you believe them. That Cabinet Committee business is the oldest joke in the place.'

'How d'you mean?'

'Come into my office and listen,' I said.

I rang up Sutton, and said, 'I believe you asked my department for some figures this morning?'

'That's right,' he said. 'Sorry to give you the trouble, but Giles said they wouldn't take long to get out.'

'D'you mind telling me what you want them for?' I said.

'For tomorrow's Cabinet Committee. Didn't Giles tell you?'

'He did, but I didn't believe him. You say the Cabinet Committee asked for them?'

'They didn't actually *ask* for them,' said Sutton. 'But we want to hand them on to the Cabinet Office.'

'Oh, the Cabinet Office asked for them?'

'No, no,' said Sutton, getting a bit annoyed. 'It's just a question of preparing the papers.'

'Listen,' I said. 'Should I be right in saying that nobody's asked you for them?'

'Not in so many words. But they might easily be wanted.'

I said, 'There's perhaps one chance in five hundred that the total stock figure will be wanted. You've got that. I gave it to you myself last week.'

'They might ask for details,' said Sutton, a bit weakly.

'Fine,' I said. 'Well, if they do, let me know and we'll get the figures out. Until then, my department's got a lot of work to do that *is* wanted. Cheerio.'

I hung up and said, 'There you are.'

'Don't really want them at all?' said Fred.

'No.'

'Well, my God, when he rang me up you'd have thought the whole Cabinet was waiting for them with its tongue hanging out.'

I said, 'You always want to check up on Sutton. He's a nasty little pip-squeak, and he's always doing that sort of thing.'

'What for?'

'God knows. He likes to load the Minister up with a pile of papers two feet thick that he'll never read and wouldn't understand if he did. Then he reckons he's done a whale of a job.'

'It takes a hell of a time too, that stuff.'

126

'Of course it does. About half the place spends its time producing stuff that somebody important might want. That's why it's never got time to do its proper job. Go and take 'em off it Fred, and get them back on to the stuff for Wednesday.'

About half past six Lennox's secretary rang up to say that he'd just come in. It was the first time he'd showed up all day. I was fed-up and tired, though I'd hardly done a thing. But I thought I'd better go down and catch him in case he went pottering off again.

Lennox was pretty hopeless. He had a mass of stuff there he hadn't touched, and he really wanted to start burrowing into that. But I stuck to him until I'd got through my stuff. It wasn't any good thinking to get decisions out of him, but at least I could say we'd discussed it. I always found the best way with him was to tell him about a thing and then go away and do what I thought. To do him credit, he'd usually back you if you did that.

I got away finally just after eight. It wasn't until I was half-way back to the Palace that I remembered it was Monday and that Marcia was going out with Stephen. It seemed to fit in very well with the sort of day it had been.

I got the key and went up to our room. Marcia had left a note on the dressing-table. It said, 'I've gone. Have a lot of dinner, sweet. I shan't be late. I love you. M.'

Jerry hadn't shown up that evening, and there hadn't been a warning for nearly twenty-four hours. I was glad about that. I washed and changed into flannel trousers and a sports coat, wondering what the hell to do with the evening. I thought of going along to Edwardes' brothel place, but that seemed to be admitting something that I wasn't prepared to admit yet. Anyhow it seemed a bit irrelevant in the middle of a war.

I went down to the bar and had a drink and looked at the evening paper. The place was full of uniforms. I tried to work out that they were all younger than I was, or else crusty old professionals, but it wasn't any good. For sheer bloody uselessness I was out by myself.

I was just thinking about dinner when who should come in but Laurie. I was damned glad to see him. I should have been glad to see anybody. We had a drink. Laurie told me that he'd got it all fixed about the Army. He wasn't going into the Guards but into the Rifle Brigade. He was as happy as a sandboy about it,

127

I said, 'It must be a nice decisive feeling.'

'There was nothing else to do,' he said. 'I'm a bit too old to fly.'

'You've always been quite clear that you wanted to do something military, haven't you?'

'Of course,' said Laurie. 'To me, a war is a thing in which you fight.' He said it as though he were repeating a lesson.

I said, 'It's rather refreshing to hear someone say that. Most of us of our age keep on pointing out that we can be much more valuable doing nice safe jobs of national importance.'

Laurie shrugged his shoulders. 'It seems quite simple to me. It's different for you, of course.'

'Why?' I said.

'It'd be absurd for you to go into the army. You're more use where you are. I'm no damned use where I am.'

'Flattering, but probably untrue,' I said.

'No. It's true of you. And of two or three other people I know of our age. The rest I'd shove into uniform tomorrow.'

We had another drink. I said, 'Just what have we lost by conscription?'

'How d'you mean?'

'It's kept a lot of people out of the Army who wanted to get in, and taken in a lot who wanted to stay out. That's a bad thing in some ways.'

Laurie said, 'Everybody says the quality's far below 1914, but far better than 1918. That's the point.'

'Conscription's the only thing which has made the position possible for people like me,' I said.

'Why?'

'My dear man, in 1915 I couldn't have sat in this bar in mufti without being presented with white feathers.'

Laurie said, 'But being a civilian was safer then. And it's safer now than it soon will be.'

'I'm not at all sure the Army won't be the safest place soon,' I said.

He wasn't doing anything, so we had dinner together in the grill room. I told him about our night out with the police and about Marcia's job.

'She's a remarkable woman,' said Laurie. He always thought Marcia was remarkable. 'But you won't let her go down there at night, of course?'

128

'I don't know,' I said.

'She ought to have gone to the States with Dolly. This country's going to be no place for women.'

I said, 'She wouldn't have gone. Marcia hates to think she's missing anything.'

I thought a bit and then said, 'That's what I dislike about my own position. I think you're probably right and that I'm most use where I am. But it'll be bloody annoying afterwards, you know, when all you people are old soldiers and I'm not.'

'Nonsense,' said Laurie rather bitterly. 'You'll be a KCB and I shall be on the dole when the thing's been over six months.'

I said, 'Aren't you thinking in rather old-fashioned terms? I doubt it'll be like that this time.'

Laurie said, 'All wars end like that if they don't end in revolution.'

'This one may,' I said.

'If it does away with a lot of the slack-gutted sentimentality it'll have been worth it.'

I said, 'I take it you think we shall win this war?'

'We can't lose it,' he said. 'There are too many people who can't afford to have us lose it.'

'The States?'

'Yes. It may easily take ten years, but we must win in the end.'

'Right. And then what?'

'How d'you mean?'

'What do we do then? You're going into the Army. What are you going to fight for?'

Laurie shut his mouth very tight and then said, 'I'm afraid that's outside my sphere.'

'But, good God, why? You'll be affected.'

Laurie said, 'I think we'd better get on and win first and then talk about that. I didn't want this war. But as it's happened I'm prepared to fight in it. I'm not interested in the theory of the thing.'

Laurie went about half-past nine. We shook hands and I wished him luck. I wondered vaguely if he'd be killed. Not a lot of people were being killed, but the thing might change at any moment. I was sorry for him. Laurie was Eton and Christchurch, and Eton and Christchurch fitted better in 1914

129

really. I thought there couldn't be much of his world left after this anyhow. There wasn't a lot before that. But he'd get a commission soon and he'd like that.

I went into the lounge and had coffee. The place was full of people. At ten o'clock the news was switched on. They sat around and listened, giving little grunts of satisfaction and grinning at each other over the good bits. It reminded me of Ted's German pals. I felt bloody lonely and out of touch, what with Laurie and all the uniforms and then this crowd.

Marcia came in about half-past ten. I was surprised that she was so early. I ordered some more coffee and said, 'Well, how did it go?'

'Oh, quite all right,' she said, rather wearily.

'Finished it?'

Marcia said, 'Yes. I finished it.'

'How did Stephen take it?'

'Oh, he was all right.'

'Not waiting on the doorstep?'

'Not as far as I know,' she said with a pretty hard-working smile.

I could see this wasn't a very good conversation so I told her about meeting Laurie. She was as interested in Laurie as if he'd been Bimetallism. Then I told her about the Foster girl and that wasn't any good either. She seemed fagged out, so I suggested bed. Marcia didn't even seem very keen on that, but she came.

We got upstairs and I started to undress. Marcia lit the gas-fire and sat down on the floor and looked at it. After a bit I began to feel a bit fed up.

I said, 'The first step in going to bed is to remove the clothes.'

She went on looking at the gas fire, but she kicked her shoes off and started to undo her suspenders very slowly. I looked at her and realized that it didn't mean a thing to me either to see her face looking like that or to see her undoing her suspenders. I was just going to take off my tie but there didn't seem a lot of point in that, so I put my jacket and waistcoat on again and went across to the telephone and asked for Stephen's number.

Marcia looked up quickly and said, 'What are you doing?'

I didn't say anything. Stephen's voice said, 'Hallo.'

130

I said, 'Stephen – this is Bill. Can you come round to the Palace? I want to talk to you.'

Stephen said, 'No, no, no.'

'I think you'd better,' I said. 'I'm getting bored. Better have a clean-up.'

Stephen said, 'I think I've suffered enough tonight.'

'Well, you'd better come and suffer some more,' I said. 'Room 527. Come straight up.'

I rang off. I knew he'd come. Marcia said, 'Just what are you doing?'

'Making it possible to go to bed,' I said.

'Well, I may as well tell you that Stephen was extremely tight when I left him. He'll be tighter now.'

'I can't be expected to pick Stephen's rare sober moments,' I said. 'I'm a busy man. You'd better put that stocking on again. We don't want to mislead him.'

Marcia looked at the fire again. 'I don't understand,' she said wearily.

'It's quite simple,' I said. 'I don't like having you around eating your heart out. It's dull and what's more, I find it rather insulting.'

Marcia said, 'Are you going to throw me out?' She looked as though she didn't give a damn if I was or wasn't.

'I don't throw people out,' I said. 'I just leave doors unlocked so they can walk out if they want to.'

'It would help if I knew what you were trying to do,' said Marcia in a dead voice.

I said, 'You go out to say goodbye to Stephen for about the seventh time, and you come back and play all broken-hearted, as you always do. Usually I've felt sorry for you. This time I don't. I'm left feeling that either you're lying to me about your feelings for Stephen most times or else acting a lie to me about them tonight. Whichever it is, I don't like it.'

Marcia said, 'It doesn't occur to you that both might be genuine?'

'It does not,' I said. 'It has occurred to me several times before. But not this time. You must remember I've lived with you for eight years. I know your technique fairly well by now.'

'What exactly do you mean by my technique?' said Marcia, getting dangerous.

'The stuff you do when you want to produce an effect,' I said, going over close and saying it in her eye. 'What the film people call "registering".'

'And what am I "registering"?'

'You're registering a broken heart,' I said. 'And a very poor performance it is.'

'Oh, bunkum!' said Marcia. 'I'm doing nothing of the sort.'

'Then why exactly the pensive gazing into the fire?'

Marcia said, 'Well, damn it, you didn't expect me to *like* this evening, did you? I've always told you I was fond of Stephen and that I hated the idea of giving him up.'

'Quite,' I said. 'And I told you not to do it unless it was worth it to you. Presumably it was. If so, why the hell should I be expected to fall on my knees and thank you?'

'What on earth are you talking about?' said Marcia. 'Nobody expects you to.'

I said, 'No. I'm just expected to maintain a decent silence and reverence in the presence of grief.'

'Well, what are you going to do now?' said Marcia contemptuously.

I said, 'I'm going to tell Stephen that as far as I am concerned he can have you, and that if you stay here it'll be because you don't love him enough to leave me.'

'He knows that already. Why say it again?'

'Because he doesn't believe it – not in the way I mean it.'

Marcia said, 'I assure you he does. I've told him myself.'

'I dare say. But I mean it all cheap and nasty – much cheaper and nastier than you two ever let anything be. So it won't hurt him to hear it at first-hand.'

About ten minutes later I heard somebody outside. There was no knock so I went to the door. Stephen was just vanishing round the next corner.

I came back in and shut the door.

'What's happening?' said Marcia.

I said, 'He's walking up and down outside trying to pluck up enough courage to come in.'

'The ass!' said Marcia. 'I'd better go and get him in.'

'Stay exactly where you are,' I said, grabbing her.

'But he'll go away or something,' said Marcia.

I looked at her for a moment. She really thought so.

I said, 'Sometimes you're so dumb that it nearly makes me

cry. You can never see that it's a play even when the scenery creaks itself hoarse.'

'I don't see what you're playing at.'

'I'm not playing at anything,' I said. 'I'm acting like an ordinary human being who's waiting for a man to come and knock at his door.'

'But why not go and get him?'

I sighed. 'Listen,' I said. 'When Stephen wants to come in he'll come and knock at the door. At present he doesn't want to come in. He wants to be all temperamental and have someone go out and get him, so he clumps about outside blowing like a grampus instead. I don't want Stephen's temperament. I want Stephen. If I go on sitting here he'll come all right and his temperament will stay outside. Part of it, anyhow.'

We just sat there and after a bit he came back and puffed about outside some more. I caught Marcia's eye and we both started to giggle. He still didn't knock so I let out a bawl of 'Stephen!' He came in then and said, 'I wasn't sure if it was the right number.' He didn't look at Marcia.

I said, 'Hallo. Come in and sit down.' He was looking extremely ill, rather handsome, and very tight. He sat down, glanced across at Marcia as though she were a part of the furniture and then leant back and shut his eyes.

I said, 'Drink?'

'No, thank you,' he said. 'I'm drunk now. What d'you want?'

I suddenly realized that the original shot I'd meant to play wasn't on the table. He wasn't in the sort of state where you could do it. I said quite gently, 'I think we ought to get this mess cleared up, Stephen. It won't do like this.'

'You talk as though someone's spilt something on the carpet,' he said wearily. 'I don't understand you. I never do.' He opened his eyes and stared at the fire. I didn't say anything. I knew he'd go on.

'It isn't a mess on the carpet,' he said. 'It's my life.' He said it just like a discontented child, and his lips quivered.

'Quite,' I said, a bit curtly. 'But I'm not particularly interested in your life. I'm only interested in Marcia's.'

'They're the same thing,' he said. 'You won't believe that, and Marcia pretends not to. But she knows it's true.' He still didn't look at Marcia.

133

I said, 'That's the point that we've got to get settled. Or rather that you two have.'

Stephen shut his eyes again. 'Settled,' he said. 'You're always settling things. How can you settle a thing like that?'

I said, 'Listen, Stephen. I've not only told Marcia that she should go to you if she wants to – I've told her that she's no earthly good to me unless she comes from pure choice. If she ever had any sort of obligation to me I make her completely free of it. I can see exactly why you attract her, and I think it's a second-rate sort of attraction. If it's stronger than her feeling for me, then her feeling for me is worth precisely nothing.'

I got up and said, 'Now I'll make you both a proposition. If you can persuade Marcia to come to you, I'm prepared to divorce her, to let her divorce me, or to stay legally married to her, whichever she chooses. Further, I'm prepared to pay over to her half of my income and to go on doing so.'

'Don't talk nonsense, Bill,' said Marcia.

I said, 'It's my turn to talk nonsense. The only difference between this and most of the nonsense I've heard from you two is that I happen to mean mine.'

Stephen said, 'It's odd how you people always think money comes into everything.'

'That view comes from having had to earn it,' I said.

'This is complete bunk anyhow,' said Marcia. 'You know quite well that I shan't go and that even if I did I shouldn't go on that basis.'

'I don't profess to know what you'd do or wouldn't do,' I said. 'I've given up reckoning I knew about you lately. I'm starting at the other end and telling you what *I'm* prepared to do. And that's it.'

Stephen opened his eyes, and looked at the fire again. His lips were curling contemptuously, but he didn't say anything.

I said, 'So there you are, Stephen. Now it's up to you. There's only one condition.'

'Well?' he said.

'You have my full permission to take Marcia away from me – if you can. But if you can't, for God's sake pull yourself together, realize that you've flopped, and stop telling yourself and her that she's really breaking her heart for you and that only your noble souls are stopping you from pushing off together.'

134

'You're very clever,' said Stephen, shaking his head. 'Very clever.'

That got me rather. I said, 'Christ Almighty, what d'you mean clever? There's nothing clever in calling your bluff – particularly when I don't even know whether it *is* a bluff. I've given you since last February to stack the cards how you wanted them. Now I want to see what you've got. You've been playing the great lover to my Birmingham stockbroker for long enough. Now let's see just what there is to it.'

Stephen glanced across at Marcia, shut his eyes and said, very slowly, 'You've brought me here when I'm drunk and you're sober. But that doesn't make any difference. I'm not clever and I can't play with words like you do. I've only got my feelings.'

His lips quivered. He blinked hard and said, 'I'm not going to give you the satisfaction of talking about my feelings for Marcia. It would only give you a chance to sneer at them, and say I was lying. And they're too sacred to have that done to them.' He stopped and gulped. It was damned good. You could see how it would go with a female audience.

'I know Marcia will stay with you,' Stephen said. 'I've accepted that in all its bitterness. A bitterness you'll never be able to imagine. I've nothing to say to Marcia but to tell her of my gratitude for all the happiness – the *supreme* happiness – she has brought into my life. She knows that.'

He threw up his head suddenly and looked at me. 'But I'll tell you this,' he said. 'You can say what you like, but she's staying with you because she won't let you down. You may not like it, but it's true and you can't alter it. Not however clever you are. She knows that too.'

I turned to Marcia and said, 'Well?'

Marcia said wearily, 'I'm staying because I want to. Nobody's making me do anything. Nobody could. You'd better go now, Stephen.'

He got up and said, 'Yes, you're quite right. You always are. Thank you for always being right.' He turned to me and said, 'You don't know. You never will. That's your tragedy. We all have a tragedy, and that's yours.'

He went out without looking at Marcia again. We sat there for a moment and then I said, 'That serves me utterly, completely, damnably and most justly right.'

'What d'you mean, Bill?' said Marcia.

I said, 'The first requirement of a tough guy is to be tough. Otherwise it doesn't work.'

'Well, anyhow that's that,' she said.

'Is it?' I said.

Marcia looked at me. 'Yes. Why?'

I said, 'A quarter of an hour ago I should have said that if you preferred Stephen to me you were cuckoo. After that completely deplorable performance of mine I could very nearly see your point of view. But you see, Marcia, he was tight, and that's cheating.'

'But honey,' she said, 'I told you he was.'

'Oh God!' I said, flopping down on the bed. 'I'm not even competent. I'm not any bloody thing.'

Marcia came over and sat down beside me.

'You're lots of things,' she said, and put an arm round me.

I said, 'But it was a bloody incompetent effort, Marcia. And I meant it to be damned good.'

She grinned and said, 'Darling, I like you much better when you're incompetent.'

'But you don't see,' I said. 'I wanted to show you an honest man dealing with a bounder. And all I've shown you is me at my worst bullying a vaguely poetical, reasonably dignified and rather pathetic drunk. What an utterly nasty and contemptible show.'

'Well, damn it,' said Marcia. 'I let you in for it. Anyhow you don't have to show me things about you and Stephen. I know them.'

'Then why are you sulking?' I said. Marcia hesitated.

'Well, it sounds silly,' she said. 'But I had an idea that not having seen Stephen for a fortnight I should find he'd got over it and that we could go on knowing him without – all the other stuff.'

'My God!' I said. 'Stephen as a platonic friend!'

'Yes. Well, of course, I found it wasn't like that and it made me a bit wretched. I hate losing people, Bill.'

'Well, why in the name of Pete didn't you say so?'

She grinned and said, 'You didn't give me much chance.'

I kissed her and we stayed there for a bit.

TEN

THE DAY raids were dying down now. I suppose the pace was too hot to last. But to make up for it the nights were getting rougher than ever. The chief difficulty was to get enough sleep to keep going. Everybody was turning up at the office looking half asleep and as sour as hell. I think it was this which led up to my row with Lennox. Lord knows there were enough reasons for quarrelling with Lennox even if you were sleeping eight hours a night. When you got down to an average of about three the thing was a certainty.

It was a completely stupid business anyhow. We'd been having a lot of trouble over finding emergency factory space for places which had been bombed. I put through a minute to Lennox suggesting that where people hadn't made private arrangements for transferring their production if their factories were knocked out, we should work out an arrangement ourselves, and simply tell them that if they were hit, their production would go to such-and-such a place. It was the obvious thing to have it worked out in advance instead of waiting till the worst had happened before we did anything. You would have thought it was the sort of idea which nobody could have kicked at.

I sent this through to Lennox and for nearly a week I heard nothing about it. Then one day the thing just arrived back on my desk. It was scribbled all over with question marks and 'Whys?' and 'I don't agrees' and so on, in comrade Harness's writing. Underneath Lennox had just written, 'As you will see your suggestion is not practicable. J. L.'

I went straight in to Lennox and said, 'This minute of yours.'

He looked up in a bleary way and snapped, 'Well, what about it?'

'Who says it isn't practicable?' I said. 'And why?'

'You see Harness's comments,' said Lennox. 'He doesn't agree with you.'

I said, 'I didn't ask for Harness's comments and I don't mind in the least whether he agrees or not. If he agreed I should think there was something wrong with the idea anyway. I happen to know more about this issue than anybody in England and if it weren't practicable I shouldn't have suggested it.'

'You seem to forget that I am responsible for running this Department, Sarratt,' Lennox said.

I said, 'Then why not run it?'

'What do you mean?' Lennox said in a queer squeaky voice, getting really angry.

'I mean that when I put up a scheme I put it up to you, not to Harness.'

'I am perfectly entitled to ask advice from whom I please,' he said. 'You know quite well that Harness is my industrial adviser. Naturally I should ask his advice on a technical matter.'

'It's not only natural, it's inevitable,' I said. 'But I see no reason why you should always take it – particularly when it's just funny.'

'You're far too fond of your own opinion, Sarratt,' said Lennox. 'Harness is an expert.'

'And what am I?' I said. 'A milliner's apprentice?'

'I'm quite prepared to admit that you have experience of these things,' said Lennox. 'But you are here as a Civil Servant, just as I am.' He said it as though that settled everything. It made me mad.

'Right,' I said. 'Then the position is that because I come and work for this damned joint for nothing and call myself a Civil Servant, any incompetent who calls himself a business man carries more weight than I do?'

Lennox said, 'Oh, be reasonable.'

'I'm being reasonable,' I said. 'I want to win the war. I put up a considered scheme to you which will save a great deal of production time. I don't mind your knowing nothing about it. It isn't your job to know about these things. I don't mind your asking Harness, though it's right outside his experience. But I'm damned if I'm going to have my ideas crabbed by Harness and thrown back at me without a word of discussion with me. What the hell d'you think I am?'

'If you feel like that about it you'd better resign,' said Lennox. He didn't say it too happily though.

'There's nothing I'd like better,' I said. 'If this were a business concern, I'd have walked out months ago. But as it is it'd be playing these people's game. Harness would laugh his head off. He'd know it was all in the bag then.'

'In the bag?'

'Listen,' I said wearily. 'What d'you think I get out of this sort of thing?'

'None of us gets anything out of it,' said Lennox.

'I wouldn't say that. But you don't get anything out of it and nor do I. You know I know my job. Why should I put up a thing like this if it's just tripe?'

'Nobody's questioning your sincerity,' said Lennox. 'It's a question of whether you're right.'

'Exactly. But why do you always assume that I'm wrong and that Harness is right?'

'Harness is an expert.'

'Oh, bunkum!' I said. 'Expert my boot. Harness has spent his whole life in two businesses, mainly on the sales side. He's never had anything at all to do with production, and certainly not with things like this. He knows no more about this than you do. Why can't you Civil Servants realize that these business men are no good at all off their own ground, and not even much good on it?'

Lennox leant back in his chair, took his glasses off and rubbed his eyes. He looked very grey and used-up.

I said, 'I can't let this rest here. It's too important, and I'm sick of being stopped at every turn. If we can't have a different arrangement I shall put in a memorandum to the Secretary on the whole thing and offer to resign if necessary. I'm just wasting my time.'

'No, no, no,' said Lennox, shaking his head in a tired way. 'That's not the way at all. There's no need to be dramatic.'

I said, 'There's plenty of need for something.'

'We're always having these difficulties between you and Harness. I know you don't like him but there's a war on. We've got to work with people, Sarratt.'

'It's because there's a war on that I'm not prepared to put up with this sort of thing,' I said.

'Well, what do you suggest?' said Lennox irritably. 'You complain but you don't suggest anything.'

'I do all the suggesting that *is* done around here,' I said.

'But over this business of Harness, I mean. What is it you want?'

I said, 'I want some assurance that when I put up a scheme to you, you consider it properly instead of asking Harness what he thinks and taking his word for gospel.'

'In other words you object to my being advised by anyone but yourself?'

'Of course I don't. You can be advised by as many people as you like. But I want you to make up your own mind on the facts, and not to turn things down simply because they don't suit Harness's book.'

'I should never think of turning anything down without the fullest consideration,' said Lennox crossly.

'Fine,' I said. 'Do you know how many factories we have had put out of action in the last month? Or what their capacity amounted to? Or where they were? Or the average time which it's taking to get them going?'

'No,' he said.

'No. And neither does Harness. But you've both considered this fully and turned it down.'

Lennox sat for a long time staring down at his pad. Then he looked up at me with a rather pathetic smile.

'All right, Sarratt,' he said. 'I'll go into it again. It's difficult to give the time they deserve to these things.' He put his glasses on again. 'I don't know about you but I find myself so sleepy nowadays. If I take work home I tend to drop off over it.'

'Tried Sanatogen?' I said.

'No,' he said. 'Is that good?'

'It works for me.'

Lennox said, 'Anno Domini. That's my trouble.'

'It's mine too,' I said. 'The other way round.'

'No, no,' he said. 'It's you young people in the thirties who have to win wars. It was the same in the last one. I was just your age then.'

I said, 'I'll bet they didn't let you do a damned thing.'

Lennox smiled at his pad. 'No,' he said. 'That's perfectly true. *Si la jeunesse savait et si la vieillesse pouvait*. It's always the same.'

He stopped for a bit as though he was winding himself up. Then he said, 'You know I think you sometimes get your sense of proportion a trifle wrong, Sarratt.'

'Yes?' I said, trying to sound all objective and interested.

'You get an idea for doing something – very often an excel-

140

lent idea in itself. But you tend to leave out of account how it fits into the general scheme – the general principle on which things are being done.'

I said, 'That's probably because I don't agree with the general principle on which things *are* being done – or not done.'

Lennox smiled. 'Oh quite,' he said rather wearily. 'Neither do I, often enough. But you and I don't decide policy. It's no good kicking against the pricks, you know.'

'Why not?' I said. 'It may hurt your feet but somebody's got to do it. Kicking against the pricks is what I'm for.'

'You like trouble?' said the old boy.

'No,' I said. 'It makes me sweat and feel sick. But I never see how to avoid it.'

'Softly catch monkey,' said Lennox with a grin. 'That's the answer.'

We parted on that. I couldn't help feeling sorry for the old boy. He looked all in. I knew I should get my scheme through but I also knew it wouldn't do any permanent good. He'd still be in Harness's pocket. They were about the same age, and that makes a hell of a difference.

We had four meetings of the Area Scheme Committee before everybody finally got tired of the joke. Pellew had never managed to get anything out of the Secretary. We just used to go and sit round a table and gas. From the start there was only one real issue. That was whether the thing was to be voluntary or compulsory. I had no doubt about it myself. If the idea was to work at all, everybody must come into it. And the only way to be sure of getting everybody in was to give them no option. Of course Harness wanted it to be voluntary. I don't think he was being particularly crooked. He just saw a chance of setting up another nice committee which would then gently remove the whole guts of the scheme. He was very clever about it. He asked a lot of questions and raised a lot of objections – most of them quite fatuous, but nice and technical sounding. Then, as I explained, he gave way on each of them in turn, started to agree, and was very complimentary about the whole thing. By the time we got down to this voluntary-or-compulsory question he had everybody feeling that he'd been most reasonable and ready to give way whenever he was convinced. The committee, of course, didn't know the first thing about it, and

I could see that they were thinking it was very unreasonable and obstinate of me to go on insisting that the thing must be compulsory. They didn't realize that what Harness was asking meant the ruin of the whole scheme. After we'd wrangled for a bit Pellew said, 'I can't help thinking, Sarratt, that Harness is right in saying that we oughtn't to wade in with compulsion if the thing can be done voluntarily.'

'Of course he is,' I said. 'But this can't.'

'Harness seems to think it can.'

'Mr Chairman,' said Harness, canting over till I thought he'd fall out of his chair, 'I'd be prepared to guarantee that we can get what Mr Sarratt wants from industry without the slightest need for any compulsion.'

'Gentlemen's agreement,' said old Parks.

'Ladies invited,' said Edwardes.

'You'll get the gentlemen all right,' I said. 'But how about the non-gentlemen?'

'Or players?' said Edwardes.

'It isn't the slightest good unless you get everybody. The thing would simply bust.'

Harness said, 'I mean everybody. We could get 100 per cent agreement.'

'How d'you know that? The liaison committees aren't the whole of industry you know.'

'Anyhow, if Harness thinks he can get 100 per cent agreement so easily what objection is there to an order?' said Lawrence, who was about the only man present who saw the point. 'Quicker and safer.'

Harness squinted round at Pellew and said, 'Well, Mr Chairman, I understood that we were *fighting* Hitlerism and dictatorship—'

That went down very big. It always did. It was the stock argument for not doing anything decisive.

'Heil Adolf,' said Edwardes turning to me, raising an arm.

Pellew said, 'I don't profess to be very expert in this, but I really don't quite see your difficulty, Sarratt.'

'My difficulty is that I want the thing to work and that it won't work on a voluntary basis,' I said.

It wasn't a very helpful remark. I could see they were deciding that I was just being obstinate.

'Harness thinks it will,' said old Parks.

'You're imagining difficulties,' said little Brooks in his perky way.

I said, 'Well, that's new anyhow. Usually I leave that bit of it to you.'

Pellew poked at his glasses, shook his head and said, 'I'm sorry, Sarratt, but on just this one point I'm afraid the finding of the committee is against you.'

'So it appears,' I said. 'I'm sorry.'

I sat back and left it at that. It was a bit awkward for them. They didn't know anything about it and it was my scheme.

'Now what?' said Pellew rather helplessly.

'I submit that the committee can only report what it thinks, Mr Chairman,' said Harness.

Lawrence said, 'Count me out. I agree with Sarratt. I've had a skinful of voluntary schemes.'

'There you are,' said Pellew. 'The committee doesn't think. It disagrees.'

'*Le congres danse, mais il ne marche pas*,' said Edwardes.

'There's a clear majority,' said Harness. 'Apart from this one point I've nothing but good to say for Mr. Sarratt's most ingenious scheme. But on this I must insist.'

That was a bad brick. He didn't mean it like that but it sounded a bit arrogant.

Old Parks said gruffly, 'I dare say. But Sarratt and Lawrence are insisting too.'

'I think the only thing is to adjourn for the moment,' Pellew said. 'And see if you three can't get it thrashed out by the next meeting. Can everybody manage Wednesday if we do that? I don't think there's much point in going on until it's cleared.'

'Sorry,' I said to Pellew as we went out. 'But that's the guts of the whole thing. If we make it voluntary we'd far better scrap it.'

He said, 'You're quite probably right. That's the trouble about discussing things you don't understand. You see *I* don't know.'

'Lawrence knows,' I said. 'He's had some. So have I.'

'Look here,' said Pellew, stopping and folding his glasses, 'is this committee being any bloody good at all?'

'It's useful to have your views,' I said.

'Nonsense,' said Pellew. 'It's a waste of time. You know it and I know it. I shall say so.' And with that he stumped off.

143

The snag about living at the Palace was that we didn't live at it any more than we could help. We just slept there and went out as much as we could. This made life darned expensive. After about a week of it we got fed up and went back to the flat.

I knew it was a mistake as soon as we were back. It was very nice in a way but the flat give us both the jitters. Too much had happened there lately. We just went dumb on each other and couldn't talk at all. We stayed in for the evening. That was the main object of going back – to stay quietly by the fire and save money. So we stayed quietly by the fire and saved money, and it was hell.

It was difficult to know what to do about Stephen. If we talked about him I hated it, and if we didn't it made an atmosphere of not talking about him. We couldn't get anywhere near one another.

After a few days it seemed to be getting better. Marcia seemed a lot happier and didn't gaze at the fire so much. She was working like a black all day now, and we were both done by the end of the day. I was a bit scared of raids in that place – there was no shelter at all. But though there was a lot of noise they weren't actually dropping much on the West End just then. We got pretty good at sleeping through it. Everything went quite well for about a fortnight. Then one Saturday evening I came home about teatime with a splitting headache. Marcia had been off duty that day and she wasn't feeling so tired. She made me go to bed and came and sat on the bed and had dinner. It was grand to have her fussing around in the pre-war style. It was the nicest thing that had happened to me for months. She lay on the bed and I stroked her hair and held her, and let it all go to hell.

About nine o'clock the telephone rang. It was for Marcia. I didn't know the voice but as soon as she took over I could see from her face that there was something wrong. I could hear the chap at the other end quacking away but I couldn't hear what he was saying. Marcia said, 'Is it bad? I mean is there any danger?'

'Quack,' said the bloke. 'Quack, quack. Quack-quack, *quack* quack.'

'Oh Lord,' said Marcia a bit helplessly. 'Has he been unconscious ever since?'

'Quack.'

Marcia said, 'Well, will you give me the address?'

The bloke gave her it and she wrote it down.

'All right,' she said. 'I'll come round.' She hung up.

'What's up?' I said.

Marcia looked at me with her anxious expression and said, 'Stephen.'

'Of course. But what?'

'Oh, a bloody mess. He's in a nursing home. He was taken in last night and he's been unconscious until now.'

'What's the matter with him? Shot at himself and forgotten to duck?'

'No. Just made himself ill. That was Woods, his doctor. He always picks up the pieces when Stephen does this sort of thing.'

'What *sort* of ill?' I said.

'Oh, apparently Stephen turned up there yesterday very drunk and nearly off his head and Woods had to get him into a nursing home and dope him up.'

I said, 'Oh, that sort of unconscious. I thought you meant unconscious.'

Marcia said, 'Now of course he's come round and started demanding me.'

'Hair of the lady dog that bit him,' I said.

'I think I shall have to go round,' said Marcia, looking worried. 'Apparently he's pretty bad.'

'Bunkum,' I said. 'You're not a prairie oyster. Forget it and come back on the bed.'

'No, I must, Bill. I said I would. It won't take a moment.'

'Don't be a sap,' I said rather crossly. 'It's only one of Stephen's try-ons. He isn't ill. He's only drunk too much and given himself a headache. Hell, *I've* got a headache, if you want one.'

Marcia said, 'But I *must*. I said I would.'

I suddenly realized that she was really thinking about it. I sat up and said, 'Look here, you don't really want to go tearing round there, do you?'

'Only for a minute,' said Marcia rather wretchedly. 'But I can't just do nothing, can I?'

'In God's name why not? Let him send for Peggy. Stephen's drunks are her affair.'

Marcia said firmly, 'No, I'm sorry, Bill, but there are some things I can't do.' She was looking obstinate.

I said, 'Well, I really am damned.' Marcia looked at her watch and said, 'If you'll just stay there I'll be back by half past ten at the latest.'

I said, 'If you go round there, Marcia, you can get back at ten-thirty, Tooting or Tuesday for all I care, and that's final. I shan't be here.'

She looked at me and her lips trembled. She said, 'You wouldn't do that.'

'I certainly would,' I said. 'What the hell d'you expect?'

Marcia looked away and said, 'I should have thought the fact that he's rather ill and asking for me would have made a difference.'

'Oh, you bloody little fool,' I said. I could have spanked her.

She wheeled round and said, 'I wouldn't care who it was, Bill, if they did that, I'd go. Anybody I knew. I wouldn't let a dog down like that. Nor would you. You want me to do things I *can't* do.'

I said, 'Sit down a minute, honey, and listen.'

She sat down on the edge of the bed as though it was red hot.

I said, 'You're still playing this for tragedy and you know it.' She shut her eyes in a patient way and said, 'How am I?'

'You're talking about Stephen being ill and being in a nursing home and calling for you and so on. That's just exactly what he wants you to do. The facts are that he's boozed until he's passed out and had to be put to bed, and now he's trying to use that as a lever to get you. If you're such a fool as not to see through that you must be even dumber than I thought. Personally I'd been expecting something like this. But I thought he'd try committing suicide by taking six aspirins. I didn't think he'd have the cheek to do it just on whisky.'

Marcia said, 'I can't *do* it, Bill. Can't you see, I know all that, but I can't *do* it. It isn't fair to try to make me.'

I said, 'I was sick and ye visited me. My God, what a fool you are, Marcia.'

'I dare say I am,' she said. 'But they thought I ought to go. They said he was pretty ill.'

'I doubt he's explained the full circumstances,' I said sarcastically. 'He's probably only called your name in his delirium. And your telephone number.'

Marcia didn't say anything.

'Well?' I said.

She said, 'I'll be back here by half past ten. I'll swear I will. And if he's all right I won't go again. Honestly. Can't I have that? It's the last thing I'll ask for.'

I said, 'You must please yourself, Marcia.'

She looked at me for a moment. Then she turned and went out quickly. I heard her go into the bathroom.

I got out of bed and dressed, and chucked my pyjamas into a suitcase.

Marcia came back. She said, 'Bill – you're not going to really?'

I said, 'I'm going to really and truly.'

'Where are you going?'

'To Ted's.'

'But you'll come back? You haven't gone – not for good?'

I said, 'Nobody ever does things for good. Good's a long time. I've gone for the present.'

She stood there with her eyes full of tears and her lips trembling.

I said, 'Pull yourself together, honey. There's only one way out of this. I've known it long enough. You've got to get this out of your system if we're to be any good.'

She said, 'But *how*?'

'That's up to you,' I said. 'From now on I don't come into it unless you want me to. And then it's on my terms. You can have the flat. I shall be at Ted's if you want me.'

'But what shall I do?'

'Go and hold Stephen's hand and cool his fevered brow until you're sure whether you like it. If you do, go on doing it. If not, stop. It's as easy as that.'

She said, 'But you'll have me back?'

'I'd like notice of that,' I said, 'when you're disengaged.'

She looked bloody miserable and about seventeen. I kissed her and she hung on to me and started to howl. I'd never heard her cry like that.

I patted her on the back, pried her loose and went out. It suddenly occurred to me that she wouldn't have any money. She never had. I went back and said, 'You'll want some money. I've only got a bit now. Use the joint account, of course.'

She was lying on the bed crying. I put three pounds in her

bag, smacked her bottom gently and went. As I went down the stairs she opened the door and called, 'Oh, Bill – Bill—!'

I was rather annoyed about it. It echoed all over the flats. I just went on.

Ted was not in. I lit the fire and started to read.

About eleven Ted came in and said, 'Well, look who's here.' He had a bloke with him. I was glad it wasn't a girl. I said, 'Off agen on agen Flanagen. Is it all right, Ted?'

'Of course,' he said. 'This is George Pine, Bill Sarratt. How about some tea?'

For a nice man Ted had the weirdest collection of friends. This bird Pine was a little thin, pale chap with a shock of black hair and a bright green tie. He was wearing a shooting jacket with leather inserts.

He said to me, 'Are you one of our great bureaucrats, like Ted?'

'I'm a Temporary Civil Servant,' I said. 'The operative word is temporary.'

'You'll be all right then,' he said enviously.

'How d'you mean?'

'They won't shift it beyond thirty.'

'What?'

'The age of reservation,' he said. 'You couldn't get me in to your Ministry, I suppose? I've only got about a month to get fixed.'

I said, 'Why should I? You've never done me any harm.'

'You all talk like that,' he said quite snappily. 'What wouldn't I give for your job!'

'Well, what would you? It's a lousy job. You work your head off, don't get paid, and get nothing done. You're welcome.'

'Better than what'll happen to me,' said Pine. He glowered at the fire and wriggled nervously about in his chair.

'You mean you think you'll be called up?' I said.

He made a face as though I'd hurt him. 'I shall unless I can do something about it bloody quick.'

'You think that'll be a poor do?' I said.

'What a question!' he said. He wriggled some more. The man seemed to be a mass of nerves. 'I've pulled every bloody wire I can think of – pulled them till my fingers are sore. It's awful.'

'Well, come!' I said. 'It may be a bit grim, but surely it's nothing to feel like that about?'

'You're all alike,' he said. 'You and Ted and all the rest of you who're sitting pretty. It isn't going to happen to *you*.'

I could swear he shuddered. I was interested. I hadn't met quite this before.

'Well, what's going to happen to you?' I said, as Ted came back with the tea.

'He's going to be fried with a flame-thrower, run over by a tank, dive-bombed and then gassed,' said Ted brightly. 'I know because he told me. Didn't you, George?'

The little squirt wriggled himself about some more.

'I'm too sensitive for this sort of thing,' he said, plaintively. 'I've got too much imagination. I don't want to have anything to do with the war. It's nothing to do with me. I should be no good to them anyhow.'

Ted had obviously had all this before. 'I've always told you,' he said firmly, 'what you want is a properly trained conscience. Then you could be a conscientious objector.'

'They have an awful time,' said Pine. 'They manhandle them. I couldn't go through that.'

'It's not easy to see the perfect job for you in a war,' I said, getting rather fed up.

'You think I'm a coward,' said Pine. 'All right. I don't care what you think.'

Ted said, 'No, he doesn't. He doesn't know you from Adam. He doesn't know what you are and doesn't care. Have some tea?'

We had tea. Ted started to talk about people they both knew. Apparently the little bloke was in the film racket, or had been. After a bit he began to cheer up and tell us stories about the film industry. They were the usual sort of thing. He told me about a time when he went over to Spain on location with a unit of about seventy. They mucked about for three weeks or so doing nothing, and then somebody suggested that they'd better get going and asked for the script. They found they hadn't got a script, so they rang up London. After about a week it turned out that the man who'd originally been working on the script was dead. He'd been dead over a year. So they wrote the script as they went along and shot each bit as it was finished.

I'd heard that story with slight variations at least a dozen times before, but he told it extraordinarily well. We all three roared with laughter. He seemed as happy as maybe. Then for some reason or other the All Clear went just after midnight and he went straight into an almighty flap again. He said, 'I can't *stand* that noise. It'll drive me mad.'

'That's all right,' I said. 'That's a good noise. Nothing to worry about in that.'

'I've got to do something,' he said, throwing himself about. 'Here I am sitting here and there's only six weeks left. Six weeks. Maybe less if they speed up.'

He looked round the room, in a wild sort of way. I shouldn't have been surprised if he'd tried to get under the sofa.

'You mean you register in six weeks?' I said.

'Yes.'

'Cheer up. I know a bloke who's been trying to get into the army for a year and they've only just taken him.'

'They're taking people fast now,' he said. 'It isn't like it was. Are you sure you couldn't find anything for me? I'd do anything. Absolutely anything. They needn't pay me.'

He went on like that for half an hour. We couldn't get him off it. Finally we couldn't do with any more of it, and Ted more or less pushed him out, saying he wanted to go to bed.

After he'd gone, I said, 'In God's name where did you get that?'

Ted said, 'Amazing, isn't it? I thought you'd be interested.'

'Look here,' I said, 'we're both possible soldiers and we aren't in the army. Do we look like that to other people?'

'I hope we don't,' said Ted. 'I don't think so.'

'It's a pretty ghastly thought,' I said. 'I'd far rather be dead than going around in that state.'

'I think he will be quite soon,' said Ted. 'He's going off his head. That's why I brought him back tonight. He's a nice little man too, is George. I was quite fond of him. But he's been like this ever since Munich. He spent hours then, rushing round trying to book a passage to America, looking as white as a sheet. When he found he couldn't, he just cracked up and had to go to bed.'

We didn't say much about my being there. I just said, 'Look, Marcia's toddled off for a bit. Can I hang on here until it all gets a bit clearer?'

Ted said, 'Sure. You know it's fine for me.' We left it at that and went to bed.

It was pretty late but it took me a hell of a time to go to sleep. The little squirt Pine had shaken me up rather. I felt sick. At one time I thought I must resign the next morning and go and join up. It seemed as though he hadn't left me any option. I must have been half asleep because that seemed quite logical in the way things do in bed. Then I started to think about Marcia, and went to sleep.

ELEVEN

THE NEXT morning Marcia rang me up and said, 'I don't want to bother you but I thought I'd better tell you where I am.' She gave me an address and a telephone number in Chelsea. We didn't talk; Marcia just said, 'I'm very sorry about last night, Bill,' and I said, 'That's all right. It had to happen sometime' – and we left it at that. I thought she seemed surprisingly calm and cheerful. I suppose it was as much a relief to her to have done something definite as it was to me.

All the same, it was rather a grim patch. I was very fond of Ted, and he liked having me. But what with raids every night and wanting to save money it was difficult to know what to do with the evenings. I thought of taking Anne out. But there wasn't much point in it unless I was really going after her, and things were complicated enough already without that. Besides, I was always dog-tired. The office just staggered on. There seemed to be an odd feeling all round of waiting for something.

Ted and I didn't have breakfast. We just drank tea and smoked a cigarette before we started out. While we were doing this on the Thursday Ted said, 'When did you last go to a party?'

'Define a party,' I said.

'I mean in the home. Thrown by somebody.'

'Not since last November, 1939, when Marcia and I had that last one of ours.'

'Well, we're invited to one,' said Ted.

'Who with?'

'Willie Hubbard.'

'Don't know him,' I said.

'Yes, you do. No, you don't though. He's an odd man. Shall we go?'

I said, 'I don't know what sort of parties Willie Hubbard gives, but I'd go to a PSA at the moment and like it.'

'He's a queer cove,' said Ted. 'I doubt it'll be the sort of thing one ought to go to in a war, but you may be interested.'

Just after I got to the office Lennox rang up and said, 'The Minister wants to see us this afternoon.'

'Fine,' I said. 'Is the department being fired?'

'It's about your Area Scheme,' Lennox said. 'He wants to discuss it.'

'But how about Pellew and the Committee?'

'Pellew's told the Secretary that he's gone as far as he can, and that it's now up to the Minister to say if he wants to do it.'

'Good for Pellew,' I said. 'Who's coming?'

'Yourself, myself, Pellew and Harness.'

I said, 'That's just seventy-five per cent perfect.' I was extremely bucked.

I had another look through my memorandum. It still looked pretty good to me. The only snag was that I was afraid Harness would start talking voluntary schemes and that Lennox would back him. While I was sweating away at this stuff someone rang up from Establishments and said, 'We haven't received your report on Mr W. J. Sayers.'

'What a horrible thing,' I said. 'What d'you want to know about him?'

'We sent you the usual note after he'd been with you a month asking if he'd been satisfactory and so on, and you haven't returned it. Will you please do so at once?'

'He's no bloody good,' I said. 'But don't take my word for it, will you?'

'What?' said the bloke.

I said, 'I haven't got a Mr W. J. Sayers. I never have had. But if I had I'll bet he'd be awful. Tra-la-la.' I hung up. I was feeling quite chirpy.

Fred Giles came in and said one of the messengers had been killed in last night's raid, plus wife, plus son, plus daughter, plus son-in-law. They were in an Anderson. It was

152

a direct hit. Fred said, 'Somebody was going to start a fund for the family and then they found there wasn't any family.'

I told him Lennox and I were going to see the Minister. I said it as though I spent most of my time with the old boy.

I had quite a needle about the meeting. It wasn't until three, and I couldn't settle down. I went out and started going round the department. Usually, I didn't see anything of it from one week's end to another. I just left that part of it to Fred.

It always felt queer to go round nowadays. There were only about three of the people left that Fred and I started with in September '39, and half of the staff I hardly knew at all. It was odd to see a couple of girls I didn't know working the indicator tabs as though they'd been doing it all their lives, and to remember the night Fred and I worked out the indicator system.

I said to Fred, 'The snag about the department is that it hasn't moved. It's just got bigger.'

'What's wrong with it?' said Fred, a bit hurt.

'There must be a better way of keeping tab of things than that damned indicator,' I said. 'It was all right when we had to vamp up something that would work in a week. But we've had over a year now. Surely we could find something less clumsy?'

'There's never any time,' said Fred.

'There wasn't then.'

'No, but we were starting from scratch. That's easier than scrapping and improving.'

I said, 'The whole bloody place is like that. You put a thing in as a makeshift and it stays, because nobody's got time to think.'

'I wish you'd got more time to think about things like that,' said Fred. 'It's not up my street. I don't have ideas much, myself.'

'Nobody does,' I said. 'I've never seen a more sterile outfit in my life.'

'Couldn't you get a couple of days on it?'

I said, 'I must try.' I knew I shouldn't. It was finished for me – that side of it. It didn't seem to matter much any longer.

At three o'clock we went along to the Minister's room. It was a real full dress show. The Minister, Childs, the Parliamentary Secretary, the Secretary, old Phillips, the financial adviser,

153

and the four of us. This was only the third time I'd had any-thing much to do with the Minister, and I'd never even seen Childs before. I thought he looked pretty dumb. Baxter himself looked all right. He always did – purely because of having that lovely silver hair.

He was very polite and dignified and charming as usual. Baxter always acted and talked as though he thought some-body was taking notes for his biography and might want to put this bit in. I always wondered how he and the Secretary got on in private. In public they made me laugh. Baxter was always looking handsome and being a great man and the Secretary was always looking an ugly little cove and under-lining the fact that he ran the place. We sat down round the long table and the Minister took cover behind about five tele-phones and posed for his portrait. I made a careful resolution that this was where I kept my mouth shut. The Secretary said, 'Perhaps I'd better explain the object of this meeting, Minister.'

Baxter bowed and said, 'If you please, Sir Frederick.'

The Secretary looked like a monkey and said, 'For some time we've had under active consideration the possibility of some sort of *grouping* of productive firms. Not mergers, of course. But groups which could be dealt with, for our purposes, collec-tively. The advantages of that would be obvious.'

The Minister nodded as though he saw. Maybe he did.

'I felt,' said the Secretary, glaring round the table as though it was everybody's fault, 'I felt that the time had come to crystallise this rather nebulous desire which had been felt by many of us. I therefore gave instructions for the setting up of a committee of which Mr Pellew is chairman, to explore the matter, and to report to me. Mr Pellew now tells me that his committee has reached certain conclusions, which I should like you to hear.'

Baxter bowed again and began to fill his pipe. Filling his pipe was one of his best bits. It showed you that the thing was just a friendly informal chat. My old headmaster used to fill his pipe just like that.

Everybody turned and looked inquiringly at Pellew. Pellew poked his glasses back on his nose and said, 'Well, Minister, the committee of which I am chairman has held five meetings in all. I think on the whole our conclusion is that, with the exception of one or two points of detail which will have to be worked out further, we agree that the proposal should be given a trial. It isn't perfect, but it's a big advance on the present position.'

'Perfection,' said Baxter with his nice smile, 'may be obtainable by heavenly Ministers, Mr Pellew, but it is out of reach of Cabinet Ministers.'

We all smiled knowingly.

'Quite,' said Pellew. 'We definitely felt that the proposal was ingenious, and sufficiently practical to be tried.'

'What proposal?' said the Parliamentary Secretary in a sullen sort of way.

'The proposal which was put before us,' said Pellew. 'I believe it came originally from Mr Lennox's department.' He turned and looked hopefully at Lennox. Everybody turned and looked at Lennox. There seemed to be a general feeling that we weren't getting on particularly fast.

'Perhaps Mr Lennox would tell us something of his proposal,' said the Minister with another little bow towards Lennox. Lennox hesitated and smiled at me, and for a moment I thought he was going to say, 'Well, as a matter of fact, it was Sarratt's proposal and he'd better tell you.' But the whole thing was beginning to be rather like hunt the slipper, so he waded in and outlined the scheme to them. It wasn't too bad. He left quite a lot out and he would talk about 'capacity' when he meant 'current production', but he did tell them what it was all about. Baxter listened very carefully and at the end he said, 'Thank you, Mr Lennox,' and bowed again. Then he sat back, lit his pipe, and said, 'Gentlemen, Ministers never know anything about their jobs. The only virtue I can claim is that I know I know nothing about technicalities, and don't even want to. That's your job. Mine is to see that, in general, we get the maximum possible production from industry at the minimum possible cost. I'm only going to ask one question, and that's a silly one. But being silly is my privilege.' He leant forward and said, 'Why is your area proposal better than the present system by which firms are dealt with individually?'

'There would be an enormous saving in administrative time and cost,' said Lennox. 'And we should be able to switch production from damaged factories much more quickly.'

'Very well,' said Baxter, smiling as though he'd got the

answer he wanted. 'Then why do you stop there?'

'Where?' said the Parliamentary Secretary, crossly.

'At dividing the country into ten areas,' said the Minister, throwing out a hand. 'Wouldn't you save even more labour by completely central control?'

'That's certainly true,' said Lennox.'

'I'm not suggesting it,' said Baxter. 'It's not my job to suggest things. It's my job to listen. Personally, I abominate centralization. But I want to hear your answer to that, Mr Lennox. And yours, Mr Pellew.'

Lennox and Pellew looked at one another. It was bone obvious that they hadn't got an answer. Unlike Fred Giles, they'd never even thought of it.

After a bit I said to Lennox, 'Shall I answer that?'

Lennox said, 'Yes, do.'

'Please, Mr Sarratt,' said Baxter with his bow.

Of course that tore it. As long as I kept completely quiet it was all right. But the thing was my baby, and once I started it never even occurred to me to stop. I woke up about twenty minutes later nearly wet through with sweat. Baxter was sitting with his legs crossed looking at me with a very nice quiet smile. Lennox was grinning in a slightly smug way that was half proud and half apologetic. The Parliamentary Secretary looked a bit asleep. I realized that I'd been lecturing them like hell. It was probably pretty good. At least I knew the stuff backwards.

Baxter said gently, 'Thank you very much, Mr Sarratt. That's extremely interesting.'

The Secretary said, 'I think you'll agree, Minister, that this is a real step forward.'

'I do,' said Baxter. 'I quite agree.'

'A lot of work has been put in on this proposal,' said the Secretary, in a way that suggested that he'd been lying awake at night about it. 'And I think the results show how carefully it has been considered.'

'I'm very grateful to those responsible,' said Baxter, taking a curtain.

'You agree that we should go ahead?' said the Secretary, wrinkling up his face as though it were indiarubber.

'Certainly,' said Baxter. 'Unless anyone has any objections?'

I saw Harness canting over and knew it was coming.

'If I might say a word, sir,' he said, 'whilst I have the greatest confidence in the general idea, I should have preferred it to be a *voluntary* scheme.'

'Yes?' said Baxter.

'One of the things which industry has always valued most, sir, was that you have always asked for cooperation whenever you could, instead of setting yourself up as a dictator.'

I was scared stiff. Harness was on a perfect wicket. Baxter was a business man himself and he was always gassing about 'cooperation' and damning bureaucracy.

But he didn't seem very impressed. Harness is a nasty looking bit of work, and that may have had something to do with it.

Baxter just looked round the table and said, 'What's the general view?'

I said, 'I'm all for a voluntary scheme if it'd work. But it wouldn't.'

Baxter surprised me by saying, 'That's what I was wondering.' He turned to Harness and said, 'I've nothing but admiration for business men, Mr Harness. I'm one myself. But there are times when I feel a little happier if I have the law of the land behind me than all the goodwill in the world.' He caught my eye. I was grinning broadly and so was he. 'Anyhow,' he said with a wave of the hand, 'that can be settled later.' He got up and started to throw us out very politely.

As we were going out Baxter came up behind me and said, 'Excellent.'

I turned and said, 'You like the scheme, Minister?'

He said, 'Yes. And I thought you put it across most ably. I'm very much obliged to you.' He bowed and smiled very charmingly.

It seemed an odd way to put it, but I was very bucked, and blushed.

As we walked back to our offices I said to Lennox, 'I'm sorry if I gassed too much. I always do.'

'Not at all,' said Lennox. 'You did it very well. The Minister was very pleased.' He seemed pleased himself. I could never quite make out about Lennox.

This man Willie Hubbard lived out at Hampstead. We went most of the way by tube. It was the first time I'd been anywhere by tube at night for several months, and I wanted to see how the tube shelter business was working out.

157

It all looked much the same, but a bit more orderly. I thought there weren't as many children as before, nor quite as many young Jew boys. But there were still too many of both, and, as Ted said, we weren't seeing the stations down East. There were still no bunks in any station we passed. I think they'd chlorinated the air a bit. Anyhow there was a strong disinfectant tang in it which I found sickening. I like disinfectant smells, but not when they're being used to cover up frowsy smells.

It was only about half past eight, and most of the people were sitting propped up with their backs against the platform wall, reading. A few were lying down with blankets over them, asleep, and others were just sitting staring in front of them. Most of them looked pretty poor, but there was one old chap at Hampstead who pleased Ted and me a lot. He had bagged a sort of corner seat up at the extreme end of the platform. He was sitting in a very expensive-looking Dunlopillo sleeping-bag, dressed in a camel hair dressing-gown, playing Archer patience. He had a silver and leather flask beside him, and as we looked he stopped playing patience for a moment and took a meditative pull at this flask while he thought it out.

Ted said, 'I suppose his valet comes and calls him in the morning.'

'And brings his shaving water,' I said. 'War's a terrible thing.'

The warning was later than usual that night. It was only just going as we came up out of the tube.

I said, 'What strikes me as odd is the different views people take of raids. Either they don't do anything, or else they go and camp in the deepest tube in London whether there's a raid or not.'

Ted told me that quite a lot of people were just staying in the tube all the time from teatime till breakfast. 'You'd think they'd get etiolated,' I said. 'All long and yellow.'

Ted said, 'They will.'

We walked along to the block of flats where this man Willie Hubbard lived. It was a big new steel and concrete affair, very expensive-looking inside. Ted said to the porter, 'Which floor is Mr Hubbard on?'

The porter grinned and said, 'Mr Hubbard? Oh, Mr Hubbard's downstairs now, sir.'

'Downstairs?'

'Yes, sir. You come with me and I'll show you.'

He took us downstairs into a basement, and then down some more stairs.

'Good God!' said Ted. 'What a cavern!'

'Safest place in London,' said the porter proudly. 'Eleven floors over you, each one made of concrete. That's Mr Hubbard's door, sir.'

There was a hell of a babel going on inside this place. We rang, and as nobody came we just pushed the door open and went in.

There was a big room about thirty feet long with a curtain across one end. It was fitted up very lushly, with close carpeting and strip lighting. You could hardly see across it for smoke, but it looked just the sort of thing you expect in an expensive block in Hampstead. There were about thirty people milling around and talking at the tops of their voices.

The man Willie Hubbard loomed up out of the smoke and fell on Ted's neck. He said, 'Teddy, my dear, I thought you'd been destroyed by a bomb.'

'Not yet,' said Ted. 'This is Bill Sarratt.'

'How do you do?' said Hubbard. 'Do have a drink. You're both horribly behind the party.'

He went over to the sideboard and poured us drinks.

'We wondered where the devil the porter was bringing us,' said Ted.

'Like it?' said the Hubbard bloke.

'I should think it the most luxurious dug-out in London. How did you get it?'

'Forethought, my dear, forethought. Just before Munich I decided that quite soon it would be healthier below ground. So I went along to the owners of this place and made them a small offer for one of their cellars. They fell for it. They've kicked themselves ever since because now they'd like it for a shelter for the whole place. I only got it furnished just before the war began. Beautiful timing.'

'It must have cost the hell of a lot,' said Ted.

'In all,' said Hubbard, 'it cost me just over five hundred pounds – excluding rent, of course. A small price to pay for the preservation of the last of the Hubbards, yes?'

I didn't say so, but personally I thought it was just five

159

hundred pounds too much. This man, Willie Hubbard, was a most unpleasant-looking structure. He was very tall – I should think about six feet two – very thin and narrow-shouldered, and about the last six inches was a bald egg of head. He had small, very dark eyes, a flowing black moustache, and he was wearing a red velvet smoking jacket and bright yellow corduroy trousers. He looked like a painting by somebody who couldn't draw and had a nasty mind.

'I like your trousers,' said Ted, who couldn't bear that sort of thing.

'A protest, my dear,' said Hubbard. 'Purely a protest.'

'Against what?' I said.

'Aha, a rationalist,' Hubbard squeaked out in his high raucous voice. 'My dear sir – my very dear sir, protests should be abstract. Leave us something abstract in the midst of so much concrete.' He was pretty tight.

We drank our drinks and took two more. By the sound of things we should need to move pretty fast to get near the field. They were making a noise like the parrot house.

'Come along,' Hubbard said, squeezing us both by the arm, 'Come and meet people. Is this one of your homo or. heterosexual phases, Ted dear? Ravishing girls or slinky little boys?'

He stopped in front of a very fat cove who was arguing at the top of his voice with a hag of a woman in glasses. 'Here's Tony,' he said. 'He's a slinky piece. Tony – meet Ted and Bill.'

'Go to hell,' said the fat cove politely, not looking round. Hubbard hauled us round and introduced me to a few people. They were all tight and all pretty awful. Ted had another drink and started to argue about the war with a hollow-cheeked man who looked like a decadent James Maxton. I found a little dumpy girl with a pink and white face and started to make passes at her. She was exactly like a rather charming little pig.

Suddenly the very fat cove bawled out, 'Willie!'

'What?' squeaked Hubbard.

'Here's somebody talking about the bloody war!'

'Take his trousers off then.'

'It's a wimp,' said the fat cove. Roars of laughter.

'Don't let that deter you,' said Hubbard. 'Anyone who talks about the war loses his, her or its trousers or nearest equivalent. Rule of the house.'

I said to the pig, 'Go on – talk about the war.' She giggled. I said, 'I don't suppose you've anything to lose anyway.' She giggled some more and said, 'Not a lot.'

Somebody else spoke to her and I sidled over to Ted and said, 'God, what a zoo!'

'You wouldn't believe it if you didn't see it, would you?' he said.

I said, 'I'm not going to see it for long. Your boy friend Hubbard makes me sick in the stomach.'

Hubbard was standing with one arm round a rather lovely young Jewess, making her drink out of his glass.

'He is pretty poisonous,' said Ted. 'I thought you might be interested?'

'I'm fascinated,' I said. 'He's like a Rowlandson brought up to date and run over by a steam-roller.'

Hubbard let go of the Jewess and squeaked out, 'Ladies and gentlemen, Tony will now sing.'

'Go to hell,' bawled the fat cove.

'You sing, Willie,' shouted the pink pig.

'The War Song,' said the female in glasses. They all took it up and began to yell, 'The War Song!'

The cove Hubbard simpered, and said, 'All right. W. Hubbard will now sing. Words by W. Hubbard. Music traditional. And if you don't sing the bloody chorus I shall stop.'

The cadaverous man rushed over to the piano and started to play the Vicar of Bray, and Hubbard began to sing. He could sing too. High tenor, very well produced. I should say Italian taught. The words were a sort of war dodger's anthem, with the chorus:

'And this is the answer I will make
To Berlin or to Rome, sir:
That whatsoever place they take
Yet I'll stay safe at home, sir.'

It was quite funny really, but for some reason it got me down. I suppose it was because they were such a poisonous lot – particularly Hubbard. I tossed up whether to do something about it, and then thought I'd better not as Ted had brought me. Hubbard had just got to the sixth verse about 'When Hitler took Aus-tra-li-a—' when I said to Ted, 'I'm going. Coming?'

He said, 'I'm with you.'

161

We went and left them at it.

When we got into the street I said, 'I like your friend Hubbard's voice, but he smells so nasty. So do his pals.'

'It was a bit like that,' said Ted. 'Sorry.'

'Not at all,' I said. 'Interesting.' We didn't say anything as we walked back to the tube. There was a lot of gunfire down East. The old chap in the tube station had stopped playing patience and was lying down in his beautiful sleeping-bag.

Ted said, 'I wonder if he got it out?'

As we stopped at Camden Town we saw a woman in the crowd on the platform sitting a small kid on a chamber-pot. The kid was crying and a lot of people were turning round looking at her in a fed-up way.

I said, 'The great thing about this war is that there's equality of sacrifice. We are all in the front line now.' I was finding it difficult to get the chap Hubbard out of my mind.

'I'd rather like to meet a *nice* cove,' said Ted a bit wistfully. 'I've had a skinful of interesting ones lately.'

I said, 'The thing that beats me is why those poor devils down in the East End stand for it – not only for people like Hubbard, but for you and me.'

Ted didn't say anything. He was a conservative cove.

'After all,' I said. 'Just what has this war meant to me? Somebody goes on paying me. I don't get conscripted. I can go and eat what I like in flash pubs and sleep under about twelve steel and concrete floors—'

'That's right,' said Ted, getting fed-up. 'You're having a wonderful time. So am I. It's a rich man's war.' But he knew there was something in it, and so did I.

TWELVE

I HEARD no news of Marcia for several days. It was a bit difficult, because there were raids every night, and I was afraid she'd be going out and gaping at them. I didn't ring her up. It didn't seem to be much good telling her to go and try living with Stephen if I was always butting in. But I went down to

Chelsea a couple of times to see that the house was still there. It was. On the day that she'd been away a fortnight she wrote me a letter. It said:

'Darling – I think I've seen all there is to see about this. I should never have come if you hadn't rather made me. I know I didn't want to be with Stephen all the time. But you were quite right. It's been a good thing, and I'm cured now I think. Stephen has started to write again, so he's all right, though of course he's making a hell of a fuss. You're right about my being bad for him. This is just to ask if you want me back. You never made it quite clear whether you did or not. You don't have to have me. I shall quite see your point of view if you tell me to go to hell, and shall be quite all right. But please, Bill, don't take me back just because you think it's your duty. It isn't, and I should hate it.

'I've told Stephen I shall go tomorrow, so will you let me know? I'm at Chelsea after six. Of course I shall go anyhow, even if you don't want me. But please try to.

'Darling Bill, I am awful.'   'M'.

This was all right as far as it went. But I liked getting it more than that.

I put it in my pocket and went off to the Ministry. There was a lot to do, and I thought I'd ring up in the evening instead of trying to get her at the Aldgate place.

Lennox rang up and said that the Minister was talking to the General Liaison Committee about the Area Scheme the next day, and would I do a brief for him?

I said, 'Hadn't somebody better be there, too? They're bound to ask questions.'

'Oh, yes,' Lennox said. 'We're both to go. The brief is just for the Minister to open with.'

I got Doris in and started to boil the whole thing down into six sentences with no word of more than two syllables. I always think the golden rule with briefs is that they should be. It was difficult to boil down a thing as wide as that without making it completely vague. Doris was looking darn pretty and more than usual, as though she was doing it on purpose, which didn't help. I found myself looking at her in all the wrong ways. I decided it was about time Marcia came back.

We got the brief down to a couple of pages eventually. I told

163

Doris to type a rough and bring it back to me to cut about.

I said, 'This young man Cyril must be a notable specimen.'

'Cyril?' said Doris.

'The one that you put those clothes on for,' I said.

Doris blushed and said, 'Oh—' Then she grinned. 'His name isn't Cyril,' she said. 'It's Bernard.'

'New?'

'Oh, yes.'

'Nice?'

'Mm.'

'I knew it,' I said.

Doris said, 'How did you?'

'You have a come-hither look,' I said. 'You practise it when I stop dictating and think. It puts me off.'

'I don't!' said Doris indignantly. 'Do you want two copies of this or just a rough?'

'Just a rough,' I said. 'And I want it fast.'

About twelve the telephone rang. I took off the receiver and said, 'Sarratt.' Nothing happened for a moment. Then there was a click and it went dead. The other end had hung up. A minute or two later the same thing happened again.

Our exchange didn't think it decent to put a call on to the right extension at once anyway. It usually rang a few wrong numbers first, just to get itself loosened up. But it didn't just ring you and then hang up when you answered without saying anything. Besides, I thought I recognized the practice-swing technique. So when it rang again about half a minute later I just picked up the receiver and said, 'Hallo, Stephen. This is Bill.'

'Oh – hallo,' said Stephen's voice. I grinned to myself and said, 'How are you?'

Stephen said, 'I'm all right, thank you.' There was a pause. I thought for a moment he was going to hang up and tee himself up all over again. But instead he said, 'I want to speak to you. Not over the telephone.'

'All right,' I said. 'How about lunch?'

He said, 'I haven't got any money.'

I said, 'Now do you imagine I thought you had? I mean come and have lunch with me.'

'All right. Thank you.'

'De Vrie's,' I said. 'One o'clock. That all right?'

'Yes,' said Stephen and hung up.

Luckily I looked to see if I'd got any money, because I hadn't, and I didn't want anything to complicate things. I had an idea what was coming, and it sounded as though it might be good. So I dashed off up to the bank and cashed a cheque. I was going to get just five pounds, and then I thought I'd make it ten. It seemed a reasonable bet in the circumstances that Stephen was going to say something about Marcia, but he was quite capable of never saying a word about her and borrowing a fiver.

I dashed back to De Vrie's, got there about ten to one, and took up a strategic position in a doorway. I knew if I went in he'd hang about outside for twenty minutes before making the plunge, if he didn't go away altogether. That was one of the snags about Stephen. You had to think ahead, and everything took such a hell of a time.

He turned up sharp at one, looked at De Vrie's doorway and then walked on past it. He didn't even stop. When he was about ten yards from me I stepped out of my doorway and said, 'What-ho, Stephen. Nice timing. Come along.'

He said, 'Oh, hallo,' and came like a lamb.

There weren't many people in De Vrie's. Tony said business was pretty lousy. Nobody was coming out in the evenings now.

I said, 'Last time I was here you were making a fortune out of being an air-raid shelter.'

'It's all different now,' said Tony. 'Too many damn' bombs. What you like, Mr Sarratt?'

When we'd ordered, I said, 'Right. Now go ahead. What's on your mind?'

Stephen looked across the place so that I got his profile, and said, 'I thought it only fair to tell you that Marcia and I had a long talk into the early hours of the morning—'

He stopped.

'That's all right,' I said. 'I never fuss about my wife talking to other men.' I was thinking it was a damned good profile but for his mouth.

'And that I advised her to come back to you,' said Stephen, taking no notice.

I grinned to myself and said, 'Oh, did you?'

'Yes,' said Stephen. 'And I think she'll take my advice. We

165

shall part tomorrow – for the last time.' He dropped his head suddenly as though his neck had broken. The boy came up with the hors d'oeuvres trolley.

'Well, well,' I said. 'This requires thought. Hang on a minute while I choose some of these. People always bring me hors d'oeuvres at important moments.'

I chose some hors d'oeuvres. Stephen was sitting like a collapsed sack looking down at his plate in a tragic way.

'Just why did you advise that?' I said.

'I'd rather you didn't ask me that.'

'Why not? It's rather relevant.'

'Very well,' said Stephen, shrugging his shoulders. 'If you insist on having it put into words – because I thought it the right and decent thing to do.'

I said, 'Oh God. This is getting difficult.'

'Why?' said Stephen.

'If you're going to start being guided by considerations like that we shall get in a hell of a mess.' I shook my head and said, 'I'm disappointed. I thought I could rely on you not to go all ethical.'

Stephen fired up and said, 'Blast your eyes, you know I love Marcia and that I'd do anything to make her happy. Yes – *anything* – even send her away.'

'And you think sending her back to me will make her happy?'

Stephen said, 'Why do we have to discuss this? I don't want to hurt you. I've told you what I've done.'

'Don't worry about hurting me,' I said. 'I like it when it's done delicately like this. Just tell me the agonizing truth.'

Stephen cleared up his food and went into profile again. It's a mistake to do that when you're eating.

'All right,' he said sombrely. 'Then I'll tell you. Coming back to you won't give Marcia happiness. She can never be happy – *really* happy – away from me.'

I saw Marcia for a moment. I damn' nearly cracked him one. But it was only for a moment.

He said, 'But Marcia isn't a person who can live for her own happiness. She's one of those people who must give all the time. And she loves you. Loves you more than you can ever realize.'

I unclenched my hand very carefully and said, 'Go on.'

'Marcia can never know complete happiness,' said Stephen. 'She'll always be pulled two ways. We have been happy. Now she must go back to the other pull – her life with you – her desire for your happiness – her delight in giving. I have accepted that.'

He took a large clean white handkerchief out of his pocket, shook it out to its full size and applied it to his eyes.

I said, 'Listen, Stephen – there's just one aspect of this that you've left out. What happens if I don't want Marcia back?'

He looked at me in surprise for a moment. Then he smiled slightly. 'You do,' he said. 'Why suppose an absurdity?'

'And the idea is that I have her back and she comes and does her duty as a wife and longs for the king over the water?'

Stephen shrugged. 'I should hate to feel that. I'd rather she forgot me entirely. If I doubt she will, it's because two people can't experience what we have experienced and forget. There are some things that remain, even if one would give anything to forget them. If I have injured you, I am sorry. I've tried not to. I may have failed.'

I said, 'You've failed all right.'

When they brought the coffee, Stephen said, 'You're not serious of course about not taking Marcia back?'

'I think that's a matter for me to discuss with Marcia,' I said.

'Of course. I only wanted to say that as far as I am concerned I shall do everything possible to make her forget me.'

I drank up my coffee. I decided that the time had come to say it. I said, 'Why try to make her forget you? A good joke's worth remembering. Lots of people write them down.'

'I do loathe this facetiousness of yours,' he said. 'Why do you do it? It's horrible. It's macabre.'

I said, 'Stephen, what I'm going to say isn't worth saying really. I've tried kicking you before, and you always wriggle round until you convince yourself that a kick up the backside was a pat on the back. But for the good of your soul I can't let you go on thinking you've got away with this.'

'I haven't got away with anything,' said Stephen rather indignantly.

'I know,' I said. 'You haven't. But you've done your best.'

'I don't know what you're talking about.'

I said. 'You may or may not have talked to Marcia last night, but you certainly didn't advise her to come back to me. And even if you had it would have been preaching to the converted, because she was leaving you anyhow.'

Stephen said, 'What makes you think that?'

'Because she happened to have written to me and said so. She also inquired if I was willing to have her back.'

Stephen smiled a rather poorish, tolerant smile.

'The truth of the matter is,' I said, 'that about a fortnight of living with you has made even Marcia see just what this great love of yours is made of – as I always knew it would. Your technique's so rich that it only works in small doses. You ought to make a note of that.'

'There's no reason why you shouldn't say all this, or even think it, if it helps you,' said Stephen.

'Fine,' I said. 'Let's do some more. You're so bloody sure that no woman can resist you that you don't realize that for Marcia you were a mixture of a sick dog and a psychological experiment.'

'I must confess that that had escaped me,' said Stephen indulgently.

I said, 'It would. But it's true. If she'd had any proper children you wouldn't have meant a thing. Marcia is nuts on lame dogs, crying children and binding up wounds. She also wanted to go on the tiles to see what it was like. Now she's got a nice lot of dogs, children and wounds down in Aldgate, and she's seen what the tiles are like, and that's that. Damn it all, do you really think I'm such a BF that I would have let all this go on if I didn't see why and how it would work out?'

That was the only time in my acquaintance with Stephen that I ever saw him on one foot. He looked at me for a second and he really wasn't sure. But it was only for a second. Then he just said, 'You do it very well. I almost wish it were true. Almost as much as you do.'

I couldn't help smiling. You can't defeat people like Stephen. Besides there was no point in it. I knew the game was up, and I knew he knew it. That was all that mattered.

I called for the bill and said, 'Well, cheerio, Stephen. It's all been very interesting. I shall ring Marcia up this evening at six and tell her to go straight back to the flat. Don't take any notice of what I said. People like me only spoil the game.'

'Goodbye,' said Stephen bowing. He looked incredibly handsome.

I got a fit of the giggles, going back to the office, though as a matter of fact I was rather angry. Somehow my real cracks at Stephen never came off properly. You couldn't hang Stephen. You could only give him a hell of a lot of rope and leave it to him. It was the handkerchief business which was giving me the giggles. I kept saying to myself, '*There's* richness,' and giggling some more. But it wasn't really satisfying. I was always all right with Stephen until I wanted to hit really hard and then somehow it never worked, and just felt rather vulgar. He was funny all right. But he ought really to have been funnier than I ever found him. In a queer sort of way he was a natural. And naturals always have some sort of dignity, even if they're only natural skunks.

Doris brought in my brief for the Minister. It was terrible. I tore it up and we started again. This time it went better and I was through it by four.

When I'd sent Doris off to type it I rang up the place in Commercial Road where Marcia was working.

I said, 'Hallo, Marcia. This is Bill. We have to acknowledge yours of even date.'

'Yes?' she said.

'And I've seen Stephen.'

'Seen him?'

'Yes. He invited me to lunch.'

Marcia said, 'Well, I'm damned.'

'It was funny,' I said. 'I'll tell you about it later. Anyhow, I'm coming down to fetch you this evening.'

Marcia said, 'Darling – are you having me back?'

'We'll go into that later,' I said. 'But I think it'd be a bit awkward for you to stay another night *chez* Stephen.'

'I've got some things there.'

'Then they'll have to stay there for a bit. I'll pick you up about half past six.'

'All right,' said Marcia. 'Do you think you *will* have me back?'

'Maybe,' I said. 'Bungho.'

Doris whistled through typing the brief. This time it read quite well. I took it into Lennox and he seemed pleased. He said, 'Well, I do congratulate you, Sarratt. I think this has been an admirable piece of work.'

I said, 'Selling it has. The idea wouldn't give a child of three a headache.'

'It's a pity the Minister is such a *weak* man,' said Lennox suddenly.

'Is he?' I said. 'He always strikes me as being reasonably good as Ministers go.'

'Yes,' said Lennox a bit doubtfully. 'I suppose so.'

'Seems to know his own mind.'

'Oh yes,' said Lennox. 'He does. He knows exactly what he thinks at any moment. But he never thinks the same thing for long. He tends to be convinced by the last man who talks to him.'

He shook his head and said, 'He's given us a lot of trouble. A *lot* of trouble. Anyhow I congratulate you on this. I think it's an admirable scheme, and, if I may say so, more *moderate* than your ideas tend to be.' He grinned and I grinned back.

'I'm learning,' I said. 'Shall I leave it with you?'

'Oh, no,' said Lennox. 'Just give it to the Private Office. I don't really come into it, you know.'

It took me a hell of a time to get to Commercial Road. I went by bus, and there was a lot of mess down in the City and even more when we got to Aldgate. They seemed to have been a lot slower clearing up than they were in the West End, and in a lot of places the whole town had a sort of frowsy look, as though it wanted its face washed and no one had time to wash it.

Marcia's joint was right down nearly in Stepney, and there it was worse than anything I'd seen so far. In some of the really slum streets the places hadn't waited to be hit. They'd just fallen down at the thought of it.

The Rest Centre itself wasn't a bad place. It was nearly new, and looked as though it had been meant for a chapel or some social do or other. There wasn't a lot happening. There were only about a dozen people there besides the helpers and they were all sitting round having cups of tea.

'Hallo, darling!' said Marcia, getting up and coming to meet me. She was wearing a white overall with the sleeves rolled up. She looked good.

'What-ho!' I said, 'Picture of vigorous social endeavour.'

'Oh, this is the slack bit,' she said rather apologetically.

'We've cleared most of last night's and now we're waiting for the next batch. The last two nights have been quieter anyhow. Come and say hallo to Estelle.'

She took me into a sort of office. Estelle was on the telephone. I hadn't seen her for about five years, but she looked much the same. She waved a hand at me and grinned and went on cooing into the telephone in her reasonable way.

'*All* right, Mr Francis,' she finished up. 'Then I shan't worry any more about it. I know I can depend on *you* not to let us down.'

She rang off.

'Wotcher, Estelle,' I said. 'Still purring the life out of them?'

Estelle said, 'Hallo, Bill. However are you?' She turned to Marcia and said, 'Francis is going to send.'

'Good,' said Marcia. 'I don't know how you do it. Listen – do you mind if I go now?'

Estelle said, 'Oh yes. You're clear, aren't you?'

'Yes,' said Marcia. 'And anyhow I'll come back if it's a rough night.'

'That's sweet of you,' said Estelle. She turned to me and said, 'I wish you knew just how much work Marcia has done here in the last few weeks.'

I said, 'I know. She's told me. Guns and drums and wounds. And then I find her sitting down guzzling tea.'

'It isn't quite all tea drinking,' said Estelle, with her professionally charming smile. 'Anyhow you ought to be proud of her.'

I said, 'People keep telling me that.'

'As though you didn't know it,' said Estelle. 'Would you like to see the place or are you in a hurry to get away?'

There wasn't a lot to see. The place was a sort of mixture of canteen, dormitory, information bureau and dressing-station. I didn't say so to Estelle, but it seemed to me that the fact that it was necessary to have a voluntary place like that at all was a criticism of somebody. Still, there was no doubt about there being a job to do. Estelle said that after a raid they often handled over a thousand people a day in one way or another.

As we came away I said to Marcia, 'I've always been afraid that if there's a clerical error and I got to Heaven it'll be full of people just like Estelle.'

'I should think it probably will,' said Marcia. 'Will that be bad?'

I said, 'It'll be awful. Because I shall feel a skunk all the time, and they'll be sweet to me.'

'It is a bit like that,' said Marcia. 'But it's quite genuine, you know. She goes on just the same right through the worst of it – perfectly kind and reasonable and gentle. It's marvellous then. The only thing is that she can't stop. She's shy of you, of course.'

I said, 'People like Estelle are the sugar of the earth. Don't think I don't realize that. But the snag about being a saint is that people don't like it except in emergencies.'

Marcia said, 'But they like it then all right.'

As we passed some of the mess I said:

'Homes that not infrequently fall down
Support the Marquisate of Underdown.'

'Yes,' said Marcia. 'Now tell me about Stephen.'

I told her about the lunch. Marcia said, 'Poor Stephen.'

'Listen,' I said. 'There's no more poor Stephen about it.'

'Yes, there is,' she said. 'Because he'd got it all wrong. And it was my fault anyway.'

'I take it that he *didn't* advise you to come back to me?'

'I wouldn't say he exactly advised me to do anything,' said Marcia. 'It went on from dinner-time till about four this morning – with intervals when he didn't say anything for about half an hour.'

'And you told him quite definitely that it was finished?'

'Oh, yes. But you know how much good it is telling Stephen things if he doesn't want to believe them.'

As the bus got into the city Marcia said, 'I rather wish you hadn't come to get me.'

'Why?' I said.

'Because I should have come by myself anyhow. And now I don't see much how to prove it to you.'

'We are rather a long way apart,' I said.

'Miles,' said Marcia. 'And I don't want to be, Bill.'

'You wrote and told me it was finished,' I said.

'But I've said that before. You can't really believe it much now. What's more, I always knew it wasn't true really. Now I know it is, and I don't see how to show you the difference.'

'It is all a bit difficult,' I said. We were acting as cold as codfish.

It was a bit better when we got back to the flat, but not much. We bought some food on the way, and it was nice to be back. But we were still walking round one another on the tips of our toes.

'Listen,' Marcia said. 'You couldn't beat me, could you?'

'Maybe I could,' I said. 'But I don't want to. You know I never want to beat you when things are difficult.'

Marcia said, 'I know. But if we go on like this I'm afraid you'll think it's nicer without me.'

I said, 'You see it's difficult for me. Of course, I take your word for it that it's all right. But if I do that and then you decide it's no good we're finished.'

Marcia faced round to me and said, 'Look here, do I mean a bloody thing to you really – now? Or are you just making it up?'

I looked at her for quite a bit, and thought about it.

Marcia said quietly, 'I trust you to be kind and tell me the truth about it, Bill. I'd far rather know now – honestly.'

I said, 'Will you tell me some things first?'

'Yes.'

'They must be straight, even if I shan't like them.'

'All right.'

'What did Stephen suggest last night?'

'All sorts of things.'

'That you should marry him?'

'Oh, yes. Or that I shouldn't, and go on living with him.'

'Why didn't you agree?'

'I didn't want to.'

'Why not?'

There was a long pause. Then Marcia said, 'Because he isn't a person you could be married to or live with.'

'Why not?'

'Because you've got to do it *all* with Stephen. It's like dealing with a child. Besides, it's utterly exhausting.'

I said, 'Are you in love with him?'

'No. I think I was at one point. But not now.'

'What point?'

'Well – that night we went to dinner with him and Peggy.'

'Do you still like Stephen?'

'Yes. I'm very fond of him.'

'Why?'

173

Marcia hesitated, 'It's difficult to say to you because whenever you see him he's just being intolerable—'

'He's different when you're alone?' I said.

'Oh, Lord, yes. Completely. Frightfully in and out and over-emotional, of course. But sometimes awfully happy. That's when I like him really. He – he's sometimes very *alive* then – feeling and seeing and hearing things very clearly. And then when he gets miserable, I'm sorry for him.'

I said, 'I think that's the trouble, you know. I'm never very alive myself. Not like that.'

'Bunkum,' said Marcia. 'Of course you are. But in a different way.'

I said, 'You would like that, of course. You always like the colours of things, and sounds and smells and the feel of surfaces and so on. They mean a lot more to you than to me. I suppose I starve you.'

'No, you don't,' said Marcia. 'It's just that you're not at all childish and I am rather.'

I said, 'Supposing Stephen were to ring up now and say he was going to commit suicide. Would you go to him?'

Marcia looked at me in a frightened sort of way.

'Would you let me?' she said in a low voice.

I said, 'Never mind if I'd let you. Would you want to go?'

Marcia's lips trembled. Then she suddenly said, 'Yes!' chucked herself down on the sofa and started to sob.

'That's good enough for me,' I said.

'But it isn't *fair*,' said Marcia, throwing her head up with the tears streaming down her face. 'It isn't *fair*, Bill. You oughtn't to have asked me that. You know it isn't fair. I've told you I don't love him. That's another thing. You know it is.' She dropped her head back on her hands and sobbed a lot.

I grabbed her and started kissing her hard. I said, 'Darling, of course it's another thing. I only wanted to see if you knew it was.'

She looked up at me. She was surprised for a moment. But she saw at once.

She said, 'You mean it's all right, Bill? Even after I've said that?'

'If you'd said anything else I'd have thrown you out here and now,' I said.

'And you won't now?'

I said, 'Please, Marcia, come back to me. Really back. It's no good without you.'

She started to cry again differently, and I held her for a long time. After a while she stopped crying and sighed. 'I don't understand,' she said.

'Of course you do. Don't you?'

'You mean you meant me to say that?'

'I just wanted to see whether you *could* play straight nowadays or whether you'd just wangle again.'

Marcia said, 'I think I'm straight now. It *feels* straight.' She sighed again and said. 'It's all very queer, Bill. I think I've been mad.'

'We've agreed on that several times,' I said.

She sat up suddenly and said, 'You asked me to come back. You *asked* me!' She was looking at me in a frightened way.

'Yes,' I said.

'You've never done that before.'

I said, 'It's no good asking for something that isn't in the shop.'

She gave a sort of sob and said, 'Oh, God, I believe you do know. I never thought you would.'

THIRTEEN

NEXT morning I told Marcia about the Area Scheme and the Minister's meeting. We made a date to meet at De Vrie's at seven-thirty to celebrate.

I said, 'I'm rather sorry you've come back just now. If you'd waited a day or two we could have had a blind on the Area Scheme going through and a fatted calf about you as well. Now we shall have to make one go of it.'

Marcia said, 'They must be pretty pleased with you about this. Will you get a knighthood or anything?'

'I shouldn't think so. Most of the knighthoods are bespoken. I might get an OBE.'

'Would you like an OBE, sweet?'

I said, 'I should like it if I could walk in a procession. I looked it up in Whitaker and it says if you get the OBE you can walk in a procession behind Masters in Lunacy and in front of the Younger Sons of Younger Sons of Peers.'

'Mopping and Mowing?' said Marcia.

I said, 'I don't know how to mop. I've always known exactly how you mow, but I don't think I could mop.'

'There's nothing in it,' said Marcia. 'Any Master in Lunacy who knew his stuff could put you in the way of it in five minutes.'

We were so early that I thought I'd walk to the office. Marcia came with me through the Park down to Hyde Park Corner. I kissed her and we reminded one another about De Vrie's. When I'd walked on across to Constitution Hill I looked back and she was still standing looking after me. We waved.

My elephant balloon in Birdcage Walk was down having his morning pump up. I thought he looked in a better temper than usual. If it came to that I was in a better temper myself. The sun was shining and altogether it looked like being one of the better days. I felt that one of the better days was due anyhow.

The Minister wasn't seeing the Liaison Committee until half past four. There was a message from Lennox saying that he wanted to see us a quarter of an hour before that.

I said to Doris, 'I expect that's so that we can remind him what he's seeing them about.' Doris still had her hair behind her ears.

Everybody seemed rather cheeful about something, except Fred Giles. Fred was getting all worried again about staff. They'd never given him a replacement for old Clynes.

Fred said, 'They say that if he never did any work anyhow there's nothing to replace.'

'Bunkum,' I said. 'He worked like a horse. He was the most valuable man we'd got. Tell them we've got nobody to make passes at Miss Chase now he's gone.'

'That's what they do,' said Fred. 'They give you some dud and then when you throw him out they reckon you've lost your place in the queue. Seriously, we're in a spot.'

'All right,' I said. 'I'll have a go at it tomorrow, Fred. I can't do anything until I've got this thing with the Minister off my chest.'

It was quite true. I couldn't settle down to anything. I did a few letters and then started to draft the circular that would have to go out after the Minister had told the committee.

I had lunch with Edwardes. He pulled my leg like hell about having got the scheme through. I told him my OBE joke and he said that personally he was sucking up to the Grand High Sponge of the Order of the Bath. Edwardes said, 'The funny thing about this stunt of yours is that the Minister and the Secretary both agree with it. It's agin nature. I didn't know there was that much money.'

I said, 'Money, hell. Baxter's straight and all the money in the Bank of England wouldn't make the Secretary do the right thing unless there were questions in the House about it.'

Lennox came in and sat with us. Edwardes bought him a pint of beer without asking him. He knew Lennox loathed beer. Lennox drank it so as not to hurt Edwardes' feelings and had a ghastly time with it. I felt quite sorry for the old boy. Edwardes told us a good yarn about Establishments. He had a spare table and the Accommodation people sent some blokes to get it. It wouldn't go out of the doorway, so Edwardes suggested that they should take the one out of the next room, which was exactly the same and would come out. They said they couldn't do that. The one they'd been told to take was the table out of number thirty-seven, and an exactly similar one out of thirty-eight wouldn't do at all. So they sent for a carpenter and cut it in two and got it out like that.

Lennox said, 'In the last war we weren't ready and we had no organization. We had to use the brains God gave us. This time we've got an organization. I think it was better the other way.'

The Liaison Committee was meeting alone before it saw the Minister. About half past three old Percy popped his head round my door on his way to the meeting.

I said, 'Hallo, sir. How's the Ways and Means Society?'

'Pretty well,' said the old boy, chuckling away. 'Going to put it across us this afternoon, eh?'

'The Minister's going to make an announcement,' I said, with a grin.

'I know,' he said. 'And I know where he got it.' He waggled his head at me.

'I suppose you know all about it?' I said.

'Outline,' said the old blighter. 'Just the outline.'

'Well, I hope you liked my English,' I said. I always found

the whole inside information thing a bit riling.

'It was pretty good,' he said. 'But you've got the first two lines misprinted.' He chuckled at my face.

'How d'you like it?' I said.

The old boy shrugged his shoulders, 'Had to come,' he said. 'I'm not complaining.'

'Good,' I said. 'I wouldn't like to think you were ruined.'

'We're all ruined,' he said, grinning. 'So what's the odds?'

He took out a big gold cigarette case and offered me a cigarette. His hands were dark red and they had big blue veins standing up on them.

'What did you want to force us for?' he said. 'We'd have worked with you if you'd asked us.'

I said, 'For Pete's sake don't bring that up. I know you're all choir boys. Harness told me.'

He gurgled to himself.

'But we would,' he said, going serious again. 'We'd have worked it and saved you all the trouble.'

'I know you would,' I said. 'With just a few little alterations to make it run easier.'

'Maybe a detail or two,' said the old boy innocently. 'But nothing much y'know. You'd have got what you want.'

I said, 'Sure. We should have got the whole thing except the guts of it. I know.'

Old Percy puffed his cigarette and grinned. 'Who wants guts?' he said. 'We'd have cleaned it and drawn it and left it all ready for the table.'

We both laughed. He was an attractive old shark.

'Where are you going after this war?' he said suddenly.

'God knows,' I said.

'How about coming to me?'

'Who'd pay my salary?' I said. 'With all the money you're losing now you won't have any left.'

The old boy laughed like hell.

'That's right,' he said. 'Cutting your own throat, that's what you're doing.'

Sharp at a quarter past four Lennox and Harness and I went in to see Baxter. He was sitting at his desk, with the sun shining in on that grand silver hair, and he was wearing a very light grey suit. He looked like the Prophet Isaiah in one of his more business-like moments. He greeted us, as usual, as though he'd never met us before but was very glad to now. Then he did his pipe-filling act and said, 'Now, just what am I to say to these fellows we're going to see?'

Lennox murmured something about a brief having been sent in.

'Let me see if I've got it right,' said Baxter. He leant back in his chair and ran through the gist of it. It was pretty good. I was rather impressed.

He opened his eyes and said, 'That do?'

'I think that's an admirable summary,' said Lennox. Baxter bowed his head. 'I know my words then,' he said. He looked round with his nice smile, and said, 'I'm always thankful that Ministers of the Crown are only called upon to recite and not to *sing*. I'm quite incapable of memorizing music.'

This rather got me, and I let out a loud snort of laughter. Baxter caught my eye and we both giggled some more.

'Now,' said Baxter, going serious again. 'The first thing they're bound to ask me is, "When does the scheme start?" What's the answer to that?'

'Well—' said Lennox a bit doubtfully, turning to me. 'I'm not sure how long Sarratt would require—'

'I'm ready to go,' I said.

'Ready to go at once?' said Baxter.

'Yes. The actual machinery is ready. We shall have the registration forms from the Stationery Office in two days, and I've drafted the circular.'

'Excellent,' said Baxter. 'Then is there any reason why we shouldn't start at once?'

'Say from the first of next month,' said Harness.

'I should have said the first of next week,' I said.

'Oh, yes,' said Baxter. 'We want to get on.'

'It gives very little time for adjustment,' said Harness.

'What type of adjustment, Mr Harness?' said Baxter sharply.

Harness looked a bit uncomfortable. 'Certain arrangements might have to be made,' he said vaguely.

'Oh, no,' said Baxter decidedly. 'I can't agree with you there. No manufacturer who's been playing the game will be a penny worse off if the scheme is put into operation tomorrow. We can't allow time for those who may be caught by it to mend their ways.'

179

'I hope you don't feel that industry has not been playing the game, sir?' said Harness rather sulkily.

'Mr Harness,' said Baxter, writing a bit of his biography, 'my experience of life is that if ninety-nine per cent of people don't play the game, then there's something wrong with the game. But if *more* than ninety-nine per cent of people play the game, then the rules are too easy. I'm a business man myself and I know.' He smiled and took a curtain as though he'd said something. 'Now is there anything else?'

'I think they're bound to raise a certain number of purely technical questions, Minister,' I said, 'Such as—'

Baxter held up his hand. 'Quite,' he said. 'And if they do, I shall suggest that they should discuss the matter at leisure with Mr Sarratt, Mr Lennox and Mr Harness, where I do not doubt that they will get all possible information.' He smiled and gave me a little bow. 'Now,' he said, getting up, 'let us go and see them.'

We trailed along the corridor to the conference room, Baxter leading the way at a proper ministerial pace, *andante pomposo ma non troppo lento*. As we passed the Secretary's office he popped out and fitted into the procession just behind the Minister. He must have been waiting with his ear to the keyhole to time it so neatly. It struck me that the Masters in Lunacy were in front all right but we were a bit short of Younger Sons of Younger Sons of Peers to walk behind, and I started to giggle rather.

There were twelve of them sitting round the conference table. Baxter made a good entry. They all got up and he said, 'Good afternoon, gentlemen – please be seated.' He said it in the sort of way that my old headmaster used to when he came into the prefects' room.

The Minister took the chair. The Secretary sat on his right looking even more like a baboon than usual, and the rest of us spread ourselves out on either side at the top of the table. The committee were the usual gang. I caught old Percy's eye and he winked.

Baxter was good at meetings. He looked good and he had a good manner with them. I don't know how he did it but he contrived to be as pompous as hell and yet to have you feeling that Ministers of the Crown *ought* to talk like that. But he was a slow starter. He began as usual with about a quarter of an hour during which he said that there was a war on and that it was all very difficult. It would have been all right if these people hadn't been to a lot of meetings with him and heard it all before. As it was, everybody got a bit bored, except one very long thin old boy with a green face and a white beard like an El Greco, who wrote it all down. I thought maybe it was the first time he'd heard about the war and that he was hoping to sell the news to the *Express*.

Finally, at about ten to five, Baxter decided that they knew enough about the war and started to talk turkey. It was nothing like as good as the rehearsal he'd done with us – chiefly because he kept stopping to say what marvellous blokes they all were and how loyally they'd helped the country and how it hurt him more than it did them. But just on five he seemed to get fed up with it and just more or less read them the summary of the scheme I'd given him in the brief. I watched their faces. It was quite all right. He'd made their flesh creep so much that they were quite relieved.

'There,' said Baxter when he'd waded through it. 'Those are the steps that I propose to take – in outline, of course. I don't doubt that there are some features about them which you regret. I myself regret any step which involves interference with industry on my part. But I am sure you will realize the urgent necessity of them, and that you will accept the scheme with that readiness and loyalty which you have always shown.'

He sat back in his chair. We all sat back in our chairs. The El Greco bloke carefully wrote down the last bit and sat back in his chair.

'Now,' said Baxter, 'I should be glad of any comments which you care to make. Perhaps as its chairman you would speak for the committee, Sir Leslie?'

Old Leslie Warks was a very short, fat old boy who looked like a bus driver and spoke like one. He looked down at the blotting paper in front of him and said, 'Well, Sir Clive, I thank you on behalf of the committee for your statement today.' He looked round rather helplessly at the rest and said, in an aggrieved way, 'Of course this has all been sprung on us.'

I caught old Percy's eye and he grinned. They'd had every word of it for at least a week, but it was always old Warks'

181

great cry that things were 'sprung on them'.

He rambled on for a bit saying they'd all be ruined, but he didn't seem very convinced about it. It stuck out a yard that he thought they were well out of it. Baxter was very polite and patient with him and when the old boy finally rolled to a standstill, bowed and said, 'Thank you, Sir Leslie,' as though we'd all been given a real treat.

A few other people asked questions. The El Greco man wanted to know the starting date. Baxter said, 'Forthwith,' and he wrote it down. A rather nasty slick little man tried to cross-examine Baxter about the details and was squashed rather curtly. He grinned and said rather impudently. 'I suppose I can't expect you to have knowledge of the details, Sir Clive.'

Baxter looked at him and said, 'No. And I'm afraid if I had the knowledge I should not have time to discuss the matter with you, Mr Steyner.'

It began to look like a pushover, and Baxter was doing a sort of going-going-gone auction to see if anybody wanted to say anything else before he wound up when old Percy suddenly said, 'I've only got one thing to say and I'm sure you'll forgive me, Sir Clive. I don't quite see why you're compelling us to do this.'

Baxter said, 'I thought I had made the necessity clear. I am asking for your cooperation because—'

'Ah, no,' said old Percy. 'You misunderstand me. I can see that you must *have* it. But I don't see why you need to get it this way.'

'What other way do you suggest, Mr Percy?' said Baxter, looking a bit puzzled.

'Why,' said old Percy, 'if I may say so, Sir Clive, your Ministry has always *asked* us to help. It's come along and told us the country needed this and that and asked us to get together and provide it. I don't quite see why that wasn't done this time. I think we can say we've never let you down.'

He looked straight across the table at me without a glimmer of expression.

'You mean you would have preferred to work this scheme by yourselves?' said Baxter. 'To put it bluntly, there's no need for me to butt in?'

Old Percy smiled. 'I wouldn't put it like *that*,' he said. 'But I think I'm speaking for everyone round this table when I say that if you'd cared to ask us to carry out this policy we would have done it – without the need for laws and enforcement and all the paraphernalia.' He looked round the table. 'Hear, hear,' they said.

'That's quite right,' said old Warks. 'We could do it without all this.'

I waited for Baxter's crack about preferring the law to a lot of goodwill, but it didn't come. 'That's a very interesting suggestion,' said Baxter. 'Interesting and valuable.' He was looking a bit nonplussed. It suddenly hit me hard on the head that he really thought it was an interesting suggestion. It had come as a brand new thought to him.

'Done like that,' said old Percy, 'you'd have the whole of industry solid behind you. As it is,' he waved his hand. 'Well – they say one volunteer's worth ten pressed men.'

'There's no need for it,' said the little man. 'No need for laws and red tape. Industry's ready to do all that is asked of it without being whipped on.'

'I see the force of your request, Mr Percy,' said Baxter. 'Personally I abominate interference. I don't quite know—'

He turned rather helplessly to the Secretary.

I said, 'If I might interfere, Minister—'

'Yes?' said Baxter, turning to me with some relief.

'The possibility of a voluntary scheme was discussed,' I said. 'But it was felt that whilst the large firms represented by these gentlemen would of course carry out the scheme, it might be difficult to deal with anybody who chose to stay outside.'

'Yes,' said Baxter. 'That's true.' I saw that he didn't remember and wasn't impressed. He turned to the meeting and said, 'There are certain difficulties about a voluntary scheme, of course, as Mr Sarratt says.'

'I don't think there's anything that couldn't very easily be overcome,' said old Percy expansively.

'If I could be sure of that—' said Baxter.

'I would be prepared to give my personal guarantee of it,' said old Warks. 'Wouldn't you, gentlemen?'

'Hear, hear!' they said.

I had a queer cold feeling in my head. I grabbed a sheet of paper and tore off a slip. I found my fingers were shaking. I wrote on it, 'I think we agreed that a voluntary scheme would be disastrous. It would have no chance of working. W. Sarratt.'

183

I folded it and passed it to Lennox and said, 'Minister.' Lennox passed it on.

Warks was saying. 'After all, we're completely in your hands. We're bound hand and foot, and none of us is such a fool as to fly in the face of what the Ministry wants.'

Baxter nodded. He had put my note down beside him still folded.

I said desperately. 'You may remember discussing this at some length, Minister, before the scheme was finished.'

'I remember discussing a good many things,' said Baxter rather coldly. 'But if these gentlemen think a voluntary scheme is workable, that is obviously important.'

'I don't think you have to worry about it being *workable*, Sir Clive,' said old Percy. 'We're unanimous about that. It's simply up to you.'

Baxter was opening my note. I watched his fingers. They were long and cool-looking.

'You've always been prepared to work by consultation and cooperation,' old Percy went on. 'If I may say so that policy has served you well. If you choose to continue it, and simply to tell us that this is what you want, we'll do it, without compulsion. We simply ask you to trust us. That's all.'

Baxter had read the note now. He frowned and put it down again. He said, 'I must confess that the possibility of a voluntary scheme has been rather overlooked—' He hesitated.

'It was raised by Mr Harness at our meeting, Minister,' I said. My voice sounded funny.

'Well?' said Baxter curtly.

I knew I'd lost. I said, 'On that occasion you didn't feel that it would be a workable proposition.'

Baxter flushed slightly and turned away. He picked up my note and folded it up again. Then he slowly tore it across and raised his head. 'Well, gentlemen,' he said. 'I'm most obliged to you for raising this point. I think there is a great deal in what you say, and certainly I've no desire to drive where I can lead. Unless there are objections which I cannot at the moment foresee, I am perfectly prepared to consider keeping the scheme on a voluntary basis.'

There was a faint stir. I looked across the table at old Percy. He was staring at me expressionlessly. Then his face broke into a smile as he turned to Baxter.

'We're much obliged to you, Sir Clive, for that,' he said.

The door was close behind me. I got up quietly and slipped out. As I shut the door behind me I heard the El Greco man speaking. Then I was in the corridor and walking away. I was nearly at the end of the corridor when I heard Lennox's voice trying to call 'Sarratt!' in a whisper. I stopped and turned. Lennox came up.

'Where are you going?' he said.

I said, 'Out of here.'

'Nonsense,' he said. 'Come back at once. The Minister will want to know why you went.'

'Then tell him,' I said, going on. Lennox grabbed my arm. 'You're being quite absurd,' he said. 'There's nothing to feel like that about. The Minister doesn't realize the point. That's all.'

I said, 'Then tell it him.'

'You're making a fool of yourself,' said Lennox.

I turned and said, 'I've sweated at that thing. I explained it to him. I warned him about this. He agreed and said all the right things. Now he's sold me down the river for two minutes' popularity. I am tired of being sold down the river. He can have it.'

Lennox said, 'You take these things too personally. What does being diappointed matter? Only the job counts.'

I said, 'Get one single man in that room to put winning the war first and I'll be with you. Cheerio, Lennox.'

I turned and started down the stairs. There were one hundred and twenty-three stairs to go down to reach the street. I walked down and left a bit of the dust of the place on every one of them.

FOURTEEN

I T was cool in the street outside. I had left my hat in the office but it was an old hat anyhow. They could have that. But they couldn't have what went inside it.

I came out into St James's Park and walked slowly up

towards Piccadilly, thinking about it. I knew it was the finish, but I wasn't angry with people any more. I remembered Baxter's grin, and what he said about Cabinet Ministers not having to sing, and laughed to myself. I liked Baxter. And I liked old Percy, crook that he was, and I was sorry for poor old Lennox, and if I didn't like Harness it wasn't because of that. I wasn't angry with them. But I was angry with the thing that was stupid and ignorant and incompetent and selfish – the thing that stopped me, not because it knew better, but because it knew worse. Maybe I was wrong. But they couldn't be right.

My balloon was right up on the end of his string, all blown up and buoyant. I thought of passing him in the morning and thinking everything was fine. I was a fool not to know that it would happen. I wondered if Lennox guessed, and whether what he'd said about the Minister the night before was a warning.

There were quite a lot of people about in the Park, sitting around doing nothing in particular. There was one really magnificent bloke who must have been all of fourteen stone. He was wearing dirty old trousers and an open-necked shirt. His face and throat were a sort of reddish walnut. He was sitting with his back against a tree doing a crossword puzzle. It seemed to me that he brought up the whole question of what I was going to do next about this war. But I looked at my watch and found it was half past six so I thought the war could keep for a bit, and walked along to Princes. I had three quick drinks and felt better. I got out some bits of paper and a pencil and started to write a letter of resignation to Baxter.

I was meeting Marcia at half past seven at De Vrie's. About seven I wandered along there and settled down in a corner of the bar with another drink. I thought I'd better make that one last. I was beginning to feel a bit tight, and it was too soon to be tight. I got out my letter to Baxter and read it through. It wasn't too hot. It read a bit small and shrill. I tore it up and started again.

Tony came into the bar for something and pitched up to me. He said business was lousy. He was shutting Sunday evenings now, and might have to close the place down altogether. Tony was very patriotic and quite sure we were going to win the war. Poor devil, I suppose he was scared stiff of being interned. Three of his waiters had been taken.

When he'd gone I had another go at my letter to Baxter. It still wouldn't come right. This time it just sounded as though I'd got a swollen head and thought I knew all the answers. I gave it up. What it came down to was that I didn't fit in and that was the end of it. Maybe they were all out of step but oor Jock but I couldn't prove it. You had to know a hell of a lot about it to see how bad the place was. And Baxter knew just exactly what they chose to tell him.

I went over to the bar and sat on a stool and had another. I wasn't really tight but things were getting a bit difficult to focus. There was no one else there but an Air Force bloke drinking White Ladies. He seemed to have drunk rather a lot of them. He suddenly said, 'So tomorrow I shall be back there. And a damn' good thing too in a way.'

I think he thought we'd been talking for quite a time.

I said, 'Back where?'

'There,' he said, 'unless Jerry's finished the job off while I've been away. Of course we're moving back. But then he's moving back from the French coast too. Bloody funny that.' He picked up a match-box and said, 'Start right back here. Hop one down to here in the afternoon. Fill up. Hop two over the ditch. Easy.'

'Child's play,' I said.

He leant across to me and said, 'I'll tell you what. The new Comets. Five hundred and twelve on the level and turn in nine miles land covered. Now the old Mess 109 takes eleven. But five hundred and twelve! I ask you.'

'Nice work,' I said.

'We had a job in 1937 that would do it,' he said. 'Two engines, one in front and one behind. Shaft between your feet. But when they spun they went on spinning. They made three and spun two of them into the ground. I don't know what they did with the third. Is this careless talk?'

'Yes,' I said.

He nodded. 'All right. I'll dry up. Thanks for the drink, o'man. Come in and see me if you're ever down there. Just ask for Paddy.'

He got off his stool with some difficulty, tipping it back behind him with a colossal crash.

'I was dive-bombed once by ours,' he said. 'Bloody good too. Better than the Germans.'

'In England?' I said, a bit puzzled.

'God, no,' he said. 'In France. What the hell should we be doing dive-bombing here? You say the bloody silliest things. Is this careless talk?'

'Pretty careless,' I said.

'All right,' he said. ' 'Nuff said. Come in any time. Just ask for Paddy. And thanks for the drink.'

He pushed off. I said to George the doorman. 'You must hear quite a lot from these boys on your job, George.'

George wiped up a couple of glasses and said, 'I do that, Mr Sarratt. But I don't reckon they know much that Jerry don't know already, if you follow me.'

'Bit dangerous, all the same,' I said.

George said, 'I keep my ears open and if they say too much I stop 'em.'

'How?' I said.

'There's ways,' said George mysteriously. 'I knew it didn't matter him talking to you, see.'

I left it at that.

As Marcia hadn't shown up at a quarter to eight I went and found Tony and ordered. I thought we might as well do it in style as it might be the last blind we could afford and I ordered a bottle of Pol Roger. Tony said the warning had gone. I was a bit worried about Marcia travelling through it, but Tony said it was fairly quiet.

At eight o'clock Marcia still hadn't turned up. I thought I'd give her another five minutes and then ring up.

A bloke came in and said, 'My God, have you seen it?'

I said, 'What?'

He said, 'The whole bloody Town's on fire.'

I knew, and I went upstairs.

I don't see how we hadn't known in there. There were two fire-engines working on stuff on the other side of the street not fifty yards away, and it was crackling like a furnace. Down East it was bright orange, and not very far away. I could see the orange against the underside of smoke that looked almost still. It was quite different from the night when the docks were fired – much brighter and nearer. I made it chiefly the City. But there were other bits all over the place. The whole town east of me was glowing. I stopped a cab and said, 'I've got to get down to Commercial Road. Anything you like.'

He said, 'Not for anything you've got. I've just come back from there. You stay where you are, guv'nor.'

I started to run towards it. He called out, 'You won't get through.'

I must have run about half a mile. There was a taxi standing by the pavement. The taxi-man was a Jew. He was standing on the pavement looking at it and talking to somebody. I thought 'He won't.' I said, 'Anything you like to get me down to Aldgate.' He looked at me and then he looked back at it. Then he said, 'OK. I don't mind a look meself.'

I jumped in. The other chap grabbed him by the arm and said something. The taxi driver said, 'You're telling me.' We started off. He pulled back the window and said, 'Aldgate is it?'

I said, 'Down Commercial Road if you can make it.'

'We'll have to go round by Birmingham,' he said. 'Veah Bristol. Leave it to me, pal.'

The taxi-man drove as though he was trying to pull the cab to pieces. He leant right over so that his shoulder was out of the cab all the time and smoked a stub. We went straight for a bit and then he was stopped and had to turn off north. He tried four right-hand turns and was stopped each time. The fifth was all right.

We were too far north, and he kept trying to turn in, but there were cordons everywhere. He found a street that was empty but a bobby in a tin helmet stopped him. The taxi-man started to argue. I got out and said, 'Listen, I've got to get through. I'm on Government business. Here's my pass.' I showed my Ministry pass. The bobby wasn't sure but he hesitated and we went on.

We were right in among it now. It was bright enough to read by and we were getting in the way and driving over hose. We came to a place where the engines blocked the street. The driver started to turn round. I said, 'It's no good. You won't get any farther.'

I jumped out and said, 'Where are we?'

We weren't far from Liverpool Street. I gave him a pound and said, 'Thanks a lot.'

I went on. It had been still before, but there was a strong breeze blowing now, rustling the paper in the gutter. There was water everywhere. I could hear planes overhead, and once or twice bombs burst not far away. They were using high explosive now. The guns seemed practically to have stopped. It smelt like the Fifth of November. I kept on being stopped but my pass always got me through. Once I showed my Ministry lunch card instead but it did just as well.

They were playing on a big square factory building that was burning with a dazzling white flame and clouds of black smoke. The middle fell in as I passed and the sparks went up to a terrific height. I saw a fireman start up a ladder and slip when he'd got up about six rungs. He slid down again, hanging on to the sides.

The breeze was blowing as though the whole thing was a blast furnace. I tripped over a hose, shoved out my hand to save myself and cut it on a broken window. It was nothing much. A shower of sparks came down and I had to brush them off. I missed one, and smelt it singeing my hair. A bobby shoved a man in a raincoat and knocked him into the gutter. The man's hat fell off. He was bald. I don't know what it was about. I had worked right round the centre of the City. I reckoned if I cut in soon I should be about right.

There was a terrific wallop quite close. I thought it was a bomb but it was a gas main. I saw the firemen run back from it. It made a sort of triangle of flame about twenty or thirty feet high. There was a lovely smell of violets for a bit. I should think it was a scent factory. My hand was bleeding, so I put my handkerchief round it and held it in my hand. The air was very hot and there was a sort of steady roar. I thought the whole place was done for.

I was working to the right and they were getting stickier about letting me through. A chap in a tin hat with a black face grabbed me and said, 'Get back. No way.'

I said, 'Government business.'

He said, 'I'm telling you. It's for your own sake.' I dodged round him and bolted down the street.

I wished I'd had a tin hat. A lot of stuff was falling in the streets and I had to keep brushing sparks away. I thought I was nearly there but as I turned a corner I saw the front of a place fall right out across the street. The inside was just a furnace.

I turned back. There was a bobby standing with his hands behind his back. He was the only bloke I ever saw doing

190

nothing. I said, 'I've got to get through into Commercial Road.' He didn't ask questions. He just said, 'Best chance is third along on the right. But I doubt they'll let you through. The rest are gone. You'll have to hurry.'

I ran along the street to the turning. It was burning on both sides and only about thirty feet wide. A whistle went and they started to come out of it. A chap was bawling, 'Get back!' and blowing a whistle. He pushed me in the chest. I dodged round him and turned my collar up. I was scared. The firemen were running up the street, except two who were still handling a hose about fifty yards down it. I bolted down the middle of the street dodging in and out among the firemen. I could feel the heat burning my face. The street was only about a hundred and fifty yards long and for the last fifty yards I was clear of the firemen. When I got to the end I stopped and looked back. It was still standing up. I dare say it stood up for hours but it may not have. I turned left and right again and got into Commercial Road.

I couldn't find the street that the rest centre was in. Everything looked queer and different in that orange light. I passed the turning twice before I recognized it. There were two houses burning quietly to themselves, one at one end of the street and the other at the other. Nobody was doing anything about them. There were a few people in a group in the middle of the street. I still couldn't quite get my bearings and I couldn't see the Rest Centre. Then I realized that that was it. The heap was only about ten feet high. It hadn't been a very big building.

There were two or three men trying to drag stuff away with their hands. I saw someone leaning against some iron railings. It was Estelle. She had a bandage round her head. I said, 'Estelle.'

She said, 'Bill – oh, Bill.'

'Marcia?' I said.

She just said, 'Oh Bill, Bill!'

I said, 'Pull yourself together, Estelle. Where's Marcia?'

She didn't reply.

I said, 'Underneath?'

'She was in there,' she said, sobbing.

I nodded. 'How long?' I said.

'About half an hour. We had them all out and she and I and Kathleen—'

'All right,' I said. 'Know which end?'

Estelle shook her head.

I went over to it. The men were just pulling at it with their hands. They hadn't got any tools. I found a place where it hadn't come down to the ground. I lay down on my face and started to wriggle in. I got a little way but I couldn't see. I backed out and shouted 'Torch!'

Somebody gave me one. I wriggled in again. There was a hell of a lot of white dust. It was like driving in a thick fog, and it made me cough.

I seemed to go a long way. I suppose it was about ten feet actually. Then it suddenly went solid and I had to stop. I started to back out, but there was a place where I had to go up and then down coming in, and I couldn't do it backwards. There was no room to turn. I thought I was finished.

There was a place to the left where a girder had come down to within about six inches of the ground. I didn't think I could get under but I thought I might as well try. I got my right foot against something solid and pushed, and my head and shoulders slid through. I had a hell of a struggle to get an arm through but after that it was easy. I came out into a sort of cave. I couldn't understand it. Then I looked up and saw I was under a table that had stood up.

The dust was awful. I couldn't keep my eyes open and I was afraid I should stifle, I yelled, 'Marcia!' and listened. Someone called, but it was from outside. I rested for a moment and then went on. The table had made a sort of channel which gradually tapered off. I went on along it.

I thought it was a lump of concrete at first and then I saw that it was Marcia's head covered in white dust. It was only about four feet away but it was on my right and for a long time I couldn't get round to it.

I said, 'Honey, I'm coming,' but she didn't speak or move. I thought she was dead.

I got round at last. Her face and head were completely covered in dust like a mask. Some blood had come out of her mouth and made a streak of black mud with the dust on one side of her chin. A girder had fallen right across her chest diagonally, so that it was on her right shoulder, but her left shoulder and arm were free. It was right down within an inch or two of the ground and I knew at once. I couldn't see the rest of her. There was a lot of stuff on it.

I was right shoulder forward. I wriggled and tore about until I could get my left hand up with the handkerchief round it. I wiped the dust off her face and eyes and the blood off her chin. Her face was drained, even her lips.

I managed to get my hand up to her arm and felt for her pulse. I thought I could feel something but I wasn't sure. I kept on saying, 'Honey, it's Bill.'

I knew she wasn't dead because her lips moved once or twice. Then she gave a sort of little hiccough and said something. I said, 'Darling, darling.'

She said, 'It hurts. Oh, it hurts. Bill, don't let it. It hurts.'

I said, 'My blessed, my blessed.' She moaned and said, 'Bill, Bill.'

'I'm here, darling,' I said.

She said, 'Don't let it. Please don't let it. Please Bill, let me go. It hurts so.' She moaned again.

I said, 'You shall have anything you want, sweet.'

She said, 'Please, please!'

I wriggled back. When I got under the table I turned round and got my head forward. After that it was quite easy, except that once the back of my jacket caught and I had to tear it free. I thought I'd come out the same way but I hadn't quite.

When I got out there were a lot more people. I said, 'Doctor.' They shoved forward a little man in dungarees. His face was yellow in that light. He wore horn-rimmed glasses.

He said, 'I'm a doctor. Have you found them?'

I said, 'Have you got morphia?'

'Yes.'

I said, 'Give me the syringe.'

He said, 'I'll come in.'

'You can't,' I said. 'There isn't room. Give me the syringe.'

He hesitated and said, 'I can't do that. It might be wrong. It all depends—'

'I know what I'm doing,' I said. 'Give me the syringe.'

He started to fumble about in his bag. Another bloke came up and said, 'Good show, but you can't go in again. That side wall's coming down at any moment.'

The little doctor brought out a hypodermic. He said, 'I must come in. It might be fatal if—'

'So what?' I said. 'Give me that syringe. It's my wife, damn you.' I took it away from him and ran back. The other fellow grabbed my arm and said, 'I tell you that side wall's coming down.'

I wrenched my arm away and went in again.

I had the syringe in my right hand and the torch in my left, but it was easier this time. When I came to the low beam I held the torch in my teeth and went arms first. I could hear Marcia moaning. I had to stop under the table for a moment to cough. Then I went on and got back to her. She was saying, 'Bill — where've you gone? Bill.'

I said, 'I'm here, sweet.'

She said, 'Bill, can't you stop it? Please stop it hurting.' She was crying in little gasps. I looked at the beam across her and knew there was no doubt. I got my right arm with the syringe forward and said, 'It's all right, honey. I'm going to stop it now. Here we go.'

It was difficult to get the needle in. I tried and tried but I couldn't get my other hand up to steady her arm and my hand was shaking. In the end I had to get her arm up against something solid, and this time I hit the vein slap in the middle and pressed the plunger right down. Then I dropped the syringe and felt for her pulse. It was still going very faintly. I wondered whether the pressure on her chest would stop the morphia from working.

She seemed to go on moaning for a long time, and I was afraid I hadn't done it. But after a while she stopped. I couldn't feel her pulse any longer and I thought she was dead, but she wasn't. She suddenly opened her eyes and did a sort of smile. She said 'Darling Bill.'

I said, 'It's all right, my sweet. Better now.'

She said, 'I never thought you'd believe it after all that, but you did.'

I said, 'Of course I believed it. You go to sleep.'

Marcia said, 'It was true, too.' She shut her eyes again. I lay there for a bit with my fingers on her pulse, though I hadn't been able to feel it for a long time. Then her eyes opened again and I knew that was that. I shut them because of the dust. I couldn't get far enough to kiss her face, but I kissed her fingers and wrist. Then I picked up the syringe and backed out.

I got out. There was a bloke who seemed to be in charge. I

think he was the one who'd tried to stop me. I said, 'Have they found the other woman?'

'They've found one,' he said. 'She's dead.'

I said, 'Well then, get them off it if it's dangerous. There's no one left alive in there now.'

He looked at me and said, 'It was your wife, wasn't it? I'm damned sorry, old man.'

I said, 'That's nice of you.' I found the little doctor in dungarees and gave him back his syringe. 'Well?' he said.

'All over,' I said. 'Thanks, doc.'

He said, 'I ought to have come in with you.'

'For what?' I said. 'There wasn't anything you could do.'

I started to cough a lot from the dust. After a bit I was sick and that made it better, but I felt pretty limp. The little doctor gave me a shot of brandy and I went to see what had happened to Estelle. They'd taken her away, I think. It was while I was looking round for her that the second bomb fell. I heard it coming and I heard somebody yell and a lot of people chucked themselves down. But I was feeling a bit muzzy and before I'd done anything about it the thing had landed. It was a couple of streets away – too far to hurt any of us. But it was too much for the wall the bloke had been talking about, and I saw the whole side of the next house fall out, rather slowly, it seemed, on top of the ruins of the Rest Centre. Nobody was hurt. But after that there didn't seem as though there was anything much more to do.

They were very nice to me – particularly the little Doc. They wanted me to go back with them and have my hand dressed and so on. But I wanted to get away now, and I wouldn't go with them. I wanted to get back to the flat. I don't know why, but I did.

I got away from them and started just walking anywhere that was in the right general direction where there wasn't a fire. I must have walked for hours. The raid was still on, and I hoped maybe I should walk under one and that would stop it all and save a lot of trouble. Once I thought that if only I'd stayed under with Marcia until the second bomb fell that would have done it, and I would have stayed with her and gone on holding her fingers and not had to leave her there alone. That got me and I sat down on some steps and cried. Crying made me cough again. I couldn't get my breath at all, and in the end I must

195

have been there half an hour crying and coughing and snort-
ing about. Finally I tried smoking a cigarette and that helped
a lot, though I still coughed my head off every now and then.

My left hand had begun to hurt like hell. It was a big deep
cut and there was all sorts of muck in it. I thought I'd better do
something about it so I went into a dressing station and they
cleaned it up and bandaged it. They also fixed up a place where
I'd torn my left ear a bit. I didn't know about that. It must
have been done when I was wriggling about underneath. It
wasn't anything.

I was rather surprised that there wasn't a bigger crowd in the
dressing station. There were quite a lot of people, of course,
but not as many as I should have thought. They told me it had
been more buildings than casualties so far.

They let me wash. I was covered in white dust.

I came out up in Islington just as a clock was striking twelve.
I saw the Tube station and it struck me that maybe the Tube
would be quite all right and that I was a fool not to have used it
going. I doubt if I could have actually, but it took me home as
though nothing were happening outside. I went to sleep on
the way.

FIFTEEN

I GOT BACK to the flat. It wasn't blacked-out, and I had to do
that first. I just did the bedroom and then lit the gas-fire and
sat down and looked at the room. I was trying to see just where
we were, but we didn't seem to be anywhere much. There were
a lot of Marcia's things about the room, of course – her pyjamas
on the bed and her things on the dressing-table and so on. I
wasn't sure whether I minded about that or not. I wasn't sure of
anything. I got up and opened the door of her wardrobe and
looked at all her things hanging up. But all it came to was that
these had been Marcia's things and Marcia was dead and so
what? When I got that far I just stopped.

My back and legs were aching like hell, and now I was sitting
down I felt pretty used up. I went out in the kitchen and blund-

ered about in the dark getting a whisky and soda. I brought it back into the bedroom and before I drank it I raised the glass and said, 'God bless my sweet.' Of course that did it and I did my crying and coughing act again for quite a while. I could see how it was. As long as I didn't start any of that stuff I was quite all right. But if I did it got me and I couldn't stop.

When I'd finished my drink I lay down on the bed and looked at the ceiling and started to work out some of the things I'd have to do tomorrow – the people I should have to tell and so on. I didn't work out anything beyond tomorrow. That seemed plenty far enough.

Telling people brought me up against the Stephen business, I don't know why, but at first I thought I wouldn't tell him at all. On the principle that it was none of his bloody business anyhow, I suppose. But that didn't seem to pass and I think I decided to write to him. Anyhow I went to sleep about then.

I must have been asleep about an hour I suppose when the telephone went. I don't know why but I was quite sure it was Stephen ringing up for Marcia. It wasn't. It was just a wrong number. But anyhow as soon as I'd put the receiver back I picked it up again and rang up Stephen's number.

It occurred to me as I did it that it was late and he'd probably be in bed, but he answered almost at once.

I said, 'Stephen, this is Bill.'

He said, 'Yes – yes . . . .'

I think he guessed.

I said, 'Marcia's dead. She was killed in the raid tonight.'

There was a long silence, and then he said, 'You say *Marcia's* dead?' As though he could have believed it about anybody else.

I said, 'Yes. The Rest Centre place was hit.'

Stephen said, 'You're quite sure? But of course you are.'

'I'm quite sure,' I said. 'I was there.'

Stephen said, 'Oh God. Wait a minute.' There was a pause and then he said, 'Why the hell are you telling me anyhow?'

'I don't know,' I said. 'I think I should have been expected to.'

I heard Stephen start to sob. He said, 'Oh God, don't let her have been hurt. Let it just have killed her.'

'It's all right,' I said. 'She was killed at once. She never knew a thing about it.'

Stephen said suddenly, 'Can I come round? Now?'

I didn't know what to say. 'I must,' said Stephen.

I said, 'You can come if you like. But there isn't anything here now.'

There was a long silence.

'You'd rather I didn't,' Stephen said.

'You can come if you like,' I said wearily. 'But what for? There isn't anything here, Stephen.'

'All right,' he said, after a bit. 'You're quite right. What's the use? Oh Christ, Marcia my darling . . . !'

The line went dead. I don't know whether he hung up or what. I found I didn't mind his feeling like that. I had thought I might, but I didn't.

I wondered if I ought to have let him come over. But what the hell should I have done with him anyway? I hadn't got anything. Then the thought struck me, and once I'd thought of it I had to do something about it. Besides, I didn't want to sleep and I didn't want to stay in the flat. I was quite glad of something to do. I brushed some of the dust off myself, put out the fire, and went out again.

The raid was still going on, and just as I started there was some very heavy gunfire. There were no cabs about so I started to walk down to Chelsea. I was dog-tired and aching when I sat down, but I was quite all right as soon as I was walking again. I could see a lot more fires up in the West End than there had been before, but on the whole it didn't look as though the thing had spread as much as it might have.

I went down Sloane Street and along the King's Road. None of the fires seemed to be as far west as that, and it was very quiet and quite dark. The glow seemed a long way away from there. I knew where the house was. I'd never been in it but I'd been down there once or twice when Marcia was living there with Stephen, to see that it was all right after raids. It was a place that belonged to some vague pal of Stephen's. I wasn't sure whether he was by himself or not. I knew Peggy wasn't there.

The street was very quiet. I found the bell in the dark and pushed, but I couldn't hear it ring. It must have been broken. I pushed the door and it opened. It wasn't even latched.

I went in. I could smell the stuff at once. I shouted 'Stephen!' but nobody answered. I found a light and switched it on. There were three doors opening off the hall. I opened the first two but the rooms were in darkness. As I came out of the second Stephen came out of the third room. He was very pale and swaying about on his feet.

He said, 'What d'you want?' in a thick voice.

I said, 'Hallo, Stephen. You've got a gas-leak somewhere. Can't you smell it?'

He didn't say anything. He just caught hold of the banister to steady himself and stood there swaying and looking at me.

I went past him and into the third room. It was full of gas. I went across to the gas-fire but it was turned off. He must have turned it off when he heard me call. He'd bunged the chimney up and put a mat against the bottom of the door. The room was in a hell of a mess. There were two or three dirty cups and plates, an empty half-bottle of whisky and three letters on the table. The letters were to Peggy, his mother, and a man in Norwich whose name I didn't know. I thought, 'He hasn't written to the Coroner.'

I heard Stephen shuffle away into the back of the house. Then I heard him retching. The gas was making me feel a bit sick myself, and I started to cough again. I pulled the stuff out of the chimney, put out the light, drew back the curtains and opened the window.

I went out into the kitchen at the back. Stephen was sitting slumped across an enamel kitchen table staring in front of him. He didn't look at me.

I said, 'Don't put on a light if you go in there. I've opened the window.'

Stephen said, 'Why did you have to come?'

'I don't know,' I said. I sat down. I was feeling a bit weak in the legs and damned tired.

Stephen said, 'I don't want to go on living. Why the hell should I if I don't want to?'

'I'd give it a day or two,' I said. 'Plenty of time, after all.'

'There isn't anything to live for,' said Stephen, starting to cry a bit.

I couldn't suggest much on the spur of the moment so I didn't say anything.

Stephen turned round and looked at me in a wild sort of way. 'It was always you,' he said. 'You never saw. You starved her.'

I said, 'I don't think we'll go into all that.'

He said, 'It's true. You know it's true.' He was shouting.

199

I felt very tired. I wanted to get it over. I said, 'You may be right. Anyhow it doesn't matter now.'

He said, 'You did something to her. She gave up everything because of you. You didn't know and you didn't care.'

He dropped his head on his arms and started to sob. I thought 'He's got to say it. Then he'll be all right and I can go.'

'I could have made her happy,' said Stephen. 'She knew that. But she wouldn't come – wouldn't take it. If she would have come, this wouldn't have happened. Now it's all wasted.' He turned on me and shouted, 'What right have you to waste life like that? You can't use it. What right have you got to stop other people from having it?'

I didn't say anything.

Stephen said, bitterly, 'You always kill everything. Nothing can live near you. You make it flat and grey and dead and sterile like yourself.' He started to shout again. He said, 'Why did you let her go to that bloody place? I always knew it would happen. Of course it would happen. Any fool could see it would happen.'

He started to retch again.

I said, 'What you want is some air. You've got a hell of a lot of that gas in you. Sit still.'

I put the light out and opened the window. Then I drew the curtains and put the light on again. He looked pretty ghastly.

I said, 'I believe milk's a good thing. Have you got any milk?'

He didn't say anything. He just lay there with his head on his arms. I found a bottle of milk that hadn't been opened and gave him a glass. He drank some of it.

He looked up and said, 'Christ, what have I been saying?'

I said, 'I don't know. It doesn't matter anyway. I'm going to ring up Peggy. Where's the telephone?'

Stephen said. 'I'm crazy. She was yours and now she's dead. What have I been saying to you? Christ, what will you do now?'

'To hell with it,' I said. 'It doesn't matter. Where's the telephone?'

'Why don't you kill me?' he said. 'You've every right to.'

'Listen, Stephen,' I said. 'I don't want to kill you. I want to ring up Peggy. Where's the telephone in this joint?'

He said, 'I don't want Peggy. What the hell's the good? She can't do anything. Christ, I'm no good. I'm no good. Why did you come? It would have been finished by now.'

200

I went out and found the telephone. It was in the first room. I rang up Peggy. She took a long time to answer. I suppose she was in bed. I said, 'Peggy, this is Bill. I'm in Chelsea with Stephen. Come along right away, will you? I'll explain when you get here.'

She said, 'Yes. Of course. Is he all right, Bill?'

'He's all right,' I said. 'But I've got to go, and I think you ought to be with him.'

'I'll come at once,' she said.

I went back to Stephen. He hadn't moved. I said, 'Peggy's coming at once.' He didn't say anything. We sat there for a long time.

Stephen said, 'Did Marcia say anything – about me?'

I would have told him something but I couldn't think of anything that helped. I said, 'She didn't say anything about anyone. It wasn't like that.'

He looked at me and said, 'But she did love me, didn't she? You know she did? She was yours. She wouldn't leave you. But she did love me?' He said it as though he were asking me for something he was afraid I wouldn't give him.

I said, 'I don't know what love is. She was very fond of you.'

He dropped his head again and started to cry quietly. We sat there for a long time. There was a tin clock on the dresser which ticked very loudly. The ticking seemed to get louder and then softer again and then louder. Stephen lay with his head on his arms. I think he was asleep. He looked very big, slumped over that small table. I could see his breath blurring the shiny enamel top of the table.

It must have been half an hour before Peggy came. She knocked at the door and the knock woke Stephen. He half got up, looking very wild.

I said, 'It's all right. It's only Peggy.' He sank down again.

I went to the door and let Peggy in. She was wearing a blue raincoat and carried a little attaché case. She looked like a dumpy little district nurse called out to an urgent case.

She said, 'What's the matter, Bill? What's happened?'

I told her about Marcia.

She gave a little groan and said, 'Oh Bill, my dear, how terrible. Oh, poor darling.'

I said, 'Stephen's had some sort of a shot at gassing himself but I came in in the middle of it. He's all right now, I think.'

She hustled out of her coat and said, 'It'll kill him. He worshipped her.' She was a single-minded woman.

I said, 'He's in the kitchen.'

Peggy bustled off out to the kitchen. I followed her. Stephen had dropped back across the table. He didn't look up as she came in.

She said, 'Stephen, darling.' He didn't move so she went across and put an arm round him and said, 'Stephen.'

I said, 'I think the best place for him is bed, Peggy.'

'That's right,' she said. 'A nice bed and some sleep and he'll feel better. Come along, darling. It'll be so nice when you get there.'

Stephen raised his head and stared straight in front of him. He never looked at either of us. Peggy was fluttering round coaxing him about how nice it would be to go to bed. He still didn't say anything or look at her, but at last he slowly heaved himself up on his feet. Peggy said, 'Can you get upstairs all right, darling? Come along and I'll help you.'

He started slowly for the door without a word, with Peggy holding his arm. As they got to the door she looked back at me and said, 'Bill, dear – are you all right?'

I said, 'Yes. Good-night, Stephen.' He didn't reply.

I heard them go slowly upstairs, Peggy talking to him all the time. It seemed all right.

I looked round the kitchen. The small clock said half-past three. I thought I could go now. As I started towards the door I saw something flash on the dresser. I looked and it was a pair of Marcia's earrings. They were just cheap things she had bought a few weeks ago. She was always buying earrings and then losing them or leaving them about.

I left them there and went out into the hall. I could hear Peggy talking to Stephen upstairs. I think he was talking too. I changed my mind and went back and got the earrings and put them in my waistcoat pocket. I wasn't really sure about it. It wasn't that I wanted them or minded Stephen having them but I didn't like them to be left lying there among all that stuff that wasn't hers or Stephen's or quite anybody's. I knew he had quite a lot of her things that she had never fetched.

I waited a minute or two longer but everything was quiet upstairs, so I put out the light in the kitchen and went.

It was cool outside and darker now. There was still the big

202

glow in the East but it didn't seem quite so bright, and when the houses shut it off it was quite dark. As I went down the steps I felt very free and empty. The whole day there had been a series of things to be finished up, and now they were done with and there was nothing left, good or bad. I knew I was very tired but it didn't matter.

I walked on down to the Embankment and leaned against the parapet, looking at the river. I could just see it glimmering in the darkness. It was very full and silent. Down to the East the buildings stood out a solid, thick black against the glow. It was very beautiful. I said, 'I didn't let you in on that. Everyone went on dead to form just as you would have expected. Nobody was kidding you.'

There were no guns firing but the searchlights flashed every now and again. I heard the queer broken throbbing of planes overhead and stared up for a long time. But I couldn't see anything but stars.

I thought about the blokes up in the planes. When I was a kid I used to pretend I was in an aeroplane when I was in bed.

I said, 'If it were only me, you could have it – whatever it is you want. I haven't got anything I care all that about. But it isn't only me. You want something that isn't there to have, and you'll die trying for it, and we shall die stopping you.'

I sat down on some sandbags and tried to think it out – what I should do tomorrow and so on. But there was too much of it, what with Marcia and the job and this and that. There didn't seem to be anything to start from. I thought, 'It's all right as long as it stays dark and I go on sitting here. But in a few hours it'll be light and I shall have to start again and I don't exist any longer. You couldn't define me now.'

I thought of Marcia under there and holding her fingers and I wished I'd stayed, but I knew I couldn't have, and I knew I couldn't do anything about it now. I said, 'Oh Christ, honey girl, I know you're well out of it, and I know you wouldn't have gone without me for anything on God's earth. But I don't think I can do much without you.'

I heard a rustling and three or four sharp smacks round about, and there was a splash in the river not far away. I only saw one of them. It landed in the road about thirty yards away and started to burn with a bright green flame. It was quite small, but the flame was very bright and lit up the road and the parapet. It wasn't doing any harm and I sat and watched it for a bit. Then it began to catch the tar on the blocks and I thought I'd better do something. I got up and picked up one of the sandbags. It was surprisingly heavy. I carried it along, holding it in front of my face, and dumped it on top of the green flames. For a bit the flame showed from underneath it. But soon the bag split open and the sand went all over it. It went out, and then it was darker than ever.